"Why are you here?" Sarah took the only other chair in the room and leaned toward her.

"You asked me to come."

"Would you like something to eat or drink? Cookies, chips, pop, wine, liquor?"

Lindsey shook her head.

"You're a good looking woman. Do you know that?" Sarah said.

She met Sarah's startling light blue gaze and blurted, "And you have Paul Newman eyes."

Sarah laughed. "I'd like to think it's a compliment to have eyes like an old man. Is it?"

"Yes. Only his have lost some of their intensity."

"I know why you're here."

"Do you?" Lindsey's heart rolled over in terror.

"You want to experiment. I'm your guinea pig."

Lindsey stood. "I should go."

Sarah got up, too. "Yes, you should, but you don't want to. Come on." She took Lindsey's hand and led her into the bedroom.

The bed took up most of the room. Lindsey was looking at it when Sarah pushed her against the wall and kissed her. Sarah's body felt almost as hard as Gregg's, except for the breasts which flattened her own. She got an instant headache and turned her head to free her mouth so that she could breathe. Sarah began undressing her adeptly.

"Wait. Slow down," she said when most of her clothing lay in a heap at her feet.

Sarah lowered her onto the bed instead, and Lindsey watched with fascination as Sarah pulled her turtleneck over her head, unhooked her bra and stepped out of her jeans and underpants. Obviously, Sarah had done this often.

Visit

Bella Books

at

BellaBooks.com

or call our toll-free number

1-800-729-4992

OBSESSION

Jackie Calhoun

Bella
BOOKS
2006

Bella Books, Inc.
P.O. Box 10543
Tallahassee, FL 32302

Printed in the United States of America on acid-free paper
First Edition

Editor: Anna Chinappi
Cover designer: LA Callaghan

ISBN 1-59493-058-9

Acknowledgments

Anna Chinappi, my editor
Joan Hendry, my first reader
Linda Hill and the staff at Bella Books

About the Author

Jackie Calhoun is the author of *Abby's Passion*, *Woman in the Mirror*, *Outside the Flock*, *Tamarack Creek* and *Off Season*, published by Bella Books; ten books published by Naiad Press, some of which are being re-released; and *Crossing the Center Line*, published by Windstorm Creative Ltd. Calhoun lives with her partner in northeast Wisconsin.

1

Lindsey leaned on the counter in the open shop, sipping luke-warm coffee, her book lying open in front of her. Her son and daughter were loading plants into the bed of the truck. Matt had taken over most of the nursery's landscaping jobs, and Natalie often went with her brother to help. Lindsey remembered when they were little and fought fiercely over nearly everything. She wasn't exactly sure when the rivalry turned into friendship. Sometime in middle school, she thought, but she was grateful for it. Less than two years apart, they shared many of the same friends.

A streak of sunlight shot through the clouds, bisecting her kids. It reached inside the overhang and fell on Lindsey's face, warming her. She wondered if Matt and Natalie felt as if they'd been caught up in the business and rendered incapable of leaving. She some-times did, despite working part time at the brass factory as girl Friday, a job she'd taken after she and Gregg had started the land-scaping and nursery business, when they'd needed the outside

1

income. She knew she could quit the other job, and wasn't sure why she kept it. She only worked the nursery after she left the brass factory and on weekends.

"We're going now, Mom," Matt called. "We'll be back late."

She waved as he and Natalie piled into the cab of the truck, first tossing the dog in between them. She was grateful for their help, but they had lives to lead. She thought it time for them to find jobs in their fields away from their father's business, yet she felt rooted to the place.

During the late-morning lull, Gregg came to the counter and poured himself a cup of coffee. He wore jeans and a short-sleeved polo shirt with Second Nature, the pine tree logo and his first name stitched on the pocket—just as she did, just as their kids did. His hands were already dirty, his gloves shoved into the back pocket of his pants. "It's finally quiet," he said, leaning against the other side of the counter.

"A reprieve. It'll be a zoo before long." The professional landscapers had already come and gone, taking away burning and snowball bushes, potentillas, yews, creeping junipers, lilacs, dogwoods and other plants and trees. This was the calm before the homeowners showed up. Unlike the professionals, they didn't always know what they wanted and often solicited advice.

Gregg squeezed her arm. "You okay, hon?"

She smiled and nodded. When he left, she turned back to her book, *Waterbourne*. She became so engrossed that she failed to hear the woman come around the side of the open-fronted shop.

"Hi, I'm looking for plants that won't die over the winter and don't demand a lot of sun or attention."

Lindsey looked up, startled to hear the voice.

"Good book?" the woman asked with a broad smile, revealing a tiny gap between her front teeth.

"Sorry." Lindsey put the novel under the counter. "I'll show you what we have." She led the woman to the rows of potted perennials arranged on boards, supported by sawhorses under a latticed roof.

2

"I've got a patch of bare earth outside my bookstore that needs greenery."

Lindsey glanced at the woman, who was taller and younger than she was, and athletic looking. Her skin was deeply tanned, her eyes a startling light blue, her curly hair bleached by the sun—or so Lindsey thought. She looked like she spent more time outdoors than indoors. "These perennials do well without much sun. The flats for the pots are stacked underneath. Just bring what you want up to the counter."

"Why don't you pick some out for me?" The woman thrust out a hand. "My name is Sarah Gilbert."

Lindsey wiped her palm on her jeans and watched her hand disappear into Sarah's. "Lindsey Stuart Brown."

"So formal, Lindsey Stuart Brown." Again the disarming grin. "Have you worked here long?"

"Twenty years." Almost as long as she'd been married. Gregg had started the nursery a few years after his parents gave them the acreage as a wedding present.

"I've been here before, but I don't remember seeing you."

"Nor I you." Lindsey picked out a few vincas, some hostas and lilies of the valley. "You'll have to water once in a while, but these are pretty hardy. You might want to put some peat moss down or loosen the earth before planting and add garden bark afterward."

Together they carried the flats and the bags to the counter, where Lindsey rang them up. She caught a glimpse of Gregg and Eddie, their long-time employee, busy with customers among the trees and bushes up near the road.

"What time do you close?" Sarah asked.

"Five-thirty."

"How'd you like to go to a movie with me?"

Lindsey looked at her in confusion. Never had she been confronted with such forwardness. She didn't know how to answer politely. Her heartbeat lodged in her throat.

"Have you ever heard of *Desert Hearts*?"

"No," she said, "but I'm pretty tired by the end of the day."

3

"Too bad," Sarah said as they carried her purchases to her station wagon and loaded them in the back. "I'll let you know how these grow."

"Where's your bookstore?" Lindsey asked with idle curiosity. She loved books.

"On Frank Street. It's called Rainbow Coffee and Books. Stop by for a free cappuccino when you get a chance." Sarah slid behind the wheel of the Escort and turned the key. "You shouldn't be hiding from the world."

Lindsey said, "I'm not."

"You're too interesting, and pretty." She drove off, leaving Lindsey standing in exhaust, her mouth open. A tingling sensation galloped up and down her skin.

Then she laughed and shrugged it all off.

That evening Matt and Natalie were playing cribbage, passing time before going out with friends. It was what Lindsey had done when she was young. Work all day and play half the night. She wished she had that kind of energy now. The sight of her son's and daughter's dark heads bent over their cards along with the sound of their laughing banter reached some sad note deep inside her. When they found jobs in their fields, they'd be gone, leading adult lives. They'd come home to visit, but it would never be the same as when they lived here.

Although Matt's degree in natural resources came in handy in the family business, he wanted to work for the Department of Natural Resources. Unfortunately, the DNR was laying off employees, not hiring. Natalie's major in journalism had led her to send an application to the local newspaper, but that was as far as she'd gone. She dreamed of becoming a writer and spent many of her free evenings in her room at her computer, her fingers flying across the keys as she conjured up stories.

Freshly showered, his dark hair still wet, Gregg came into the room. Strands of gray at his temples gave him a distinguished look. Gray had crept into her hair, too, sort of helter skelter. Salt and

4

pepper, Gregg called it. He didn't want her to color it, said he liked her just as she was. Where would she find a better friend? That's what they had been from the beginning, when they'd met her second year of college and his third. He'd made her laugh.

It was true that one choice led to another. She'd attended college in southern Wisconsin, met Gregg there, gone steady with him most of her sophomore and junior years. She'd finally given in to his pleas and her own sexual urges after graduation, when he visited her at her mother's home. Impregnated during that first sexual contact, she'd married him, and moved to the city in southern Wisconsin where he grew up, several hundred miles from her home. It was a common story. Most of their friends had gone to the altar for the same reasons, although Gregg had asked her to marry him when they were still in college. She'd broken up with him instead.

He turned on the TV and sat on the sofa next to her. "Tired?" he asked, gently squeezing her knee.

The newspaper had fallen to her lap. She picked it up and tried to concentrate on the front page. "A little." Then she remembered *Desert Hearts*, and turned to the entertainment section. There was no movie such listed.

"Want to go to a show?" Gregg asked.

"Not really. Just looking."

"I'm getting garbage for cards," Matt complained. His dark blue eyes looked black, just like his sister's and father's. Lindsey's were hazel. "I haven't had one double run."

"The luck of the draw," Natalie said.

"It is just luck, you know," Matt insisted.

"I'd agree, but you're not even pegging. I count first, and I'm out." His sister laid down her hand.

Matt laughed. "She skunked me. I think she stacked the deck." He tousled his sister's hair, and the dog under the table began to bark.

The two young people stood up, faking punches, while the dog jumped up and down, yipping.

"Okay, okay. Shut the dog up, will you?" Gregg said, looking mildly amused.

5

Natalie picked up the small black, curly haired dog and held him close. "Shush, Willie." The animal panted and yawned, his little pink tongue unfurling between tiny teeth.

Matt and Natalie flopped on chairs to watch TV with their parents. A National Geographic special about wolves on some Canadian or Alaskan island was partway through. The wolves swam for miles, sometimes attacked grizzly bears, and caught and ate spawning salmon. Even the dog was watching.

The business phone in the kitchen rang in the distance. They ignored it, knowing a message would give the business hours. When it began to ring again after the message was over, Lindsey went to answer it.

"Want me to get it, Mom?" Matt asked as she left the room.

"Let it ring, Lindsey," Gregg said.

"I'm going to the kitchen anyway," she called and picked up the receiver on the fourth ring, before the answering machine kicked in again. "Hello."

"Hi. Sure you don't want to see *Desert Hearts*?" It was the woman who'd bought the perennials.

Her heart bounced off her ribs. "I looked in the paper. It's not showing." Something very strange was going on. She, who usually struggled to remember names, easily recalled Sarah's.

Sarah laughed. "Not in the theaters. It came out years ago. We're having our own private showing on video here at the bookstore."

Impulsively, she decided to get the video and watch it at home when Gregg was in bed and the kids were gone. Something told her this was not a movie she could share with her family. "I can't get away."

"Come on over to the bookstore when you can. We have it for rent here."

"Maybe I will. What are your hours?"

"We're open till eight Friday night. Otherwise, we close at five, except when something like this is going on."

"I'll try to make it there sometime. This is the business phone. We don't usually answer it after hours."

6

"Well, I'm just lucky then. What's your home number?"

"It's unlisted," Lindsey said.

"Well, mine's in the book. You can call me anytime. Got to go. The movie's starting."

Lindsey hung up, filled a glass with water and took it back to the living room.

"Anything I should know about?" Gregg asked.

"No," she said, sitting down. Now restless, she found herself unable to concentrate on the program or the newspaper.

II

As a senior in high school, Lindsey had been enamored of her best friend, Julie Kapinski, without recognizing the tenor or depth of those feelings. They spoke on the phone every night and were inseparable during the day until Julie began dating Ron Williams, a basketball player. Lindsey understood then what it meant to be broken-hearted. Unwilling to be a threesome, she'd fallen into a new friendship with Kim Kettering and Lois Stepanovich.

The three of them made a name for themselves as the wild ones. They skipped school whenever one of them had the family car. They smoked in the school bathrooms and closed up the bars for eighteen-year-olds. Lindsey drank herself into a stupor on graduation night. The rental cottages on the Waupaca Chain-of-Lakes were filled with high school graduates. She was staying in one with Julie and Kim and Lois. One night after heaving up beer after beer, Julie shoved her face close to a mirror.

"Look at yourself."

That summer she started going out with Steve Randolph. He wasn't into sports. He wasn't into anything. He already had a mill job. She didn't intend to marry him. She just wanted to have a good time.

He picked her up at home after dinner, drove her to the marina where he kept a small motorboat, thirteen feet long with a thirty-five horsepower motor, in which they shared a bottle of vodka while pounding twelve miles to a bar across the treacherous lake. A storm could and would quickly churn the water into mountainous waves. Once they'd gotten caught in such a storm. The boat shipped water over the stern, the wind forced them onto the sandbars near shore, and the motor became ensnared in fishing nets. They'd been lucky to land safely on a stranger's beach where they'd phoned for a ride.

When Steve took her home nights, she let him touch her intimately, giving her quick gratification before getting out of the car and stumbling to her bed. She never wondered what he got out of the one-sided relationship.

During the day that summer she packed cheese wrappers in the paper mill where her father worked in sales. All her life she would remember the smell of the ink, the heat and the noise. There were three women on her machine. One unpacked the Kraft wrappers, one fed them into the machine that creased them, and Lindsey stacked them in bunches of ten and re-boxed them for shipment. The women she worked with were permanent employees. If they knew she was going on to college, they didn't envy her. They teased her when she came in looking sickly after a night out.

When the summer ended, Julie and Ron left for the University of Wisconsin in Madison. Lois and Kim were already working in one of the mill offices as secretaries. Lindsey's parents drove her to the small university in southern Wisconsin where she met Gregg.

What she didn't know was how much she would miss home—her parents, the lake, the hangouts, her friends, even her brother and sister who were five and seven years older and already gone from home. She felt displaced.

Her father died her senior year in college, felled at work by a massive heart attack. She took a bus home and arrived in the dark of a January evening. Her brother, Hugh, met her at the bus station. He picked up her bag and carried it to the car. Dirty clumps of snow hugged the gutters.

"Why?" she asked, shaking a cigarette from the pack in her jacket pocket.

"Because of those," he said, taking the cigarette from her and putting it in the ashtray. "No smoking in my car."

"I quit last week. Really." It was difficult when so many kids smoked at school.

He gave her shoulders a squeeze. "How's school?"

She shrugged. "Okay. How's work?"

"That about sums it up, doesn't it? Okay, huh? Are you serious about this guy, Gregg?"

"He's just a lot of fun. How's Mom?"

"She's holding up. It was Dad's third heart attack. That's usually the killer." Hugh's voice broke.

The funeral went by in a blur. She and her sister held their mother's hands during the service. It felt odd to be the comforter. Suzy had been the good sister, the one who got As and worked on the yearbook and the school paper. She was an attorney for legal services in Milwaukee. Hugh worked for a Democratic assemblyman in Madison. Lindsey was the pampered baby of the family, the one they loved without expectations.

By now Lindsey knew her brother was gay. She had worshipped him as a kid. When he brought a friend, Ray, home from college, she walked in on their embrace. After Ray left, Hugh came out to his parents. Their dad took it badly at first, but in a few months he came to accept his only son's lifestyle. If their mother was disappointed, she failed to show it. Lindsey figured she'd guessed long before Hugh told her.

Lindsey graduated with a degree in languages, nothing useful like Suzy's law degree or Hugh's master's in political science. She went home and interviewed with the same paper company she had worked for between school years, the one where her dad had died. They hired her as an interpreter for their foreign subsidiaries.

She spent a lot of time translating orders and letters. Sometimes she sat in on meetings with visitors from German, French or Spanish speaking countries, the only three languages she spoke outside of English. She liked the job, liked living at home near the lake, liked going out with her unmarried friends from high school, but there was always something missing that she couldn't quite put a finger on. It made her lonely.

Gregg persisted in his pursuit of her, and she caved in to desire one night. She hadn't planned to marry him. She felt she'd barely begun living herself before she was saddled with babies.

She loved her babies from their beginnings, though, even before their tiny fingers closed around hers. Maybe she hadn't planned either one, but she found them adorable, was enamored with their first words, their first steps, cheered them on as they made their way to adulthood. Just as she hadn't imagined life with them, once they were born, she couldn't imagine life without them.

Her mother had died a year ago in the bitter cold of January. She missed her terribly and dreamed of her regularly. There were questions she should have asked and now never could. She wished she had been a better daughter, had gone home to visit more often, had taken more trips with her mother, had told her how much she'd meant to her. It was only after her mother's death that Lindsey experienced restlessness. Death had come to her doorstep and, combined with her own age, caused her to take a critical look at her own life.

Some would call it a midlife crisis, her sudden dissatisfaction.

It was in this frame of mind that she drove to Sarah's bookstore. Parking a block away, she walked on the opposite side of the street until she stood directly across from the small building. A rainbow colored flag flew from a staff next to the door of what had once been a modest Cape Cod type home. She walked past the building, noticing the women going in and out of the front door. Fascinated and fearful—of what, she wondered—she crossed the street and approached the bookstore from the other direction.

A group of five women stood on the sidewalk, talking, animated. A woman about her age nodded and smiled as they moved over to let her pass. She nodded in return but couldn't think over sudden panic. What was she doing here? She wanted to turn and run, but she'd already been noticed. Besides, she knew if she left, she'd never return. She paused to look at the plants in the small patch of earth sandwiched between the pavement and the building. A curled hose lay nearby.

She climbed the steps to the stoop and opened the door. In what must have once been a living room were shelves of books, prints, CDs, videotapes, DVDs. There were a few chairs in the room. Music played over a speaker system. In the next room was a bar with stools behind which hung a sign with the prices of coffee, tea, hot chocolate, bagels and sweet rolls or muffins. On the wall next to the door she'd come through was a bulletin board with announcements on it. She studied it for a moment, stalling for time to gather her wits.

On it were the dates for a book discussion group, announcements of meetings on gay and lesbian political issues, pamphlets from two churches that welcomed everyone despite their sexual orientation—the Unitarian Church and the United Church of Christ. And there were ads by singles wanting to hook up with other singles. She read a few of these hopeful listings.

Thirty-some SWL looking for SWL of same age who likes to bike, hike and watch movies. Twenty-five-year-old SGM searching for someone who enjoys good food, good books and bodybuilding. SBL wants companionship. Call if under thirty. There was one from a woman in her forties, like herself. *MWL interested in meeting someone for an occasional rendezvous.*

She was committing the last number to memory when a loud voice called her name.

"Lindsey Stuart Brown. Don't move." It was Sarah's voice.

Lindsey turned to meet her, her face heating up.

"Aw look, she's blushing. That is *so* cute."

Lindsey desperately wanted to shut her up. She felt exposed and uncomfortable, and chewed on her lip when Sarah approached her.

"I'm just so glad you came. I didn't mean to embarrass you. Let me show you around." Sarah grinned widely, showing white, straight but slightly chipped teeth, along with the small gap.

Lindsey noticed these things even though she had momentarily lost the ability to speak.

Sarah took her arm. "My God, woman, you are thin. You must be working too hard and eating too little. Come on, I'll fix you the best cup of cappuccino you ever drank, and we've got bagels and sweet rolls. Anything you want." She led Lindsey into the next room, where Lindsey managed to speak.

"Decaffeinated or I'll be up all night."

Sarah threw back her head and laughed as if Lindsey had said something terribly funny. "She speaks. Did you hear that, girls and boys?"

Heads turned in their direction. "Quit embarrassing her, Sarah," a familiar voice said.

Lindsey turned toward the man. "Hugh!" she said in complete surprise. "What are you doing here?"

Hugh arched one thin eyebrow. "More to the point, why are you here?"

"How about that. You know each other," Sarah said enthusiastically.

"This is my little sister, whom I thought was happily married."

Feeling as if she were about to experience instantaneous combustion, Lindsey managed to say, "I came to get a video."

"*Desert Hearts*," Sarah said. "I'll get it for you. Then we can all sit down and talk."

"I have to go." Lindsey spoke in a quiet voice.

"Oh, no you don't. You just got here." Sarah still held her arm.

13

Hadn't Sarah heard what Hugh had said? She was a happily married woman. What was she doing in a gay bookstore? And why was Hugh here? He could get any gay book or movie he wanted in Madison, where he now worked for a Democratic state senator.

She pulled away and started for the door. Hugh followed, stopping her. "You may as well get that free cup of cappuccino. We can talk." He led her to a stool. "I'll tell you why I'm here."

Handsome, dapper Hugh was aging, too. She studied her brother. How little she knew of his life. Sarah brought her a cup of cappuccino and her brother coffee.

"I'll show you around later," Sarah said, going behind the sales counter to wait on customers.

"I invested some money in this store when I was dating someone from around here."

"You dated someone here and never came to visit?" she said.

"It was awkward," her brother explained with a shrug of his shoulders.

III

She hadn't thought to invite Hugh or Suzy to her home except for events like the kids' graduations. Lindsey hadn't believed they'd want to visit her and Gregg on a regular basis. Life at the nursery and landscaping business was so hectic, so busy, especially on weekends. She thought they'd be bored. When her mother was alive, the family had come together in her home.

Suzy and Hugh had always indulged Lindsey's children with lavish gifts. Suzy had never married, although she had a long-term, live-in lover. After Ray, Hugh had never brought his boyfriends to his mother's home or talked about them when he was there. Lindsey had thought her life was humdrum compared to theirs. She'd imagined them going to plays and concerts every weekend, when she and Gregg were too tired for such things except during the off-season.

She was thinking of how to put these thought into words, when Hugh said, "It was easier not to let you know I was in town. I still see this guy. It's the longest relationship I've ever had."

"Is he here?" she asked, curious to see him herself.

"No. He's busy." He fiddled with his cup. "I think it's over." He raised a hand. "It's okay. I don't care that much. Really. Now tell me why you're here."

"I don't know," she said honestly. "Sarah stopped by the nursery to buy some perennials and asked me if I wanted to come here and see a movie that night. Then she called and asked again. I was curious, I guess."

"*Desert Hearts* is a lesbian movie, and not a very good one," Hugh told her. He smiled and the dimples on his cheeks deepened.

"Oh," she replied. "I didn't know."

"You guessed, though, didn't you? Have you got the L gene, Lindsey?" His eyebrow arched again. A lock of his steel gray hair hung over his forehead. She wondered if her hair would be like his in a few years.

She frowned. "I'm married with children. How can you ask that?"

"You're here," he pointed out.

"Yes." She lifted her cup to drink. "I think I should go home. Do you want to spend the night with us?"

"Thanks, but I have to find out what's going on with the boyfriend here." He looked in her eyes. "Be careful, Lindsey. Don't do anything you're going to regret."

"Do you regret anything?" she asked.

"I'm not married with children."

When they both got up and Hugh put money on the bar, Sarah joined them. She handed a DVD to Lindsey.

"Bring it back when you've had a chance to see it. No hurry."

Lindsey looked at it as if it were a dangerous thing. "Another time." She tried to hand it back, but Sarah wouldn't take it."

Hugh said, "You can watch it at my place."

"Your place?" Lindsey asked. "In Madison?"

"I have a small apartment here," he said. He scribbled the address on the back of a business card and gave it to her. "I'll take the DVD. Come over tomorrow night. We'll watch it together if you can get away."

Lindsey felt disoriented. Her brother had an apartment here, and she didn't know about it? She turned to leave and felt a hand on her arm again.

"Come back," Sarah said. "Soon."

Then Lindsey was outside with Hugh, taking long strides through the warm October evening.

"You're upset," her brother said.

"I feel like I'm in some kind of dream where nothing makes sense. My own brother has an apartment only a few miles from me and has never told me. I have a hard time believing any of this."

"I'm sorry, Lindsey. I thought maybe it was better the kids didn't know about me and my boyfriend." He laughed harshly. "It always sounds so strange calling a fifty-one-year-old man a boyfriend." He fell silent, and for a moment their footsteps were the only sounds in the night. "You know, I like Gregg."

"I love him," she said.

He walked her to her car, a Chrysler van that in a pinch could be used to haul plants.

"See you tomorrow night?"

"I'll try," she said. "I'll call you if I can't make it." It would be hard to explain. It had been difficult enough getting away alone this evening. She had told Gregg she was going to the library and had stopped and picked up a book on hold. If she said she was going to see a movie, Gregg might want to go with her. Kohl's had one of their many sales. She could say she needed a new pair of jeans or something, and Gregg would gratefully stay home. The kids would have their own plans.

She pulled into the separate driveway that led only to the house they had built when they started the business. It was a basic four-bedroom ranch with a full basement and a sunroom.

A wiggling Willie greeted her at the door. She scooped him up and carried him into the living room where Gregg had fallen asleep in front of the TV. Setting the dog down, she turned off the television. The sudden silence wakened Gregg.

"You're home." He said the obvious.

She sat down next to him. "Anything on that's worth watching?"

"Friday nights are a bust."

"Most nights are a bust, unless it's public TV."

"Nothing good on public television tonight. I'm ready for bed. Did you get some good books at the library?"

"Just this one," she said, holding up Dan Brown's latest novel. "I'll put Willie out for a minute and then come to bed, too."

"Can I read it first?" he asked.

"Sure. I haven't finished the book I'm reading. I can always go back to the library." Maybe next Friday night, she thought, already scheming ahead. She had never had to find reasons to be gone at night or during the day, but then she had never felt the need to hide her movements—not since her wild youth.

Saturday was usually the busiest day of the week, and this Saturday proved no different. Cars and trucks lined up along the curb, waiting for someone to open the gates. Their one permanent employee, Eddie Johanek, let them in. Eddie knew as much as Gregg and more than she did about plants and trees and shrubs. Lean and muscular, despite his age, he had skin made leathery by the sun and a kind, homely face. He worked long hours, was patient with customers and never complained. Gregg depended on him.

Lindsey spent the day in the open-air shop with Natalie, helping customers select plants and flowers and ringing up purchases. The overcast sky threatened rain, and a chill tinged the air, but she was too busy to pay much attention. She almost hoped the clouds would spill their contents, so that they would have a breather.

When they closed, the three older people gathered in the shop for a few moments. Matt and Natalie had gone inside the house to shower. Lindsey was exhausted. Gregg was jubilant. It had been a busy day.

Gregg slapped Eddie on the back. "Time to go home. Thanks."

"See you tomorrow," Lindsey said.

"Yep." Eddie started slowly off toward his pickup truck.

She watched the older man, wondering how Gregg would replace him when he retired. She hoped it wouldn't be with Matt.

"I'll turn on the sprinklers," Gregg said. "You go on in."

Inside, Lindsey hurried to get dinner on the table. She wanted to arrive at Hugh's early enough to get home shortly after nine. Hamburgers tonight, she thought, and beans and leftover potato salad—an easy meal.

"Where are you going, Mom?" Natalie asked when Lindsey pulled on a light jacket.

"Shopping," she said. "What are you two up to tonight?"

"Matt has a date. I'm going out with friends."

"Carolyn?" she asked Matt. Carolyn was his latest love interest. He had even brought her home. She was a nice young woman, about his age, attractive, but Lindsey didn't think he was serious about her.

"Yeah. We're going to a movie."

"We're going to the same movie." Natalie made a face. "Why aren't the two of you going out?"

Lindsey looked at Gregg and lifted an eyebrow.

"No thanks," he said, to Lindsey's relief. "Shopping's not my thing."

She drove the Chrysler van, following Matt down the driveway, then heading in the general direction of the nearest Kohl's department store. She had studied the map in the phone book, so she knew where she was going. Hugh's apartment was on the north edge of the city.

Parking in front of his unit, she pushed the buzzer under his name in the building's foyer. He buzzed her in. She hurried up the carpeted stairs to the second floor, where he stood in the hall, holding the door open for her.

"Would you like anything to drink?" he asked once they were inside. He clinked the ice in his glass and took a sip.

"What do you have?"

"Vodka and tonic."

"I'll have one," she said. Gregg wouldn't detect vodka. How would she explain liquor on her breath when she'd supposedly been shopping?

He mixed her drink. "What did you tell Gregg?"

"That I was going to Kohl's." She sat on the davenport in front of the TV and looked around the studio apartment. She assumed the bed was upstairs in the loft. "Nice little place."

"It's my second home."

Still unsettled by his duplicity, she asked, "How long have you rented here?"

"Three years." He saw her face. "I know. I should have told you. Forgive me for being so secretive, but you probably understand why now."

"I knew you were gay. Why hide from me?" She took the glass he handed her and drank.

"Let it go, Lindsey. I came here on weekends. There was never much time."

"Time enough to invest in a bookstore."

"Yes, okay." He threw up his hands. "I'm at fault. I admit it. I'm sorry."

She wouldn't have had time to be a good hostess anyway had he visited her during the spring, summer or fall. He would have been a worry. "Okay. Good drink. Thanks." She looked into his eyes and smiled, glad to be there, at last comfortable with him.

"Want to see the movie?"

It was past seven-thirty. "I better. I have to be home shortly after nine."

"Ah, the price we pay for cheating." He switched on the TV and DVD player.

20

"I'm not cheating," she said indignantly.

"You're considering it."

The movie, as hokey as it was at times, stirred her and made her squirm with embarrassment at the same time. She found the sex scenes riveting. When she said good-bye to her brother, he handed her the DVD and a key to his apartment.

"Do you want me to water your plants or something?" she asked jokingly. There were no plants.

"You can use the place during the week. Watch whatever you want. Bring someone here if you like. This is against my better judgment, though. I like Gregg, and I love the kids and you. I don't want you to make a mistake you'll regret the rest of your life. I always thought you and Gregg had a good marriage." He arched an eyebrow in question and smiled.

IV

She and Gregg did have a good marriage. That was the confusion in all this. Yes, she hadn't wanted to marry him, but she hadn't wanted to marry anyone. However, she'd liked him from the beginning, and over the months and years, that liking had grown into love. Not an intensely romantic love, but a deeply caring one. Why wasn't that enough? He was her best friend, the father of her children. She trusted him, confided in him. She wasn't comfortable with this secrecy. She had to put this aside. She decided to take the movie back next Friday and walk away from any disloyal thoughts.

Willie met her at the door, so excited to see her he couldn't stand still long enough to be patted. "Silly dog," she said, picking him up while his tail whacked away.

She found all but one light out, which surprised her, because it meant Gregg had gone to bed before ten. They didn't open till one on Sundays and closed at five. They slept in, read the newspaper, drank coffee and ate a big breakfast. She'd planned to hide the

DVD in one of her dresser drawers. Instead, she stuffed it in the closet in a box with their winter caps, gloves and scarves.

Gregg was sitting up in bed, reading. The nutty, dusty, dry smells of fall filtered through the screens. She shivered. The dog wriggled to be let down, and she set him on his pad.

"You can shut the windows if you're cold." His eyes appeared almost black. She'd read somewhere that one's pupils dilate when looking at a loved one. "Willie wouldn't come to bed. Guess he was waiting for you."

"I'm not cold. What did you do tonight?"

"I walked the grounds with Willie and watched a little television. I just climbed into bed a few minutes ago. How was the shopping?"

She turned away. "I didn't find anything." Another lie. "Sometimes it's just good to get out and do something." That at least was true. She undressed, feeling disloyal and guilty, and slipped between the sheets.

Gregg moved closer, until his leg and arm were touching hers. Heat radiated off his body, and she smelled his familiar odor. It reminded her of the bond they shared—molded by children, joined finances, years of intimacy, families and friends. She was jeopardizing a relationship crafted through twenty-four years of marriage.

She picked up her book and began to read, too. This is what they did before going to sleep. When she switched off her light and turned on her side away from Gregg, he folded himself around her, and she fought off tears. It was only when he rolled away from her and his breathing evened into sleep did she relax enough to drift off.

Monday evening she found herself in the van parked in Hugh's spot behind his apartment building. She'd fought the urge to see *Desert Hearts* again, and lost. She'd gone to the grocery store after work, fully intending to go straight home, and now she'd have to take the perishables and put them in Hugh's fridge till she left.

She grabbed the bag, dropped *Desert Hearts* in it, and let herself inside the building. Glad to find the halls deserted, she climbed the stairs to the second floor, put the food in the refrigerator and the movie in the DVD player and sat down. Mesmerized by the two women's dance toward intimacy, one denying her sexuality, the other sure of it, she ignored the stiff dialogue. When it was over, she wanted to watch it again. Instead, she retrieved her groceries and the DVD and left.

At home, the lights were on in the shop, and the pickup was gone. She knew the kids were meeting friends tonight for pizza and a movie. She would have stayed home had not Gregg said he needed to work on the skid loader.

She put the groceries away and went out to the shop, a steel pole building that Gregg and Eddie had built years ago. The radio played softly, and Gregg was whistling to *September Song*. He swept her into his arms and danced her around the only uncluttered part of the concrete floor. His sweatshirt and jeans were filthy as were his hands.

"We can take a shower together." He grinned at her.

"We're going to have to," she agreed, laughing. "Do you need help out here?"

"Nope. I'm just finishing up." He let her go. "I'll be in soon."

"Okay then. I'm going."

Outside, she breathed in the crisp, cool night air and gazed at the stars flung across the black sky. The traffic, muffled by the buffer of plants between the buildings and road, sounded far away. She sometimes thought of their patch of land as an oasis in the middle of the city. A family of foxes hung around, showing their faces only at night, as did the more common raccoons and possums. The possums were slow, the raccoons nervy. They met her eyes and held their ground when she tried to shoo them away. They were after the seeds she put out for the many birds. They growled and fought among themselves after dark. Sometimes deer wandered onto the property and ate the plants, also mostly at night.

It was a great place to live. Was she willing to give it up? What about the kids? And Gregg? She'd be crazy to risk losing their love and respect. Wrapping her jacket around her, she went inside.

She'd picked up *Other Women* at the library, a book she'd seen in Sarah's bookstore. Sitting down with a glass of wine and Willie at her feet, she opened the book and immediately found herself drawn into the story. She put the book down when Gregg came inside and then opened it again in bed. She was still awake, reading, long after Gregg had turned off his light. She heard the kids come home. Willie heard them, too, and wanted out. Willie slept around.

When she did try to sleep, images of *Desert Hearts* kept her awake—the seduction scene, the two women making love. She tossed until she took a sleeping pill and fell into a dreamless sleep.

She awoke to *Morning Edition* on public radio. Gregg was nestled up against her, one arm thrown over her waist. He stirred and pulled her close. They lay there, listening until six-thirty.

Gregg made the coffee. She fixed oatmeal and toast. They talked about the news on the radio and their coming workday until it was time for Gregg to go outside. Matt and Natalie still slept, but one of them had let Willie outside. He barked to be let back in.

Eddie opened the gate when he arrived at seven. Lindsey stood in the sunporch, drinking coffee and watching the sun peep over a bank of clouds. Before getting into the van, she swore to put all this nonsense about women out of mind. Her life was full enough.

When she arrived at the small brass factory, she printed the e-mail orders and put them on John Hoffman's desk. John owned the business and was usually on the factory floor first thing in the morning, talking to his foreman. She also took orders over the phone and through the mail, handled the bookkeeping, answered letters and the phone and was the first person to greet anyone who walked through the door. She had held the job for fifteen years, working thirty hours a week.

At noon she went home for lunch, which she often ate alone on the sunporch. She was reading when Willie, who was lying beneath the table, barked sharply. She looked up from *Other Women* to see Sarah smiling at her through the screen door. It took a moment for her mind to let go of the novel and take in who stood before her, and then heat suffused her body.

"Good book, isn't it?" Sarah nodded at the book as Lindsey closed it.

"Yes." Her eyes felt like live coals. What the hell was the matter with her anyway?

"Have you read *Curious Wine*?"

She shook her head. "I'll go get your DVD," she said. It was in her dresser drawer beneath her underwear.

"Don't bother now," Sarah said. "I've got more than one copy. You can bring it back to the store when you're ready."

"No, I'm ready now. I'll go get it." She fled to the bedroom, where she stuffed the DVD in a paper bag and hurried back to the porch.

Sarah was standing inside the sunporch when she returned.

Lindsey paused, trying for composure. She thrust the bag at Sarah. "Here."

"I just stopped in for some advice. I think the plants I bought need a little fixer upper."

"Go out to the shop for fertilizer or plant food. I have to leave in a few minutes. How did you find me anyway?"

"I was in the shop. I bought some fertilizer." Sarah bent over to pat Willie, who had followed Lindsey to the bedroom and back. "What a cutie."

Willie dodged her hand. He was a one-family dog. Behind Sarah, Lindsey saw her daughter and son walking toward the porch.

Natalie glanced curiously at Sarah. Matt nodded and said, "Hi, Mom."

Lindsey introduced them to Sarah, and they went inside to the kitchen with Willie on their heels.

"Nice kids," Sarah remarked.

"Yes." Frozen in place with embarrassment, Lindsey only later wondered why.

26

Sarah said, "I'll bring the book over." And when Lindsey looked puzzled, she added, "*Curious Wine*."

"Oh, no. Never mind. I'll get it from the library."

"I doubt if they'll have it." Sarah smiled as if at a joke. Her electric blue eyes held Lindsey's.

"They'll find it for me," Lindsey said, "but thank you anyway."

She felt as if she had turned her back on something dangerous and exciting when Sarah drove out. On the way to work, she worried about her physical reaction to Sarah, how she literally turned into a weak-kneed sweat-ball. No one had ever affected her that way.

Two days later she received a package in the mail. She noted the rainbow flag with the name of the store and address in the upper left-hand corner of the brown, padded envelope. The handwriting with her name and address was bold. She should return it unopened, she thought. That would let Sarah know she wasn't interested. Or she could open it and never respond, which would give the same message.

When she was alone, she tore open the flap and pulled out the contents. Along with the book was a note, inviting her to the bookstore Friday evening for hors d'oeuvres and a movie—*Bound*. She wouldn't go, of course. She put everything back in the envelope and hid it in her dresser drawer.

Going to the kitchen, she started supper, a casserole. She was putting it in the oven when Natalie came inside with Willie.

"Need help, Mom?" Her daughter was taller and slimmer than Lindsey. She wore her thick, shoulder-length dark hair pulled back in a ponytail. Her dark blue eyes studied her mother.

"You can feed the dog. I'm about done here."

Natalie filled Willie's bowl while he jumped up and down in anticipation. "I'm going to shower now," she said, setting the food down.

Lindsey went to the bathroom off her bedroom and locked the door. She heard the water running in the other bathroom down the hall. Sitting on the john, she paged through the book Sarah had sent until she found the scenes she was looking for, and read them. Stuffing the book back in the envelope, she looked out the window, wondering why this was happening now instead of before the kids were born, before she married Gregg?

She couldn't begin to explain her feelings to anyone, and what would she say anyway? She hadn't really done anything, except go to the bookstore, watch a movie a couple of times and read a book. But it was a lesbian bookstore, a lesbian movie and a book with lesbian content. Did these things make her a lesbian? Even thinking the word made her cringe. She had to put a lid on these feelings. No one would understand, least of all her kids and Gregg.

The water stopped running, and she heard someone in her bedroom. Assuming it was Gregg, she shoved the padded envelope in the cupboard with the towels, and opened the door. Natalie was sitting on her bed, reading *Other Women*.

Her daughter looked up at her. "Can I read this when you're done with it?"

V

She couldn't recall how long she'd known she was different without knowing why or how. She had a crush on her first grade teacher, her first best friend. When her girlfriends talked about boys, she felt left out. She found most boys in elementary and junior high school silly. When a boy asked her out in high school, she sometimes went but never felt the way her friends said they did. Kissing wet mouths left her cold. She got excited when a boy's hand found its way to her crotch, though, but by then she knew how to please herself. She felt uncomfortably constrained by a boy's arm around her shoulders, and holding hands only made her palm and his sweaty. Her crushes had always been on girls and women.

Sitting on the bed after Natalie left, she thought about these things. There was one experience, though, that she clung to as a sign that she was like other girls. At nineteen, between her freshman and sophomore college years, she had fallen in love with a married man, Pete Stafford. He worked in the same department as her dad. He took her out on the huge lake in his sailboat, just the two of them, after work and on weekends, and taught her to sail. He said his wife was afraid of the water and their child was too young. He wasn't even good looking, but he was fun. Nothing physical had happened between them, not even a kiss exchanged. In the backdrop of her memories of that summer were the green-gray waves, white sails and blue skies punctuated by puffy clouds.

She'd returned to college in the fall and begun dating Gregg. When she came back to the paper mill the following summer, Pete had been transferred to New York. She never saw him again, but she never forgot him either or how he'd made her feel. Her intense attraction to Pete gave her hope that she was like other girls. Instead, it seemed her feelings for him were the aberration.

She had intended to leave Gregg after Matt was born, and hadn't. When the two children were toddlers, she told Gregg she was leaving. When he cried, she realized how unfair it would be to take his children from him. Perhaps she would have gone anyway had she had a good job and a place to live. As it was, she took the easy route. She stayed. Since then, she hadn't had time to think about leaving.

She and Gregg shared the same religious and ethnic backgrounds, had the same amount of education, enjoyed many of the same interests, had come from upper middle class families. If their marriage had been arranged, they would have been chosen for each other.

As the kids and the business grew, her feelings for Gregg became stronger, too. Still, she'd fallen for her best friend, Carol, who was married to Gregg's best friend, Theo. They saw a lot of Carol and Theo, sharing dinners in each other's homes, playing cards, going to movies together. The two couples and their children had gone on winter vacations when the nursery was closed. She thought of phoning Carol and confessing, but she couldn't bring herself to do that, even knowing Carol would tell no one. She was too ashamed.

She considered these things as she looked out the bedroom

window at the backyard, where the goldfinches fought with the chickadees over perches on the tube feeder.

She called Carol from the bedroom phone.

"Just last night Theo and I were talking about you two. Want us to bring pizza tomorrow night? I've got a meeting tonight."

"We'll pay if you pick it up," she said.

"We'll split the cost. How about a bakery cake for dessert?"

"Well, I've got a bit of a bulging belly," Lindsey said.

Carol scoffed. "I'm the one with the bulges, not you."

"Okay. Let's just eat and not think about the consequences."

"Sounds like a plan."

She needed a diversion, she thought as she hung up.

Theo and Gregg had been friends in high school. She and Carol had met at their wedding, where Gregg was best man. They'd hit it off immediately. In the early years of their marriages, when Lindsey had a crush on Carol, the two of them had gone on short trips with their toddlers—to the zoo, to parks, to the children's museum, to the public swimming pool. Even after the last of the kids started school, they still took time off for what they called educational excursions. However, when their youngest children reached middle school age and would rather be with their friends than their mothers, the two women changed their outings. Now they went to museums, plays and concerts, usually at night, sometimes with their husbands, sometimes not. The guys went to see the Packers or the Brewers together.

"It seems like forever," Carol said as they sat around the table, eating.

The windows were black with night. Willie sat at Lindsey's feet, ready to catch any food that dropped. The kids had gone to McDonald's with friends, one of them Carol and Theo's son, Teddy.

"I know," Lindsey murmured. They rubbed elbows, side by side. The touch comforted her.

Across the table, the men engaged in car talk. Theo was thinking about buying a new vehicle.

"Let's go on a food excursion," Carol suggested.

"Where to?" Lindsey said.

"The Wine Bar."

"How about Friday night?" That would put the possibility of going to the bookstore out of reach.

"I wish we could. Megan's school play is Friday. Saturday would be better."

"Making plans without us?" Gregg asked.

"Without consulting you," Carol said. "Dinner at the Wine Bar Saturday night. Seven o'clock sound all right?"

Gregg and Theo shrugged and went back to their conversation.

Carol leaned against Lindsey, her expressive, brown eyes intent on Lindsey. "Now tell me everything." When Lindsey foundered for words, Carol said, "Let's go have a girl talk."

Gregg had been listening. "Take her away, Carol, and find out what's going on. She's got wandering feet."

"Oh, sure. Going to the library and shopping translates into wandering feet," Lindsey retorted.

"Come on. Let's fix another drink and get cozy." Carol put a warm hand on her arm.

"Well?" Carol demanded when they settled in the kitchen nook by the window.

Lindsey shook her head. She would say nothing that might jeopardize their friendship. "I can't put it into words," she finally said. That much was true. What was there to tell? Only unsettling emotions that were pulling her in different directions.

"If you can't tell me, I know a good counselor. The one Theo and I went to last year."

Lindsey's mouth fell open. "What?"

"I never told you this, but Theo was seeing somebody on the side. I couldn't talk about it, either." She jotted down a name and number and shoved the paper at Lindsey. "Call her. She's good. She saved us from a divorce."

Lindsey still couldn't speak, so surprised was she by this news.

Carol was tall and shapely, if a little on the heavy side, with coppery colored hair. It was Theo who was nothing to look at. Skinny with a slight stoop and thinning hair, he looked at the world myopically through thick wire-rimmed glasses. His sharp wit sometimes tired Lindsey.

"Shut your mouth, sweetie." Carol laughed. "I should have told you."

"How did you find out?"

"The usual way. He wasn't coming home nights and was going to too many conferences. I followed him one day."

"What did you see?" Lindsey cringed from the hurt of it.

"I saw him having lunch with the other woman outside a hotel and later confronted him with it."

"Oh, Carol." Lindsey covered her friend's hand with her own.

"A midlife crisis." Carol's eyes glittered. "There were the kids to think about."

Maybe hers was a midlife crisis, too. "Do you still love him?"

"Yes, but it's slightly tarnished. If it happens again, there'll be a different ending. Now do you want to talk?"

Lindsey glanced toward the other room where the men were. "Really, there's nothing to say." She picked up the piece of paper and put it in her pocket. Maybe talking to a professional would help.

Carol's smile almost loosened her tongue, but then the men came into the room. "Guess it's time to go home."

They hugged at the door and stepped outside as Carol and Theo walked to their car. It was nearly November. The leaves were mostly gone. A chilly wind blew out of the northwest. The sky had clouded over. Lindsey was ready for winter, when they operated out of the winter office with a rotating staff of one.

During the winter months, Gregg plowed snow, and he and Eddie worked on machinery. Lindsey finished out the books for the accountant who figured their taxes, and Gregg ordered spring seedlings and started the flowers and plants in the greenhouse. They also went on vacation somewhere warm.

The next day she looked at the health insurance policy, saw that visits to a state certified counselor were covered. She called and made an appointment for Wednesday at three-thirty and hung up in a sweat. She had never gone to counseling, but she knew she would have to be honest or there would be no point.

Hugh called late Friday afternoon on his cell phone. He was in his car heading south on Interstate 51. "Thought I'd give a jingle and find out how things are going."

It seemed like a month, instead of less than a week, since she'd gone to his apartment. She thought maybe he was just making sure she wouldn't be at the apartment. "Will I see you?"

"I have plans with my friend, Jimmy. Have you ever been to a gay bar?"

"No." She laughed shakily. "And I don't want to. I've been invited to see the movie at the bookstore. I'm not going there either," she said in a low voice.

"Back-to-back lesbian flicks. I think I'd better complain. Why aren't you going?"

"Why would I be going? I'm not interested."

"Oh," he said. "Guess I read the signals wrong. Well, I'm glad—for your sake, for Gregg's, for the kids. I'll talk to you later. Maybe we can get together Sunday. Okay? Traffic's gnarly so I'm going to hang up."

She wrapped her jacket around her, wishing for the long afternoon to end. She had plenty to read tonight. She had also picked up a couple of DVDs.

When the kids left for the evening, she put in one of the movies—*The Deep End*. She and Gregg sat close together on the sofa. She watched with horror as the housewife mother tried to deal with her son's homosexuality. The boy had hooked up with a nasty opportunist who wanted money from the mother in exchange for the videotape he'd taken of him having sex with her son.

As the sleazeball showed the mother the video, Lindsey apologized. "I didn't know." There hadn't been time to read much of the blurb.

Gregg hugged her shoulders. "It's okay, hon. It's just a movie."

The housewife mother sank deeper into what was becoming a hopeless situation as she tried to protect her son, who was clueless as to what was going on. Then the blackmailer experienced a life changing moment. Lindsey felt as if everything she touched these days had gay overtones.

Maybe she should just experiment a little and get it out of her system. The thought made her squirm with excitement and anxiety.

VI

Lindsey gulped down two glasses of wine at the Wine Bar Saturday night.

"Whoa, darling," Gregg said. "You'll fall asleep during the movie."

"I don't get out much," Lindsey said with a silly smile, "and the wine is so good here."

"Ditto." Carol lifted her glass and drank.

"Not true," Theo said, ordering another beer. "Carol's a social butterfly."

"Oh, sure. Mostly I go to meetings. Why don't you and Gregg come on some of the Sierra Club outings, Lindsey? It would be so much more fun."

"We could try cross-country skiing again," Theo suggested.

They'd gone north to ski several years ago. Lindsey remembered the cold, the long trails and steep hills. She wasn't a good skier and had been terrified at times. Since, she'd only skied on boring tracks in the parks and nature centers around town. Nevertheless, she enthusiastically said, "Let's," remembering the fun afterward—sitting in the motel's hot tub and eating out.

After the third glass of wine, she laughed at Theo's and Gregg's jokes that would have brought a moan from her lips had she been sober.

"Hugh!" Gregg said with surprise, jumping to his feet. "How are you? Do you remember Carol and Theo Carrollton?"

"Of course, I do. This is my friend Jimmy Tyler."

"Care to join us?" Gregg invited, still standing.

Hugh glanced at Jimmy, and made the decision. "Love to." The waiter pulled over chairs and space was made between Lindsey and Carol.

The conversation lagged for a moment, but Hugh picked it up and ran with it. He talked about his job as an aide to a Democratic state senator—listening to lobbyists, keeping track of legislative bills and meetings, taking notes during sessions, handling publicity.

"Are you thinking about running for office?" Carol worked in the Democratic office during campaigns and confessed to be fascinated with politics.

Hugh laughed. "I did once. Now I'm only interested in engineering change behind the scenes. I'm too much of a target."

No one said anything. It was easy to guess that Jimmy was gay. He played the part. Lindsey didn't think it was obvious with Hugh, but it was guilt by association.

It was Jimmy who made them laugh. He gave convincing imitations of the president and vice president.

Their food came, and they fell to eating. They left for the late movie after dinner. Lindsey dozed off after seeing the opening credits, waking often enough to get the gist of what was going on.

"Seeing Hugh was a surprise," Gregg said on the way home.

"Yes," she remarked, not telling him she had seen Hugh at the bookstore and been in his apartment.

The next morning Gregg pressed against her back and cupped

her breast. She turned toward him, even as she wondered how the softness of a woman would feel. They had always had a good sex life. Sundays they usually made love upon waking.

By Wednesday she felt ready to talk about her obsession. Her mind was cluttered with sexual images about women, mostly Sarah Gilbert. She was unable to hold the thread of a conversation or the meaning of the words she read.

The reception room in the Mental Health Clinic soothed her—the neutral colored walls, the Berber carpeting, the comfortable chairs and indirect lighting. The colorful prints on the walls created a needed contrast. There were plenty of magazines lying about. On the counter were two coffee urns with cups, creamer and sugar. A small table with toys and books for toddlers took up one corner.

She gave her name to the woman at the desk behind the counter whose homely face broke into a smile. "Help yourself to coffee. I've got some paperwork for you to fill out." She handed Lindsey a board with medical history forms clipped to it.

Lindsey poured herself coffee, sat down, and filled out the forms. Then she picked up *Other Women*. She was rereading the book, so it didn't matter if she missed whole sections. There were still certain parts that stopped her in her mental tracks and held her rapt.

"Lindsey?"

A woman about the same size and age as herself stood in the inner doorway. She smiled and walked up to Lindsey.

"I'm Kate Flanagan."

Lindsey shook her hand firmly, nearly dropping her book as she stood. Then she clumsily gathered her purse and followed the woman into her office.

The office had the same carpet, comfortable chairs and bright prints on off-white walls as the reception room. Here there were also windows with potted plants under them.

38

She sank into one of the chairs and placed her purse and book on the floor. Her heart raced behind her ribs. She couldn't think of how to start.

Kate settled herself at her desk and swiveled her chair so that she faced Lindsey. "What brings you here?"

"A friend of mine, Carol Carollton, recommended you."

Kate glanced at the novel, which lay cover up. "Good book," she said.

"You read it?" Lindsey asked.

"A long time ago, but it remains one of my favorites."

"Why did you read it?"

"It was recommended to me by a friend. Have you read *Kinflicks*? Same author."

"No, but I will." She took a deep breath and met Kate's gaze, noting the light brown color and the pupils made tiny by the sunshine flooding through the windows. "I think I might be a lesbian."

There was a pause while Lindsey waited for a reaction. The woman hadn't looked at the forms Lindsey had filled out. She did now. "I see that you're married with two children. I suppose that poses a problem."

"Yes. I haven't told anyone, certainly not Gregg. He loves me. Everyone thinks we have this great marriage, including him. I thought we did, too, until a few months ago, when I started thinking things I shouldn't."

"Wait a minute." Kate held up a hand to stop the flood of words. "Thoughts are not something we censor."

"If I don't act on them, they're okay, I guess." She sighed. "That was easy before I met this woman." She talked about Sarah, about going to the bookstore, the phone calls and invitations. It led her to Hugh and his apartment and watching *Desert Hearts* over and over. "It's not even a good movie. The dialogue is clumsy, the acting stiff."

Kate leaned forward a little. Her legs were crossed, her hands clasped in her lap. She looked very earnest. "You can try to suppress your feelings. It works for some people."

39

"I love Gregg and the kids. He would be so hurt, and my kids would never forgive me. They'd be disgusted." She was sure they would react with anger and loathing, especially Natalie.

"Do you think you're disgusting?"

She wasn't sure what she thought and said so. "It's different when it's not myself. I don't have a problem with gays and lesbians."

"That's a bit patronizing," Kate said in a mild tone.

She nodded. "Yes. I'm wondering if I should just confront these feelings."

"You could, but there might be no turning back."

"How am I going to find out if I don't do anything?"

When Lindsey left, she had convinced herself that she should face her fears. She'd go to the bookstore Friday night.

Parking around the corner from the bookstore, she sat in the van for a few moments, composing herself. She was nervous, unsure of what to say, wondering what her welcome would be. When they last met, she'd virtually told Sarah to get lost.

The night was cold, the sky clear. It was the first week of November. Pumpkins were still in place on doorsteps and in windows. She'd dressed in new jeans and a mock turtleneck with a sweater over it. No one stood outside the bookstore. The door jingled when she opened it. Groups of men and women talking and laughing met her eyes and ears. She looked around, hoping Hugh had changed his mind about not coming this weekend. She didn't see him.

Some of the women glanced at her curiously, and went back to chatting among themselves. She felt uncomfortably out of place and would have turned to leave had not Jimmy stepped out of the crowd.

"Lindsey?" he said.

"Jimmy! Is Hugh here?" she asked.

"No. Did you think he would be?"

"I guess not."

"Come sit with me. We're having a discussion on the proposed anti same-sex marriage amendment. No movie tonight."

She followed him. They sat in the first row of the folding chairs that had been set up. She felt as if she didn't belong there. She was against changing the state constitution to include a discriminating amendment that forbade same-sex marriage, but she wasn't passionate about it. Her causes had always been environmental ones.

Jimmy was talking to the man seated on the other side of him when Sarah spotted her. Lindsey felt as if she'd touched a hot wire. Her face and body flushed, and she looked away.

"Hey, it's good to see you here." Sarah said, standing beside her. "Save this place for me. I have to set up more chairs. I'll be right back. Don't move."

Lindsey laughed, relieved not to be shunned.

After the meeting, Sarah tried to slip away several times from the people surrounding her, but couldn't.

Lindsey was nervous about getting home. Gregg would be worried. She had gone to the library at seven. It was now after nine. "I've got to go," she said to Sarah as soon as there was an opening.

"Excuse me. This is important," Sarah said, separating from the small group. She took Lindsey's hand and led her outside. "Will you come back?"

Lindsey shivered, but it wasn't from the cold. Her hand actually tingled. "Yes. I don't know about next Friday. Maybe I can get away sometime Sunday."

"Call me," Sarah urged.

"Okay." Lindsey turned to leave. "It's better if I call."

"How about a hug," Sarah said.

Lindsey hugged her awkwardly and left.

VII

The week dragged by. Thanksgiving was around the corner. Gregg's parents were coming as was Hugh. Jimmy had been asked and had said he'd let her know. She'd invited Suzy and her lover, but they were going elsewhere. She needed to plan, yet she couldn't think beyond Sunday.

When Sunday arrived, she packed her gym bag and told Gregg she was going to the Y, something she said she seldom had time to do. Gregg was working in the shop. They were no longer open Sundays.

Driving to the bookstore, she again parked around the corner. It was a rare November day, warm and partly sunny, but Lindsey was so unstrung she hardly noticed. The bell above the door jangled as she stepped inside. The place was virtually deserted. Someone she didn't recognize was at the computer. Two women browsed through the books on the shelves, giggling over something.

She went to the sales counter and asked for Sarah. The woman smiled at her.

"Hi. I'm Lorrie West. She stood and shook Lindsey's hand. "I'll give Sarah a buzz."

Lindsey's face flooded with color. "I don't want to get her from home or someplace else."

"She lives upstairs. May I tell her who's here?"

"Of course," she stammered. "Lindsey Brown."

Sarah came down immediately. "Lindsey Stuart Brown. I just went upstairs for a minute. Want to see my place?"

The directness caught Lindsey off guard, as before. "Sure, I guess."

"We'll have tea or something." Sarah grinned as if she'd just told a joke. "See you, Lorrie."

Lorrie turned back to the computer. "Nice to meet you, Lindsey."

"You, too," Lindsey said, trying to ignore the distress signals rippling through her body. She followed Sarah up narrow, enclosed stairs.

Upstairs, the rooms were cramped but cute. Those were the adjectives that registered in Lindsey's brain. The place was small and cluttered, and cozy in a way. A collection of Hummels lay behind glass doors in a hutch that took up most of one wall. Light flooding into the rooms saved her from feeling claustrophobic.

A CD of old songs sung by k.d. lang and Tony Bennett played softly. Lindsey realized she was humming along when Sarah pointed it out.

"You know these songs?" Sarah asked.

"Yes," she answered.

"Why don't you sit down and tell me about yourself?"

She sat on the edge of a recliner. "You know I'm married. You met my daughter and son. You were at the nursery and landscaping business my husband owns. I'm office manager at a brass factory. That's about it." Condensed into a few sentences, her life sounded incredibly boring. "Not very exciting," she admitted.

"Why are you here?" Sarah took the only other chair in the room and leaned toward her.

"You asked me to come."

"Would you like something to eat or drink? Cookies, chips, pop, wine, liquor?"

Lindsey shook her head.

"You're a good looking woman. Do you know that?" Sarah said.

She met Sarah's startling, light blue gaze and blurted, "And you have Paul Newman eyes."

Sarah laughed. "I'd like to think it's a compliment to have eyes like an old man. Is it?"

"Yes. Only his have lost some of their intensity."

"I know why you're here."

"Do you?" Lindsey's heart rolled over in terror.

"You want to experiment. I'm your guinea pig."

Lindsey stood. "I should go."

Sarah got up, too. "Yes, you should, but you don't want to. Come on." She took Lindsey's hand and led her into the bedroom.

The bed took up most of the room. Lindsey was looking at it when Sarah pushed her against the wall and kissed her. Sarah's body felt almost as hard as Gregg's, except for the breasts which flattened her own. She got an instant headache and turned her head to free her mouth so that she could breathe. Sarah began undressing her adeptly.

"Wait. Slow down," she said when most of her clothing lay in a heap at her feet.

Sarah lowered her onto the bed instead, and Lindsey watched with fascination as Sarah pulled her turtleneck over her head, unhooked her bra and stepped out of her jeans and underpants. Obviously, Sarah had done this often.

In the other room, Melissa Etheridge replaced k.d. lang and Tony Bennett. Lindsey struggled to get up, but it was a half-hearted attempt and too late. Stretching out next to Lindsey, Sarah began kissing her neck and nibbling at her lips. She pressed their bodies together, unhooked Lindsey's bra, bent to taste her nipples, and slid her hand into Lindsey's underpants. Her fingers began a slow caress. Electrified by the touch and helpless to stop it, Lindsey gave in to pleasure.

Lindsey knew how to please herself, so it was easy to satisfy Sarah in return. She had dreamed about this, but the reality overwhelmed her. She realized quickly that this would be hard to give up.

After, she lay on the bed a few moments, catching her breath. Sarah had jumped up to make coffee or tea or something. Lindsey looked at her watch and knew she had to leave. She got up reluctantly—already she wanted more—and dressed. Looking up, she saw Sarah leaning against the door frame, smiling knowingly.

"Leaving so soon?"

"I have to go. I've been gone three hours." Her gaze swept down Sarah's body, dressed in sweatpants and T-shirt. In that glance she relived every intimate moment. It couldn't be called love. She loved Gregg. No one could be expected to change allegiance with one act of sex. This had been an aberration that must not be repeated.

"Did you like it?" Sarah asked, then without waiting for an answer, "When are you coming back?"

Lindsey grabbed her purse from the next room. "I don't know. I'll call you. Okay?" She started toward the door.

Sarah blocked her path, a lazy, knowing smile on her face. "Don't make it too long. How about a kiss?"

The kiss weakened Lindsey's resolve, and she looked away afterward. "I'll see you."

Gregg and Matt were watching a Packers game when she walked in. She heard the familiar commentators, the roar of the crowd, and wondered why Sarah hadn't had the game on. Weren't lesbians football fans? She was.

Willie met her at the door, snuffling and wagging his body in welcome. She picked him up and carried him with her down the

45

hall to her bedroom and set him on the braided rug her grand-mother had made.

Taking off her clothes, she threw them in the wash and stepped into the shower in the bathroom attached to the bedroom. Her hair was wet with sweat as were her armpits and between her legs. She was terrified Gregg would smell sex on her.

After, she dried her hair and dressed in sweatpants and sweat-shirt and went downstairs to start dinner. During a commercial break, Gregg came into the kitchen and put his arms around her.

"You smell good enough to eat," he said, kissing her neck. "Speaking of eating, let's go out. We deserve it."

She didn't deserve him, she thought with a stab of guilt. Sneaking around behind anyone's back was a terrible thing, but to do it to someone who'd faithfully loved her for twenty-four years was hateful. Did the fact that she was involved with a woman make it any less detestable? Would he be less hurt or angry?

"Where do you want to eat?" she asked.

"How about the Indian place? That's always a favorite of yours."

"Let's go Mexican. The kids like that best. They're going, too, right? Where's Natalie?"

"She's watching the game. I'll fix us drinks. We'll leave when it's over."

Natalie and Matt each had a beer in hand and were sprawled on the floor with Willie. Lindsey stretched out on the couch. Gregg handed her a vodka and tonic, sat down, put her feet in his lap and began massaging them.

She wanted back the contentment she would have felt a year ago. Her thoughts kept straying to Sarah's bedroom. She felt drugged with remembered lust. When Gregg and the kids cheered a Packers touchdown, she started and almost spilled her drink.

At the Mexican restaurant she and Gregg sat on one side of the booth, facing Natalie and Matt. The waiter brought their drinks and chips with salsa.

46

"Were there lots of people at the Y?" Natalie asked.

"Lots of kids," Lindsey said, knowing there would be.

"What machines did you work, Mom?"

"All the upper and lower body ones, the treadmill and the stair stepper." That would account for the time. Her heart pounded with each lie.

"That's what keeps your mother in shape. You two should go more often."

"Tomorrow morning," Natalie said. "Early. Want to go with, bro?" She tossed her long ponytail and eyed her brother.

He stuffed another chip in his mouth. "Sure. Six early enough?"

"I'll wake you," Natalie promised.

"Send Willie in," Matt suggested.

Lindsey sipped her margarita. Inwardly, she cringed at the thought that her kids might somehow find out about this afternoon. She was pretty sure Gregg, although wounded, would forgive her, but it would be different with Natalie and Matt. They'd feel betrayed, then angry, then repelled.

Two of Natalie's college friends were lesbians. Natalie had hotly defended their sexual orientation. Lindsey was less sure where Matt stood. If they lost love and respect for her, it would be because she'd cheated on their father.

"You're awfully quiet, Lindsey," Gregg said. "Tired?"

"Nope. I'm fine." In fact, she felt oddly energized. She swore to herself that she wouldn't call Sarah, wouldn't go back, but even as she made these promises, she knew she would break them.

She had another appointment with Kate Flanagan on Wednesday at four-fifteen. She arrived five minutes early, poured herself coffee, said a few words to Margaret and sat down with a book. Her attention span lasted about five minutes, after which the replay of the afternoon with Sarah kicked in. She couldn't let it go.

In Kate's office she said quietly, "I went to Sarah's Saturday, and it happened." The last two words were nearly inaudible.

Kate leaned forward. "You had sex with Sarah. And?"

Lindsey glanced at Kate, saw no sign of surprise or repugnance. She wondered if Kate was a lesbian. "I'm going to try to stay away."

"Do you think you'll be able to do that?"

"No," she whispered, looking away. "I'm so ashamed."

Kate took a deep breath that sounded like a sigh. "Why exactly?"

Startled by the question, she said what she thought was obvious. "Because of Gregg and Natalie and Matt." Her heart actually hurt for them, for herself. "I'm terrified they'll find out."

"You think you'll be able to live a dual life?"

"Maybe till I get this out of my system."

"Lindsey, you don't have the flu. You were probably born this way. Do you remember earlier experiences that might be revealing?"

She recalled her crushes on her best friends, her female teachers, Carol. "Yes. What should I do?"

"I can't tell you what to do. I wish I had an answer. Some people manage to stay together even though one is gay. It takes a special partner to take a back seat to someone else and remain married. Is Gregg that person?"

"It wouldn't be fair, would it?"

"That would be up to him. And your children?"

"They would never completely forgive me."

VIII

She could tell no one else with the exception of Hugh, of course. The thought of confiding in Gregg, who had been the repository of her ideas and thoughts all these years, made her feel ill. She had no intention of leaving him. Where would she go? What would she do? She would lose him, her children, her home, even her dog.

Natalie found her in the kitchen, making dinner. "Need help, Mom?"

Lindsey had been so deep in thought that she let out a little cry of surprise.

"It's just me, Mom. You're so jumpy these days. What can I do?"

"Peel some potatoes and make a salad."

"I've got an interview with the local paper and the one in Centralia."

"Good!" Lindsey said with enthusiasm. "It's time you started working in your field."

"They're looking for copy editors."

"Well, I don't expect you to have your own byline yet."

Natalie laughed. "That'll be the day." She became serious. "If I take a job in Centralia, I'll probably move there."

Lindsey hugged her daughter and buried the relief she felt. If any of them guessed her involvement with Sarah, it would be Natalie. "Hey, you moved out when you went to college. We'll miss you, but it'll be good for you. Have you told your dad or brother?"

"Nope. You're the first one."

She smiled to herself. Natalie had been her daddy's girl. It was Matt who had shadowed Lindsey as a toddler and little boy. That Natalie had confided her news to her mother first made Lindsey feel good, but only for a moment.

"Mom, you know Stacey, my friend, was at the Y Sunday. She didn't see you there." Natalie sent peelings flying.

For a moment Lindsey thought her heart stopped but then it raced along without a pause, leaving her breathless. "I didn't see her either," she said as calmly as she could.

"She was in the fitness room. How could she have missed you?"

"I don't know. Maybe she just didn't expect to see me, nor I her. Like ships passing in the night."

"Only it wasn't night," Natalie muttered, and stopped flaying the potatoes. She cut them up and put them in a pan with water and got the salad makings out of the fridge.

Shaken, Lindsey checked the roast in the oven and stirred the beet soup on the stove. Hot food tasted good when the weather turned cold as it had early in November. She forced herself to think about Thanksgiving dinner, which was now a week off. She had ordered a fresh turkey.

"Look at my Thanksgiving list, will you Nat? See if I've missed anything."

"We're having the usual?" Natalie asked, wiping her hands on her jeans.

"Yep. Turkey and dressing, white and sweet potatoes, fruit salad, green bean casserole, rolls, pumpkin and mincemeat pies."

"Makes my mouth water. I don't see the pumpkin on here."

"That's because we have two cans of it."

"Who's coming besides Grandma and Grandpa Brown?"

She still added the last name as if Lindsey's mother was with them, Lindsey thought with a twist of pain. Her mother had been living last Thanksgiving. She wondered what she would have to say about Sarah. Her mother had been more than fond of Gregg, had dearly loved her grandchildren. She wouldn't like the cheating, the lies. Nor would she want to see the marriage end.

"Let me know when you go to the Y next time. I'll go with you," Natalie said. Her dark blue eyes briefly met her mother's. Her lips and smooth-skinned cheeks, reddened by the heat of the oven, gave her a healthy look.

"That'll be nice," Lindsey replied. She would have loved to have her daughter exercising at her side a few months ago. Now she felt as if she were being watched, her movements limited. But that was good, wasn't it? It would keep her away from Sarah.

Saturday, Lindsey and Natalie used the treadmills at the Y, while Matt lifted weights. Gregg said he got enough exercise at home. He answered Sarah's phone call Sunday afternoon when Lindsey and Natalie were swimming laps. He'd just come in from outside and was warming coffee in the microwave.

"I offered to answer any business questions, but she wanted to talk to you," he told Lindsey when she returned home.

"I'll call her tomorrow," Lindsey said, her heart jumping around like a yo-yo. She was just glad Natalie and Matt couldn't hear.

The phone rang twice after supper. No one answered it, and it rolled onto the answer machine. Lindsey went to the kitchen to see if there were messages. While she stood there, the phone began to ring again. She jumped, and ignored it.

On Monday Sarah walked into her place of work. Her boss had left for an early lunch, and Lindsey was putting data into the computer.

"Why don't you work at the nursery?" Sarah asked.

"What are you doing here?" she said.

"Where were you yesterday?" Sarah walked around the small reception room.

"At the Y, swimming with my daughter. You can't just show up, Sarah. I work here. Besides, I can't do this anymore."

"I thought you liked doing it." Sarah picked up a brass fitting on an end table between two chairs.

"It just isn't going to work."

"Okay, but I bet you'll come back for more," she said, and left, passing John on his way in.

"Who was that?" John asked. "A friend?"

"Yes."

When she went home, Natalie said, "That woman, Sarah, was here looking for you. She's a lesbian, you know."

"Is she? How can you tell?"

"I can tell."

"And if she is, so what?"

"I don't want her hanging around with my mom."

"Didn't you hang around with your lesbian friends?" Lindsey asked, before letting it go. "How was the interview?"

"I got the job."

"Congratulations! When do you start?"

"Next Monday. I'm going to look for an apartment in Centralia. I'll come home weekends when I can."

Natalie went to change clothes and Lindsey was left alone, drained and shaken.

Her appointment with Kate fell on Tuesday, because of Thanksgiving. She sat in the counselor's office, feeling safe for the first time since last Wednesday. She told Kate about Natalie's suspicions, about Sarah's phone calls on Sunday and her showing up on Monday.

"So you think I waited till my mother died last January to do what I did? Do you think her dying freed me somehow?" she asked.

"Possibly. I think parents have more influence on their children than anyone else does."

Lindsey wasn't sure she wanted that much power over her kids' lives. She'd been a good mother. She'd participated actively in their growing up. Most of all, she'd loved them.

Kate continued, "There's another side to this. If you do make mistakes, you free your children to make theirs. Some kids feel as if they can't live up to their parents' achievements or their expectations. Parents are human, after all. It's okay for their kids to know that."

After, on the way to the grocery store, she remembered her mother's death and funeral. Suzy had been with their mother when she died. Lindsey had driven through a winter storm, trying to get there before her death, and arrived too late. Hugh had driven through the same storm and also missed her death. The three of them had stood beside their mother's body, trying to absorb the loss.

Suzy handled the details of the funeral and the will. Numb, too exhausted emotionally to offer comfort to anyone else, Lindsey sat with her family at the service. Natalie sobbed uncontrollably, twining her father's handkerchief between her fingers. Matt sat stoically silent. Lindsey stiffly leaned away from Gregg's encircling arm. She had feared comfort might cause her to break down and wail.

She parked in Woodman's Grocery parking lot without remembering the drive there. The place was packed. She ran into Carol in front of the lemons and limes.

"Fancy seeing you. Picking up last minute stuff? This is probably the third worst day to shop." Carol glowed with color.

"I know and yes. Do you have a full house Thursday?"

"My parents and Theo's will be there, as will my sister and her family, and me and Theo and the kids. It'll be a zoo. And you?"

"Gregg's parents are flying in tomorrow. My brother is coming and his friend, Jimmy. You remember him?"

"Sure do. Could we have lunch next week, Tuesday?"

"I'd love to."

On Thanksgiving eve, the talk swirled around Lindsey. Images of the afternoon in Sarah's bedroom swept everything else from her mind. Her actions shocked her. She hardly knew this woman and by going to her place, she'd asked to be seduced. She'd warned her kids about sexually transmitted diseases, about rushing into intimacy without knowing the person, about not using condoms—although condoms were not relevant in this case. She tittered a little and the others turned toward her.

"Private joke, hon?" Gregg asked.

She nodded with a smile and returned her attention to those at hand. She liked Gregg's parents. They were kind, generous people.

"Have you been golfing every day?" she asked. They all looked at her strangely, and she knew the question had already been asked. "Sorry. I must have been somewhere else."

"Yeah, Mom. Where?" Natalie asked.

"We want you to come down over Christmas. The lodging's free. You may as well take advantage of it," Gregg's father offered.

Lindsey lifted her eyebrows at Gregg, who asked, "What do you think, hon?"

They usually went to visit Gregg's parents during the kids' spring break. Phil and Darlene lived on Merritt Island in a doublewide trailer set in a grapefruit and orange grove with other trailers. Their home was close to Cape Kennedy and a national seashore. It was far enough south to be on the warm end of Florida.

She would miss the snow, but the past few Christmases there had been no snow. "Sounds like the thing to do. What do the rest of you say?"

"I say yes as long as I can get off work," Natalie said.

"We might have to fly back early," Matt warned. He was starting a temporary job at Kohl's on Monday.

"Lindsey and I can stay longer," Gregg said. "There's no reason for us to come back early. We'll take Willie with us. That okay? Mom? Dad?"

Willie was sitting on Gregg's mom's lap. It was a rhetorical question.

Lindsey excused herself and went to bed. She existed in a sort of daydream, consumed by lustful remembrances. She couldn't even concentrate on a book, something that had never happened before. Her mind was filled with images of the few hours in Sarah's bedroom. She was disgusted with herself.

The next day she rose early, leaving Gregg to sleep, and went to the kitchen to make the stuffing. At one time she was so organized that those closest to her joked about it. Now she had to make lists and carefully follow directions or she forgot ingredients or part of the menu.

She turned on public radio and let Willie outside. Stepping onto the patio, she breathed in the chilly air. November was usually a dark month, its dreariness broken only by Thanksgiving and the slowing of business at the nursery.

With help from Darlene, Natalie, Hugh and Jimmy, dinner was on the table at four. Gregg, his dad, and Matt would clean up. That was the unspoken agreement.

Gregg's dad offered to say grace and his mother, Darlene, made them all hold hands. Matt and Natalie rolled their eyes, and Hugh raised his brows.

"And we're not even going together," Jimmy said as he took Phil's hand.

Lindsey caught Gregg's grin, and smiled, but the comment made her uneasy.

Phil looked at Hugh with interest. "You've gone political, Hugh. I hear you're working for a state senator. Republican or Democrat?"

"Democrat, sir," Hugh said politely. "I couldn't work for a Republican. We don't agree on the issues."

Lindsey shot a warning look at her brother. She wasn't sure where her in-laws stood politically.

"You agree with your boss?"

"Most of the time. He's not perfect, but he's better than most."

"Glad to hear that." Phil began eating with relish.

"Do you have any children, Hugh?" Darlene asked.

Oh, God, Lindsey thought.

"Nope," Hugh said. "Never wanted any either."

Natalie and Matt laughed. Neither knew their uncle well, but they did know he was a gay man.

"Little buggers cost a lot of money and are seldom appreciative," Jimmy remarked.

"Are you two partners?" Darlene ventured.

Hugh and Jimmy looked at each other as if appalled. "What? And ruin a great friendship?" Jimmy said.

Darlene laughed and so did everyone else. Lindsey relaxed. She felt thankful toward her mother-in-law for easing the tension. She wondered how they would regard her if they only knew. They would side with Gregg, of course. Even if he didn't want anyone to take sides, everyone would, except maybe Hugh and Carol.

She wanted to talk to Hugh alone.

IX

After Gregg chased them out of the kitchen, Jimmy and Hugh sat with Darlene and Lindsey and Natalie in front of the blazing fireplace. A football game was in progress on the TV.

"Are you Packers fans?" Darlene asked the two men.

"I'll watch any guy in tight pants run up and down a field," Jimmy said.

Hugh gave Jimmy an admonishing look, but Natalie and her grandma howled with laughter.

Lindsey put a hand on her brother's shoulder. When he looked at her questioningly, she jerked her head toward the door. He got up and followed her out of the room.

"Want to take Willie for a walk?" At the word "walk," Willie jumped for his leash hanging by the door and tugged on it.

Matt overheard and said, "I'll take him, Mom."

"Thanks, but we want to get a little fresh air. It's hot in here."

"We do?" Hugh asked, looking back toward the cozy living room with its roaring fire.

"Yes," Lindsey persisted, making Willie sit so she could put the lead on him.

"Okay." Hugh took his jacket from the hall tree.

They went outside through the porch off the dining room. The room was cold and unfriendly this time of year, shut off from the heat of the house. However, in the spring, summer and fall, this was where she spent most of her free time.

"What's up?" Hugh's breath formed a little cloud when he spoke. "I bet I can guess."

"Go ahead," she said, "know-it-all."

"We're into name calling, are we?" He shoved his hands in his pockets and pulled up his collar. A cold wind bore down on them out of the north. "You want to talk about Sarah Gilbert. Have you seen her?"

She told him, leaving out the intimate details. "I can't get her or what happened out of my mind. I live in a dream world."

"I noticed," he said. "It probably would have been better had you not seen her again, much less had sex with her, but you did. It's hard to deny your sexual orientation."

Lindsey looked around to make sure there were no prying ears. "I'm not a lesbian," she said flatly.

"I think you just proved that you are, Lindsey. Be honest."

"Maybe I'm bisexual."

He shrugged. "I don't believe anyone's really bi. I think it's a cover to hide same-sex orientation, but I've been known to be wrong." He put an arm around her shoulders. "Are you going to see her again?"

"I don't know."

"Look. There are other women who might be better choices."

"What's the matter with Sarah?" she asked, shivering. Willie leaned toward the house, his ears floating in the wind.

"She'll cheat on you, Lindsey."

She stared at him. They were near a streetlight. Shadows played across his features. "I don't care. I'm not going to leave Gregg anyway."

"You want to have your cake and eat it, too, do you?" her

brother asked. "It won't work." He sighed as they started back. "I love you anyway, little sis. Remember that. I'll always be on your side."

"That's a comfort," she said. "If I get thrown out, can I come to you?"

"I'll help you find a place to live."

"Well, I'm not going anywhere." She meant it, but the conversation made her want to see Sarah again. One more time, she told herself. "Let's go have dessert." They had saved the pies and coffee for later in the evening.

"You just twisted my arm," Hugh said, taking hers and hurrying her toward the warm house.

Phil and Darlene flew back to Florida Sunday morning. Gregg and Lindsey took them to the airport in the van and drove home afterward.

"Want to go to the Y with me?" Lindsey asked, as they drove up the driveway.

"I thought maybe we could exercise between the sheets." He grinned at her.

"When I get back, I promise." She gave him a disarming smile and wondered if she would really go from one bed to the other. Could she be that despicable?

Matt had gone with Natalie to look at apartments in Centralia. The house was empty except for the dog, and Gregg looked sort of forlorn.

"Okay. Let's have at it." She couldn't go off and leave him like this.

They had always had a good sex life. His body—its odor and feel—was as familiar to her as her own. He knew how to please her and she him. When they were done, he rolled onto his back, and the sun streaming through the windows covered them. She pulled the blanket up and curled against him while he lazily scratched her back.

He would fall asleep, she knew. When he did, she slipped out of

59

bed and took a quick shower before pulling on jeans and a sweat-shirt. Her gym bag was in the van.

Parking around the corner from the bookstore, she walked quickly toward the building. There were a lot of vehicles lining the curb and in the small parking lot. Something was going on.

She opened the door carefully, to stifle the bell, and slipped into an empty chair. A woman, sitting at a table with books on it near the checkout counter, was reading poetry. She listened intently. The poem was about making love—legs and arms entwined, breasts and bellies touching, the feel of skin, the slipperiness and suck of sweat. It was very erotic, and she responded to it physically.

"Glad you came," Sarah whispered in her ear, and slid into the chair next to her.

A nearly painful electric-like charge shot through Lindsey, almost as if she'd touched a hot wire. Whatever the woman poet said after that, she missed. She was acutely and only aware of Sarah next to her, their arms and thighs lightly touching.

Sarah's breath felt warm on Lindsey's cheek. "Are you all right? Your face is flushed."

She nodded, her eyes on the woman poet. "Who is she?"

Sarah said her name, which Lindsey immediately forgot. "The books are for sale. We have a reading about once a month."

Lindsey attempted to listen, but her concentration was shot.

"It's good to see you," Sarah said quietly.

"Yes," she murmured back.

The poet signed her slim books while Sarah and some others folded chairs.

"Go buy a book," Sarah urged Lindsey. "Just don't leave. This place will clear out soon."

Lindsey tried to calm herself, to stop the pounding of blood. It was unhealthy, and she was too old for someone to affect her this way.

The woman poet, whose name NoraLeigh was one word, asked her how she liked the reading.

"Very much." There were many questions she wanted to ask,

like how long it took her to write a poem, was it hard to get it published, did it pay well. She didn't ask any because there were people waiting in line.

She picked up the slim volume and found a chair to sit on while she paged through the poetry. She knew she'd have to hide the book. It was too sensual, but it was the sensuality that held her attention.

When she looked up, she noticed that the people in the bookstore weren't thinning out very fast. They stood or sat in groups, talking and drinking coffee. When NoraLeigh left, though, it was as if they all decided it was time for them to go, too.

She glanced at her watch, and saw that it was three. She'd have to leave. Getting up, she started toward the door. Sarah stopped her.

"Where are you going?"

"I have to go home."

"Not yet. Come on." She led Lindsey toward the stairs.

Feeling eyes on her, Lindsey flushed, but she couldn't walk away, even though she knew she'd have no excuse for being so late. She felt momentary resentment that she had to account for her time.

Upstairs, the sun flowed through the windows, light without heat. Lindsey stood in the sitting room, still wearing her jacket and gloves, carrying the book of poetry under her arm.

"There isn't time for . . ." she faltered, unable to finish the sentence.

Sarah faced her, hands on hips, her grin crooked, sexy. "We'll make it quick." She winked at Lindsey and closed the distance between them. "I know you want it. I can see it in your eyes."

She let Sarah lead her to the bedroom and undress her, this time folding her clothes neatly on a chair.

"You have a beautiful body," Sarah murmured. "Do you know that?"

Lindsey shook her head. "Yours is better," she said in a throaty voice unlike her own.

Sarah laughed. "Is this a contest?" she asked, pulling back the covers.

Lindsey sat on the bed, one arm covering her breasts, one hand over her crotch.

"I've seen you already. You don't have to hide yourself." Sarah carelessly dropped her clothes on the floor. "Come on, get under the covers. I'll warm you up." Slipping into the bed, she wrapped Lindsey in her arms. She kissed her on the shoulder, the neck, the cheek and eyes and nose, the mouth. Her tongue touched the end of Lindsey's. "You are the best kisser."

The touch of tongue released Lindsey from her inhibitions. Her passionate response surprised even her. They rolled back and forth across the bed, first one on top, then the other—until Lindsey could no longer hold back.

After, Sarah rose on an elbow and smiled lazily at Lindsey. "Sure you haven't had a woman before?"

"Never." She glanced at her watch, saw it was slightly after four, and leaped from the bed. "I have to go."

"Okay." Sarah got up herself. "See you next Sunday?"

"I don't know."

"Try?"

Lindsey nodded. Dressed and out the door, she hurried down the stairs.

Sarah's voice followed her. "You forgot your poetry book. I'll save it for you."

Outside, she nearly ran to her car and drove home too fast. She worried that she smelled of sex, that Gregg would notice. Arriving home, she saw with relief that the truck the kids had driven was still gone.

The television in the living room was tuned to some football game. Hurrying to the bedroom, she locked herself in the bathroom and took a quick shower.

When she came out, Gregg was sitting on the bed. Her heart twisted. "Where did you go besides the Y?"

"A bookstore," she replied, turning her face away.

"I went to the Y when I woke up. You weren't there."

"What time was that?" she asked, pulling on clean jeans and a sweatshirt. She sat beside him to put on socks.

"Two-thirty." She felt his eyes on her.

She couldn't meet his gaze. "I didn't know you were going there. I would have stayed."

"I read that people who suddenly begin exercising are probably having an affair."

Her stomach churned, her heart raced. "I don't get much exercise now that we're not busy."

He stood up, still looking at her. "Want a drink?"

"Yes. Where are the kids?"

"They took some stuff to Natalie's new apartment."

So they'd come home while she was gone. Feeling out of touch and guilty, she said, "She's moving out?"

"Yes. I'll go fix drinks."

"Thanks." She returned to the bathroom to blow dry her hair. Wiping the steam off the mirror, she noticed her lips, slightly swollen and red.

In the kitchen, Gregg put her vodka and tonic on the table and sat down with his. "I want to tell you something."

She wasn't cut out for cheating, she thought. She'd end up with a heart attack or an ulcer.

"You don't have to tell me where you're going," he said. When she opened her mouth to protest, he raised a hand. "Just don't lie. It harms all of us." His tone became upbeat. "I stopped and bought steak for supper. I'll grill it. You can do the side dishes."

Tears clogged her throat, preventing her from speaking.

X

At Applebee's on Tuesday, she watched nervously as Carol walked toward her booth. She'd been prepared to level with her friend, but now was having second thoughts.

"Just like old times," Carol said, sliding in across from her, and Lindsey smiled in reply.

They ordered coffee and the waitress left them with menus.

"You know, it's really good to be able to talk to you, knowing you won't pass on anything I tell you," Carol continued.

It occurred to her that Carol might be trying to prime her into talking. No matter. She couldn't bring herself to admit to betraying Gregg for a woman. However, that wasn't what Carol had in mind.

"My son's screwing around with his girlfriend. She's eighteen, too. I know I can't stop them, but I'm terrified she's going to get pregnant, and he'll never finish college."

"Do you like her?" Lindsey said, knowing that wasn't the point, but surprised by the unexpected turn of conversation.

"I do. We do. We just don't want him to marry so young. Teddy says she's on the pill, but she's the one in control. I suggested he use condoms. He won't, I know."

Lindsey fell silent, thinking about Natalie and Matt and how lucky she and Gregg had been so far.

"It makes me frantic," Carol added.

Carol's son had taken accelerated courses in high school. He was planning to major in physics. His girlfriend was going to the same school.

"I'll bet," Lindsey said, covering Carol's hand with her own. She felt guilty for feeling somewhat relieved. Her plate was full of her own misdeeds.

The waitress took their orders, salads for both, filled their coffee cups, and left.

Carol sighed. "Theo offered to send Teddy to MIT. Of course, he won't go without his girlfriend." With a scoffing laugh, she said, "Megan said if we're willing to send Teddy to MIT, she'd like to go to UCLA."

"It'll be another year before she goes anywhere," Lindsey pointed out.

"I know. We'll worry about that then. She's not serious about anyone anyway." Carol looked at her over the brim of her coffee cup. "You're so lucky. Your kids are out of college."

"True. Natalie has a job on the Centralia newspaper. She and Matt found her an apartment there Sunday."

"Good for her, but not so good for you, huh? You'll miss her."

"Yes," she said. She would, but Natalie wouldn't be looking over her shoulder. "I'm sorry about Teddy." She wondered how sexually active her own two children were. She had no illusions about whether they'd experimented sexually, but they'd never dated the same person for more than a few weeks. She gave up all thoughts about sharing her infidelity. It seemed irrelevant and selfish.

⁓

On Wednesday when she met with Kate, she told Gregg where she was going. He offered to come along.

"It's something I have to do alone." Instead of freeing her, his unquestioning acceptance was having an adverse effect. She felt more tied to him than ever.

She told Kate that he was too good for her.

"My guess is he doesn't want to lose you."

"How could I leave now?"

"Do you want to?"

"No. I don't know what I want anymore. I can't stay away from Sarah, and I can't leave Gregg. I'm too old for this."

"You're too old to feel desire and loyalty?" Kate asked.

"You make it sound almost respectable."

"I wouldn't go that far, but often the most respectable people have never been tempted."

"And sometimes they're respectable because they're decent," Lindsey said.

"It's very hard to deny one's sexual orientation once you've let it out of the bag. It's like being starved for years and suddenly being offered a feast. Are you going to eat or walk away?"

"I wasn't starved," she said indignantly. "Gregg and I have a good sex life."

"Tell me what it's like with Sarah. Was it ever as exciting with Gregg?"

"No," she said sadly, "but that's no reason to cheat on him."

"Do you think you can stop this thing with Sarah?"

"Not yet," she said honestly.

"Do you think Gregg wants to know?"

"No." It seemed so unfair.

She grocery shopped and then went home to an empty house. Not even Willie greeted her. He must be with Gregg or Matt. She was putting together lasagna when the phone rang from the winter shop.

"Mom, some woman named Sarah has been trying to reach you." Matt gave her the bookstore's phone number. "It's something about a book."

"Thanks, Matt. I thought you were starting at Kohl's today."

"Tomorrow. I thought I'd be helping Natalie move today."

"You're moving the rest of her stuff on the weekend, right?"

"Yep. She's worried about you, Mom. I told her you're a big girl."

She laughed. "Worried about what?"

"She wouldn't say."

"Sounds serious."

"I gotta go. Someone just came in. What? Hang on, Mom. It's this Sarah. Should I send her to the house?"

"No. Tell her I'll call when I have time." Her heart took off running again. It wouldn't do for Sarah to show up at the house whenever she wanted to.

"You don't have time, Mom? What are you doing?"

"I'm busy, Matt. I don't want just anyone coming here. Tell her I'll call."

"Okay. Later." He hung up.

The doorbell rang as she was putting the lasagna noodles in the boiling water. "Fuck!" she said, sucking her fingers.

The bell rang again, and she went to answer it with her hand wrapped in a cold dishrag. Sarah stood in the opening.

"What's wrong with your hand?"

"I burned it when you rang the doorbell. I told Matt to tell you I'd call." Her voice shook with anger.

"I didn't want to wait. I was here. Can I come in?"

"No." She stepped outside and closed the door behind her. It was a cold gray day, and she wrapped her arms around herself.

"If you call me on my cell phone, I'll leave." Sarah handed Lindsey a card.

She went back to the kitchen. The water was boiling again. Turning it down, she set the timer before calling the number on the card.

67

Sarah answered immediately.

"Don't do that again," Lindsey said.

"Why not? It's okay for you to drop in at my place when you feel like it, but it's not all right for me to come to yours."

"I won't come then. You can't just show up here. I told you I'm married."

"So, what do you want with me?" Sarah asked.

It was a legitimate question. "I don't know. I'll stay away. It's better that way."

"No, it's okay. Truce. When you feel like it, come to the bookstore. I won't bother you at home."

"Thanks," she said. The door opened, and she spun.

It was Matt, who stuck his head in the fridge.

"I'll talk to you later." She hung up, and shoved the card into her pocket.

"Who is Sarah?" Matt asked, cutting a chunk off a piece of cheddar cheese. He alternated bites of it with an apple. "Where'd you meet her?"

"Here," Lindsey said, studying her tall son. He was a handsome sight, even in baggy jeans and sweatshirt. Although his hair was cut short, it curled, and his long sideburns reached below his ears. Young people often wore their hair in bizarre styles. At least his was its natural color.

"What did she want?" He slumped in a kitchen chair, his large booted feet sticking out from under the table. How did they both get to be so tall, she wondered. Gregg wasn't quite six feet, and she was probably less than five foot three. Natalie was nearly as tall as her father. Matt was at least six two.

Lindsey shrugged. "I don't really know." Another lie to add to the impressive stack.

"I think she's a lesbo."

Lindsey's pulse leaped. "Why would you make such an assumption? And the word is lesbian."

"She's interested in you, Mom. Just tell her you're a happily married woman."

She laughed, in spite of being so alarmed she could barely breathe. "Okay. I will if I see her again. I still want to know how you can tell someone's a lesbian."

"Vibes. Besides, Natalie said some lesbian was after you."

She turned her back to him. The noodles were more than done. She poured the water off into the sink, wreathing herself in steam.

"Well, I'm glad you two are watching out for me."

"Aw, Mom, we just love you." He put an arm around her and kissed her on the cheek. His charm had always worked its wonders on her, but this time she stiffened.

"I'm an adult, Matt, and your mother. Show me some respect." She felt like a hypocrite. Was Sarah's interest and her own so obvious?

She told this to Kate at their next meeting. The words poured out of her. "You and Hugh are the only people I can talk to about Sarah, and Hugh's not around. I sent Sarah away when she showed up at the house. The kids have guessed she's a lesbian and think she's after me." She sighed. "I hate all this lying."

"Didn't Natalie move out?"

"Yes, but she's not really moved yet. She'll probably come home weekends. I know I'm going to lose everything and everyone if I don't stop this, but come Sunday, the urge to go will be almost impossible to resist." She covered her eyes with one hand. "Maybe Sarah won't want to see me anymore. There must be a lot of women interested in her."

"Only you can decide if it's worth the risk, Lindsey."

"I thought you said it wasn't a choice."

"I said sexual orientation isn't a choice. I don't know if you can resist it or if you should. I know one woman who chooses to stay with her husband, even though he's a gay man and active sexually."

"Do they have children?"

"Yes."

"Do you know any women in my position?"

69

"No. They come to see me after the divorce to learn to live with their homophobia and guilt."

"Something to look forward to," she said gloomily. Divorce seemed too risky, too final. Besides, this thing with Sarah had just begun. She could end it.

All Things Considered was on the radio when she left, but only bits and pieces of it registered. She stopped at the grocery store to buy salmon, fresh green beans, red potatoes and a warm loaf of Italian bread to make Gregg's favorite meal.

When she pushed her grocery cart outside into the damp, overcast December day, she literally ran into Sarah, who stopped the cart with a hand.

"Excuse me," said someone behind her.

"We're blocking the door," Lindsey pointed out.

Sarah let go the cart and walked with Lindsey to the van. "Come home with me. It won't take long."

"I can't. I've got perishables."

"It's cold enough for them to sit in the car for a while. I'll ride with you." She got into the front seat when Lindsey unlocked the doors to put the bags inside.

"I need to go home," Lindsey said, her resolve faltering. "I'll come tomorrow."

"If you don't, I'll be at your door." Sarah got out of the car. "What time?"

"After work, after three."

"Okay. I'll be waiting." A crooked smile tugged at the corner of Sarah's mouth, crinkling the skin next to her bright blue eyes. "I'll make it worthwhile." She closed the door and pushed Lindsey's empty cart toward the store.

Waiting for the adrenaline rush to go away, Lindsey watched Sarah in the rearview mirror. Now there was no choice. If she didn't go, Sarah would come for her. Intense excitement gripped her. No one had ever been so insistent or demanding before. She wasn't fooled into thinking this was a good sign. She knew it smacked of harassment. She should be discouraging it. Instead, it aroused her.

Willie waited at the door, ecstatic to see her. "You'd think I'd been gone a week, instead of a day, you silly dog." She put down the groceries and picked him up. As always, bits of garden bark clung to his curly hair. "You're a mess." She picked a few pieces off him before he struggled to get down. "You need a bath."

She gave him a dog treat and put away the groceries before taking him into the bathroom. He saw the tub and turned to run, but she caught him, set him inside it, and turned on the water while holding his collar. "I know, I know," she crooned, "but doggie needs a wash."

Gregg walked in while she was carrying on this one-sided conversation. "How'd it go?" He smiled at the sight of Willie, wet and bedraggled and looking miserable. "Poor Wee Willie."

"All right," she replied, knowing he was referring to the session with Kate. "What time is it?" Her watch lay on the countertop.

"Five-thirty."

Willie shook, spraying the walls and Lindsey. "Hey, cut that out." She gripped his collar more firmly. "Time to get out."

Gregg handed her the towel on the floor. She hung onto Willie as he jumped out of the tub, and wrapped him in it.

She told Gregg what she'd bought for dinner. "Hungry?"

"I am now. Want me to dry him off?"

"Sure. Should we open a bottle of wine? Red or white?"

"Whatever you want," he said. "Hang on there, dogaroo. You can go in a minute."

Willie would run wildly around the house, shaking and rolling on the area rugs. She went to the kitchen where she wouldn't be sprayed.

After breaking the beans and putting the red potatoes on to steam, she glazed the salmon and placed it in the oven to bake. By then Gregg was there to open the wine and pour them each a glass.

"How was your day?" she asked, putting the beans into another steam basket.

"Productive. I worked on the skid loader. Eddie was in the winter shop. How was yours?"

"Same old, same old. Did Matt call?"

71

"Yep. He won't be home for supper. He's stocking shelves."

"Have you heard from Natalie?" Their daughter was staying at the new apartment, where she and Matt had taken a cot and sleeping bag and pillow, clothes for the week, a small TV, her computer and desk and a chair. They had made two trips late Sunday.

"Nope."

"I suppose that's a good sign," she said. It would mean Natalie was settling into her new life.

XI

The day at work seemed endless. John spent most of the day on the factory floor. She brought the accounts up-to-date, took orders via e-mail, fax and phone, keyboarded John's dictation. She wondered why she stayed at a job that now seemed so monotonous.

She left at three, wondering how she was going to get through all the tomorrows of winter.

She had told Gregg she would be home around five-thirty. Parking again around the corner from the bookstore, she hurried toward it with her head bent against the wind. For once she was not pressed for time, although she knew the hours would fly by without notice.

When she thought about this affair, it made no sense. Why would she chance losing her family for someone she didn't know, whose interest in her was probably passing? So instead of thinking about why she was involved with Sarah, she thought about what they did together.

The bell jangled as she entered. The smell of coffee greeted her. Lorrie was ringing up a sale and threw her a glance and smile. "Sarah's upstairs. I'll let her know you're here in a minute."

Lindsey's face flamed with embarrassment as the two women buyers turned to look at her. She remembered Matt's comment about lesbians, but she wouldn't have guessed the short, slender woman with a ponytail and a purse slung over her shoulder was gay. The other one, though, wore her hair in a crew cut, which wouldn't necessarily label her. Lindsey had met straight women with hair that short, but she knew no heterosexual women who shoved their wallets into their hip pockets, although that was not to say there weren't any.

When Sarah came toward her, she realized she'd guessed at their first meeting that she was a lesbian. Why? It wasn't the hair-cut—curly on top and down the back, sheared at the sides. Was it the athletic physique? Or the way she moved with almost no sway to the hips? Or was it the stance? Hands on hips or crossed arms, a cocky smile. It was more likely Sarah's interest in Lindsey that had clued her in.

It wasn't fair to categorize people. Did she herself look gay? Her hair was cut short—a thick, wavy, graying, dark cap. She wore slacks and a sweater and flats, work attire, and a leather jacket for warmth. Her purse was slung over her shoulder.

Sarah spoke to the customers, but didn't introduce them. When the two women left, she said, "I can't remember their names. That is so embarrassing." She turned toward Lorrie, who was busying herself at the computer. "We're going upstairs. If you need any-thing, don't call me." Then she laughed.

"Barb and Jody," Lorrie said.

Sarah slapped her forehead. "Of course. How could I forget? They come to all the readings." She smiled at Lindsey. "C'mon, woman. You look good enough to eat."

Lindsey thought of Gregg saying the same thing and flushed darker, as did Lorrie. Sarah took Lindsey's hand and started toward the stairs. "Time's wasting."

She noticed again that there were no books in Sarah's rooms. "How did you happen to start a bookstore?" Lindsey asked.

"It's my house, left to me by my grandpa. Your brother and Lorrie put up the money. They approached me. I said I could live on the second floor and help manage the place for a cut in the sales. I'm more like the advertising manager." Taking both of Lindsey's hands, she walked backward toward the bedroom.

As before, Lindsey was breathless with excitement. She moved as if without will, but inside she was alive with anticipation.

Sarah threw the stuffed animals on the bed onto the floor and began to undress Lindsey. Again, Lindsey stood motionless and let her. Somehow, it made her feel less culpable.

They were still standing when Sarah slid a hand between Lindsey's legs and began that slow caress that drove Lindsey wild with desire. She leaned her head back against the wall as Sarah kissed her neck and eyes and mouth. "Tell me you like it."

"Yes, I do."

The phone rang, startlingly loud, two, three times before Sarah picked it up. "What?" There was a pause while she listened, then said, "Look, I'm busy. Don't call me. It's over. Let it go." She hung up and detached the telephone cord from the wall.

"Where were we?" she asked with a grin, as if she'd forgotten. She lowered Lindsey onto the bed and took off her own clothes, dropping them on the floor.

Suddenly self-conscious, Lindsey slid under the covers. She shivered, but not from being cold.

"Don't hide. I love to look at you." Sarah stripped off her last piece of clothing and slid in next to Lindsey. "Have you lost your voice or something? You've hardly said a word."

"You're sort of overwhelming."

"Is that good or bad?"

"A bit intimidating."

Sarah laughed and laughed. "Nobody's ever said that to me before." She covered Lindsey's body with her own, holding Lindsey's forearms down. "Now I've got you where I want you."

Her blue eyes darkened, and Lindsey thought she saw the face of desire. She wondered if hers looked the same.

Lindsey moved under Sarah's touch and became frenzied under her mouth. There was a point when neither could hold back, when desire reached its highest point, leaving them gasping for breath as it began to ebb.

Sarah rolled off her and pulled the sheet and a blanket over them as they cooled. "This is not something I want to give up."

Lindsey glanced at her watch. It was quarter to five. She had to go, and began to slide out of the bed.

Sarah grabbed her, cupping her breasts. "Where are you going?"

"Home," Lindsey said, unable to pull free.

"Stay the night. I've got a couple of steaks in the fridge and a bottle of wine. I want to sleep with you."

Lindsey thought how nice it would be to not have to hurry home. What would she tell Gregg? She'd have to tell him something. "I can't."

Sarah released her, and she stood up. Sarah watched, her arms behind her head, and Lindsey felt shy about her nakedness.

"Feel free to take a quick shower."

"I will, thanks." There might not be time to shower at home before seeing Gregg. She was thankful for the chance to wash off.

Sarah was holding a towel when Lindsey stepped out of the shower. "When will I see you again?" she asked, drying Lindsey off.

"I don't know." Lindsey hurriedly pulled on her clothes.

"Better dry your hair."

She saw her flushed face in the mirror.

"Call my cell phone number," Sarah said.

Natalie phoned around seven that evening. "It's okay," she said when her mother asked her how she liked working at the paper. "Actually, it's not the most exciting job."

"It's a start," Lindsey said.

"Give it time," Gregg added from the phone in the living room.

"I will." She sounded a little annoyed at the parental advice.

"Are you coming home this weekend?" her dad asked.

"Yes. Saturday afternoon. I have to pick up more clothes. You and Mom could drive back with me on Sunday and see the place."

Lindsey pushed away her first thought, that she wouldn't see Sarah, and said enthusiastically, "Sounds like a plan."

"Sure does," Gregg added. "Can't wait to see you, honey."

She was at work the next day when Sarah phoned. "Hi. Are you busy?"

"I'm at work. That means my time isn't my own."

"You haven't called."

"I just saw you yesterday afternoon. My daughter's coming home this weekend to get some of her things, and we're driving back with her on Sunday to see her apartment."

"So I won't see you over the weekend. How about this afternoon or tomorrow?"

"I can't. I'm busy." It was a lie. She planned to Christmas shop when she left work. That's what she'd told Gregg that morning.

"Let's go away for a weekend. Aren't there any conferences you go to?"

"No."

John came to the door of his office.

"I've got to go. My boss needs me." She hung up.

"There's an order here I don't understand. Will you explain it to me?"

She followed him into his office and looked at the order, which she'd taken by phone. She couldn't make sense of it either. "I'll call." There was a number on the order form.

"Are you all right, Lindsey?"

Did her anxiety show? Her lack of concentration certainly did. "I'm okay. I'm sorry, John. I'll straighten this out."

"I know you will," he said.

She gave him a strained smile, and taking the form, she left his office.

77

It wasn't hard to find out how the order should have been written. She took it back to John. He was a short, portly man, kind and decent. As with everyone else these days, she wondered what he would think about her behavior. She knew she wouldn't be able to face him if he found out.

"Thanks. This must be a pretty boring job for you."

"No. I'm glad to have it," she said. She'd need it if she had to leave home.

She meant to go to Kohl's Department Store when she left work, but found herself driving to the bookstore instead. She pulled up across the street and sat there, chewing on her lip, wondering why she was there when she'd planned to go elsewhere.

After a few moments, she got out of the van. The wind tunneled down the street, and she hurried across, pulling her leather jacket close. Inside, warmth and the smell of coffee engulfed her. A few people browsed the shelves. They turned to look at her, and returned to the books.

Lorrie was making coffee. "Want some?" she asked with a smile.

"Sure. It's cold out there." She sat on a stool.

"Sarah's not here." Lorrie's level blue-gray gaze studied Lindsey from beneath dark curling lashes that nearly brushed her wire-rimmed glasses.

"I didn't expect her to be. I'm going shopping. I don't really know why I'm here."

Lorrie poured two cups of coffee and set one in front of Lindsey. "I'll keep you company." Her movements were economical and graceful. Her thick, coppery colored hair was pulled back in a ponytail, accentuating high cheekbones. Freckles dotted her nose.

When two of the women who had been browsing came to the front with books, Lorrie went to check out their purchases. She chatted to them as if they were old friends.

Lindsey felt foolish, sitting alone as if waiting for someone. For Sarah. She began to wonder where Sarah was, but decided against asking. It was none of her business. She had no hold on Sarah, or

Sarah on her. She put down more than enough to pay for the coffee and headed toward the door.

"Leaving?" Lorrie called out.

"Yes. Thanks, Lorrie."

"See you next time."

Kohl's parking lot was already crowded when she got there. Forced to park at the far end of a line of cars, she walked through the icy wind to the entrance. Calling Gregg on the cell phone, she left a message telling him to call if he wanted to meet her at Chef Hunan for supper.

The cell phone rang while she was looking at sweaters. "Gregg?" she said.

"Nope. Sarah," came the answer.

"How did you get this number?" She didn't remember giving it to her. Gregg used the cell phone more than she did.

"It's in your address book."

"When did you see my address book?"

"It fell out of your purse last time you were here."

She tried to recall where she'd dropped her purse, but couldn't. Sarah must have found the book when she was in the shower. It made her nervous to think of Sarah going through her things. "Gregg uses this phone. I'm waiting for his call." And then in spite of intending not to, she asked, "Where were you this afternoon?"

"Out with a friend."

"Anyone I know?"

"Our poet. Why?"

"I was at the bookstore."

"I know. Lorrie told me."

"I've got to go. I'm waiting for a call from Gregg." Jealousy churned inside her, both appalling her and making her angry.

Gregg phoned shortly afterward. They agreed to meet at six-thirty.

XII

"Did you find any buys?" Gregg dipped a tuna sushi in mustard sauce and took a bite. Eyes watering, he grabbed his water glass.

She watched with a wry smile. "You know how hot that sauce is."

"I forget," he said when he could talk again.

"Mostly I just looked at things. There were some great bargains, though. Somebody isn't making much money. Seems like everything is from China these days."

"We're flying to Florida. We can't take a lot with us."

"There isn't going to be a lot. The trip is the big present."

"What little present would you like?" he asked.

She dipped her sushi into soy sauce. Whenever anyone asked her what she wanted, she always met up with a blank. "I can't think of anything."

"Neither can I," he said, "unless it's a swimsuit. Mine's a little faded. And maybe some sandals," he added. "And, of course, you."

He studied her out of the same dark blue eyes he had passed on to their children.

She looked away. "You have me. We're married."

"Yes," he said, picking up another bit of deep fried crabmeat, his gaze boring into her. "Are you happy, Lindsey?"

"Don't ask me questions like that, Gregg. No one's happy all the time."

"Where do you want to go on our winter trip? I've heard good things about the Dominican Republic."

She hadn't given it any thought. All her energy had been going to Sarah. It took a real effort not to meander into daydreams about their afternoons together. She sometimes ran her hands over herself to see what Sarah felt when she touched her. She remembered all too well the feel of Sarah. "You choose."

"There are all-inclusive resorts in the Dominican Republic, five-star resorts that only cost nine hundred a week apiece, including the flight. All the food and drink you want, when you want it. I picked up some brochures from Apple Vacations." He pulled them out of the inside pocket of his jacket and spread them on the table.

The bright colors jumped out at her. She wondered what it would be like to spend a week at one of these places with Sarah. She pushed the disloyal thought away. It would never happen, unless she left Gregg. No one was free, least of all herself. She was tied to this marriage in so many ways, and she shuddered at the thought of her children finding out her secret.

Looking through the pamphlets, she tried to show interest. It would be nice to get away. Maybe she could rid herself of this obsession. That's what it was, she thought. It dominated her waking thoughts.

Gregg smiled. "What do you think, honey?"

The plate of sushi was gone. The waiter brought them each another glass of wine and their first course. She spooned up the wonton soup. "You pick the resort. My only condition is that it be on the ocean."

"How about the second week in February?"

"That should be all right," she said. Sitting in the hot shade, reading, swimming in the ocean, eating good food and drinking pina coladas appealed to her. She had always loved the smell, the sight and the sound of the ocean. Breakers rolling in and breaking on the beach, walking on the sand, looking in tidal pools at the life left behind by the retreating tide.

"The Dominican Republic is known for its rum and its coffee." He sounded happy.

She smiled back. This was the boy she had liked so much in college, the man she had come to love over the years. He was her best friend, the father of her children and right now he was desperate to please her. She ached for him, for herself, for what was happening to them, to her.

The waiter set their dinners down and removed the soup bowls. She had ordered pork with vegetables. Gregg had chosen pan-fried noodles with shrimp, chicken and mixed vegetables. They shared their food, eating quietly for a few minutes.

"Do you want me to make the reservations?"

She looked up with a frown. What reservations? Then remembered, the Dominican Republic. "Sure, or you can give me the information, and I'll do it."

"I'll do it," he said quickly. "It'll be nice to have some time alone together."

She was seized with jealousy every time she thought of Sarah with NoraLeigh. The sexual images from the poetry reading became embodied as Sarah and NoraLeigh in her mind. She pictured them naked, breasts and bellies pressed together in sweaty embrace, mouths and hands exploring. It drove her wild, making concentration impossible.

After work she drove home, changed her clothes, and went to the winter shop that Eddie was manning. He looked bored. "You can leave if you want, Eddie."

"I've got some errands to run," he said, his homely face lighting up as he smiled.

She sat behind the checkout counter with a crossword puzzle. Snow began to fall, and tiny, wind-driven particles rattled the windows. The shop was heated by baseboard electricity. She dressed warmly when she was there.

Looking around at the Christmas cacti, the poinsettias and other plants, she wondered why they had never put up a tree. They could sell the ornaments used to decorate it. She would say something to Gregg. Maybe she should work more at the nursery. Gregg would love that. There was no need for her to have an outside job now. Most of her salary went into a retirement fund.

She could quit her job and never tell, too. That would free her to see Sarah during those hours. No one would be the wiser, unless Gregg called the brass factory, but he never called.

Daylight was gone when Gregg showed up. She was still working the crossword.

"Want to go out for fish?" he asked, snow glistening on his dark hair.

"Let's." She made her suggestion about the tree.

"Sounds like a good idea for next year. We'd have to find a source for the ornaments, but that should be easy."

Gregg and Eddie had put white lights on the trees along the driveway after Thanksgiving. They gave the place a tastefully festive appearance.

Lindsey made Natalie's favorite meal Saturday—pork tenderloin, mashed potatoes, gravy and a spinach salad. Natalie talked about her job and the people she'd met. Her apartment building was across the street from a park, part of which had been flooded for a skating rink. She planned to take her ice skates back with her. When she was younger, she had taken lessons. She'd been good enough to skate competitively, but had lacked the passion to practice. She skated for fun.

"Sounds great," Matt said. "I'll bring my skates when I come. We can chase a puck around." He had been on the hockey team in high school.

"Sure, it's kind of lonely there right now."

Lindsey listened without adding much to the conversation. She had always loved hearing her kids talk about their lives. She glanced at Gregg at the end of the table. He smiled and lifted his wine glass to her as if to commend them on their offspring.

Matt and Natalie went out with friends later in the evening, leaving about the time she and Gregg were getting ready for bed.

The next day Gregg and Lindsey followed Matt in the truck and Natalie in her Honda Civic to Centralia. Willie rode with Natalie. The back of the van was filled with Natalie's clothes and the drawers from her dresser. Her mattress and bed and the rest of the dresser were in the back of the pickup. They had no room for the couch or the table and chairs stored in the basement. Matt would take them over during the week.

The newer, brick apartment building was made up of twelve units. The tenants had keys to the inside door. Speakers with buzzers lined the entryway under the mailboxes.

They carried the furniture and clothes up the stairs to Natalie's second-floor apartment and arranged everything to her liking. Then they took a walk in the park. The day was bitterly cold, and they hurried back to the apartment after a half hour had passed. Before driving home, Gregg and Lindsey took Natalie and Matt out to eat at Applebee's. On the way, their daughter showed them the newspaper office and the rather abysmal downtown.

"Everyone shops at the mall," Natalie said.

The oncoming headlights on the way home put Lindsey to sleep. Her forehead bounced lightly against the cold glass, keeping her level of consciousness just under the waking point. Gregg had put a Chris Botti CD in, and a trumpet wailed in the background of her slumber. When they hit a bump, she awoke.

"Sorry," Gregg said. "Are you all right?"

"Yes. Where are we?"

"Close to home." It was only a forty-five minute drive. "I felt good about the apartment. Did you?"

"Yes. It's secure and in a nice location, and it's pleasant. So many apartment buildings are dark and smell of food." It was the kind of place she would look for if she had to leave.

"Exactly," he said. They turned into the driveway with Matt and Willie in the truck behind them.

It was only nine o'clock, but she was as exhausted as if it were after midnight. She took a couple of ibuprofen and went to bed.

Even so, she slept lightly. She'd decided to give John two weeks notice at work tomorrow. It would free her during the week, but only if Gregg thought she was still working. She'd have to get up, dress like she was going to work, and leave at the same time as she always had. A dangerous deception, easily exposed.

XIII

The next morning she arrived at the factory early enough to write her letter of resignation before John walked in.

She handed it to him when he paused at her desk. "It's time to do something different."

He reacted characteristically, telling her he understood. He would put an ad in the newspaper. She promised to stay on till he found a replacement. He went into his office, and she felt both terrible and relieved.

Before she left work, though, he made an offer. "What if we just cut your hours? Think you can manage the office working three six-hour days a week instead of five? I may need you a few hours more at the end of each month, though. Think it over." He disappeared into his office.

She thought about five minutes, and then told him she'd give it a try. They decided on Monday, Wednesday and Friday starting the next week. She left the office with a feeling of exhilaration. She would still be working, just less hours. No one would be hurt by this change. She could see more of Sarah without having to lie. And maybe she wouldn't lose her to someone like NoraLeigh.

Sarah's wagon was parked next to her van in the lot. She unrolled her window. "Get in. I want to talk to you."

Lindsey's pulse quickened, warming her. She opened the passenger door and slid inside. "What are you doing here?"

"I haven't seen you since last week."

"I'll only be working Mondays, Wednesdays and Fridays starting next week," Lindsey said. "You can see me then."

A smile spread across Sarah's face, showing the tiny gap between her teeth. "You did that so you could see more of me?"

Lindsey nodded.

"Next Tuesday's a long way off," Sarah said. "Can you come before then?"

Lindsey chewed on her lip. "I'll try. Maybe Saturday."

"Saturday is five days away," Sarah said. "Let's just go have a cup of coffee. That's not a crime, is it?"

"I have to be home by five-thirty." They had leftovers from Saturday's meal, which meant she didn't have to cook.

She followed Sarah to the bookstore. There, she sat on a stool at the counter, while Lorrie poured her a cup of coffee.

"Come on," Sarah said. "You can drink your coffee upstairs."

Lindsey smiled apologetically at Lorrie. "Where's yours?" she asked Sarah.

"I don't want one."

"We're going to talk. Remember?"

But, of course, they didn't just talk. When they were upstairs alone, Sarah took the cup of half drunk coffee out of Lindsey's hands.

Lindsey glanced at her watch. It was quarter to four. Maybe there was time.

"We'll make it quick," Sarah assured her, kissing her as she backed into the bedroom with Lindsey in tow.

When it was over, Lindsey took a hasty shower. Sarah warmed her coffee in the microwave and took it to the bathroom.

"Now you can drink it," she said with a lazy smile.

She took a gulp, scalding her mouth. "Goddamn!" she said. It was now five. If she hurried, she'd be home by five-thirty.

She and Carol sat across the booth from each other, sipping coffee over lunch the next day.

"What's going on, Lindsey?" Carol looked at her intently.

"What makes you think something's going on?" she asked, wondering why she cared if Carol found out? Carol would never tell.

"You're different."

"How am I different?"

"Forget it." The waitress brought their sandwiches and more coffee. "I'm not playing this cat-and-mouse game. If you don't want to tell me, don't. I'm just consumed with curiosity."

She opened her mouth to talk, and couldn't. "I'm seeing the counselor."

"Is she helping you?"

Was she? "Yes. I think so." She would see Kate tomorrow. It seemed like they went over the same territory every time. "Natalie came home to get the rest of her things Saturday, and we drove over to see her place on Sunday. It's nice. She seems happy."

"And Matt?"

"Well, he's working part time at Kohl's." She shrugged. "He wants to work for the DNR, but they're laying off people, not hiring. Maybe he'll stay on. Gregg needs him during the busy season." She wanted to turn the spotlight away from herself. "And you and Theo and the kids?"

Carol smiled. "Trying to change the subject?"

"Yes. Are you ready for Christmas?"

"As ready as I can be. Teddy's girlfriend is coming after Christmas for a few days. He wants her to sleep with him. Should we let them? That's the conflict right now. There's Megan to think about. She doesn't need to be exposed to her brother's sex life."

Matt's girlfriends had bunked with Natalie and Natalie's boyfriends had slept in Matt's room, but neither Matt nor Natalie had insisted differently. "Put her in the guest room if you're not comfortable with them sharing a room. They'll probably end up in Teddy's room anyway, but you won't have compromised your principles."

"What principles? Theo and I were sleeping together before we married."

"So, do whatever you're comfortable with."

"We need the guest room, but we could put Diane in with Megan."

"You could. It's such a farce, isn't it?"

"Yes." Carol looked away. "If they didn't hang on each other like they were grafted together, I could tolerate it better."

Lindsey laughed. Her back was to the door, and Sarah caught her by surprise when she appeared at the table with NoraLeigh. A blush suffused her body. Even her eyes felt hot. She stammered an introduction.

Sarah nodded at Carol. NoraLeigh shook hands. The two women moved on to another table.

When Lindsey looked back at Carol, she saw the astonishment on her face. "Are you all right, Lindsey? You're so flushed."

Lindsey dropped her eyes to the table. Her appetite was gone. She felt nauseated. "I'm all right."

"Are you good friends with those women?"

"With Sarah, yes. I met NoraLeigh at her poetry reading."

"Where?" Carol asked.

She felt the flush draining away, and raised her eyes. "At a bookstore."

Carol stared at her for a moment, her sandwich hanging between her fingers, apparently forgotten. "I'm so dumb," she said.

"No, you're not."

"I never guessed."

"Why would you? But are we talking about the same thing?"

"You can tell me anything," Carol said. "Only torture would get your secret out of me."

"I feel like I should tell Gregg first."

"Does he want to know?"

"He said rather than lie, it was better not to tell him where I was going. I've been lying a lot lately."

"You've been going to see Sarah?" Carol asked.

Lindsey nodded. "Starting Monday I'm only working three days a week. I haven't told Gregg that either. Kate said sometimes people manage to stay married when one of them is gay." There, she'd said the word. She'd implicated herself.

"You want to stay married?"

"I can't tell the kids." She shivered. "They'll detest me. I disgust myself. This sneaking around is so deceitful."

"Is it your actions that disgust you or the thought of being a lesbian?"

"Both. You sound like Kate."

Carol covered Lindsey's hand with her own. "Your kids will forgive you. You've been a good mother. And I love you, sweetie. No matter what."

"Thanks," she said wryly. "You're not afraid of me?"

"It's not catching," Carol said with a short laugh. She glanced at her watch. "Time to go. I'll take my sandwich with me."

As she left with Carol, Lindsey caught Sarah's gaze, but only nodded a good-bye.

In bed that night she felt the heat radiating from Gregg's body. He was propped up on pillows, reading, and she reached out and touched his arm. The muscles bunched under her hand.

He turned toward her.

"Why did you say I didn't have to tell you where I was going?"

"Did I say that?"

"Yes."

"Maybe I didn't want to know."

"Why?" she asked anxiously.

"I didn't want you to lie. I've done that, and I hated it. You do what you have to, Lindsey. I'll be here." He sounded angry.

He must think she was having a fling and, when it was over, it would be as if nothing had changed.

"Besides, I know where you go. I followed you."

Horrified, she asked, "When?"

"Yesterday. I was going to pick up a part, and there you were a few cars in front of me. I'm not proud of it. I tailed you to that bookstore."

"You didn't say anything." She tried to remember how he'd acted when she came home last night. She hadn't noticed any change.

"I didn't know what to say. I still don't. I wish I hadn't seen you. I don't want to talk about it."

"I don't want a divorce," she whispered.

"Neither do I. Do you think it's a passing phase?"

"I don't know," she said, although she doubted it. "You won't tell the kids?"

He snorted. "I'd rather cut out my tongue."

Amazingly, she slept well. It was as if she could finally relax her vigil. She had worried so long about getting found out, and now she was, and there was only one worse thing that could happen.

She told Kate the next day. Three people knew, and she hadn't died of shame. "Do you think you and Gregg will be able to live together?"

"Not if the kids find out. And if I leave without telling them, they'll never understand. Either way they probably won't forgive me."

"Would it be better to tell them?"

"Are you serious? They'll think my marriage was a mistake, and so were they."

"Do you?"

"How can I when they came out of it?" she asked, annoyed by the questions.

"How do you feel about yourself?"

"Not good. I should have told Gregg I was attracted to women. I should tell the kids. Instead, I sneak around behind everyone's back."

"I wonder how many people are upfront when they want to leave a relationship? They often have an affair, forcing the issue."

But she hadn't wanted Gregg to find out and didn't want her marriage to end. What did she want?

"When I told Hugh I thought I might be bisexual, he said there was no such thing."

"Oh, I don't know," she said. "I think some people are bisexual. They sometimes use marriage as a mask, though, something to hide behind."

Lindsey stared at her. "I didn't marry Gregg for that reason."

"I know. You were in denial all these years. It's a common way of life. It shows how strong society's condemnation is."

She thought of the gatherings at the bookstore, small though they were. "The gay community is something of a subculture."

"Yes," Kate added, "tolerated as long as no one clamors for equal rights."

"They're clamoring now."

"As they should," Kate said. "It's hard enough to be in a minority, but when there's so little acceptance, it's no wonder so many hide their sexual orientation."

"It's not hard to hide when you look like everyone else."

"Perhaps to come out is to accept yourself."

She guessed she wasn't ready for that yet. She felt like a pariah.

XIV

Thursday morning Gregg told her he had hired a woman to run the winter shop, so that it could stay open.

"What about Eddie?"

"Eddie wants time off. He's in his sixties, Lindsey."

"Well, why don't you hire someone who can take his place?" They were eating breakfast. She was dressed for work.

"She can take his place for now. Are you of all people discriminating against women? Besides, Natalie won't be working here anymore."

"What's her name?" She realized she was jealous. "How old is she?"

"Her name is Toni Fields, and she's thirty-five. She's got a lot of ideas on how to make the winter shop profitable."

"I had some ideas. I told you about them. Have you forgotten?"

"No. I said we'd have to wait till next year. Remember?" he said sharply.

"Is she married?"

"Divorced." He raised his dark blue eyes to hers, and she saw anger in them.

"Great. Already you've got someone to take my place," she muttered, putting her bowl and plate in the dishwasher.

"You only work here part time," Gregg pointed out. "Speaking of work, I have to get out there. Eddie won't be here today."

They'd get along without her just fine, she realized. There were plenty of people to take her place.

When she came home from work, she went to the winter shop. A slim woman with light brown hair and eyes and a pleasant face greeted her. Her smile radiated warmth.

"Hi. Can I help you?"

Lindsey couldn't resist the smile. "I'm the boss's wife."

"Oops." The woman started to introduce herself.

"Gregg told me your name. Did he tell you mine?"

"I have a short memory. I'm sorry I forgot."

Lindsey guessed Gregg hadn't even told her he had a wife. "It's okay. I'm Lindsey." She shook hands. "I think you'll do well here. I hope you're not bored. This time of year I bring crossword puzzles and a book to read. Come spring you'll be too busy to do either."

"I love growing things."

"Then you're in the right place. Excuse me. I have to fix dinner."

She felt shut out and hurt. By hiring this woman, Gregg had told her she wasn't needed at the nursery. He'd be spending a lot of time with Toni Fields, time when she wasn't around. Well, that was okay, wasn't it? She was seeing Sarah. What did she expect?

"Hey, Mom. What's up?"

She hadn't heard the door open. "Not a thing," she said, "and you?"

"I didn't mean to scare you. See the chick Dad hired?"

"Her name is Toni Fields. She's not a chick."

"I guess she's too old to be a chick."

"Matt! Don't talk about her like she's a commodity. And thirty-five isn't old."

He sprawled in one of the kitchen chairs. "I have to stock shelves tonight after the store closes. Man, I hate that job."

"Why don't you start looking for work in your field?" She popped a baking pan with chicken legs and thighs in the oven and began cutting up potatoes for french fries.

"That's my favorite meal. Want some help?"

"I'd like an answer to my question."

"I have looked, Mom. The state is letting people go. I'm waiting to hear from this environmental consultant company in Madison. I'd have to move and wouldn't be able to help Dad at the nursery anymore."

"He'd get along."

"I know. He'd hire some high school or college kid to take my place. We're all expendable, aren't we? It's kind of sad."

"It's good. If someone couldn't take your place, you'd have to stay."

I guess. He put an arm around her. "What about you, Mom? Do you feel expendable?"

"No," she said, although she was feeling that way. "You can set the table and tell me what's going on in your life. What's the name of this consulting company?"

"Green Earth. Both of your nestlings will be gone if they take me on."

"Yes. Have you seen Teddy?"

"Not for a while. He doesn't come home on weekends. He and his girlfriend stick to each other like ticks on a dog. Don't mean to insult you, Willie. You don't have any ticks."

Willie lay in the middle of the floor, hoping some morsel would fall his way. His tail whacked the floor at the sound of his name.

"That conjures up a lovely image," Lindsey said.

"He's too young to be so involved. He'll never know freedom," Matt said in a spurt of wisdom.

"I'm glad neither you or Natalie got so attached while you were in school."

"I'm waiting for the right girl, so we can be like you and Dad—made for each other."

95

Appalled at his faith in her, she forgot which ingredient she'd put on the potatoes after the chili powder. Was it salt or cumin or garlic powder? The containers were lined up in a row. She guessed salt and added the others, then shook the bag with the potatoes in it.

"You and Dad made it when nearly all my friends' parents are divorced."

She couldn't bring herself to say they hadn't made it yet. "Carol and Theo are still married. Staying married if you're unhappy shouldn't be a goal."

"Aren't they happy, Theo and Carol?"

"Yes, as far as I know."

"You never know what goes on behind closed doors. Right?"

"That's for sure."

"Are you telling me something, Mom?"

If she had any courage, now was the time to tell him the truth. Instead, she laughed nervously. "No, honey." A telltale flush began to climb up her spine.

Apparently he didn't notice. "I'm going to catch the news."

"It's on public radio," she pointed at the radio on the counter. "You'll get more news in depth from *All Things Considered*." She sounded like a fundraiser.

"Yeah, but I want to watch the sports." He disappeared toward the living room, and she heard the sound of the TV.

Weak with relief, she guessed her kids didn't really want to know what was going on with her. Why would they? It would change their lives.

When the business phone rang, something made her snatch it up. "Lindsey speaking." She heard someone else pick it up elsewhere, then hang up. She assumed it was Toni.

"What are you doing?" Sarah asked.

"This is a business phone," she said. "I can't tie it up."

"You've never given me your home phone number. Isn't it time you do?"

"No. It's too risky." She cupped the phone between her hands, muffling it.

"Why? Can't I call as a friend?"

"It's better you don't."

"When will I see you?"

"Next Tuesday. I told you," she said, exasperated.

"Saturday, or I'll come and get you."

"I've got to go now."

"I mean it."

"Good-bye." She hung up and willed the phone not to ring. It did, almost immediately. She let someone else answer. When their private phone rang, she let Matt answer.

"It's for you, Mom."

She picked up.

"Your husband's much more accommodating. He gave me the number. Now I can call you whenever I want."

"I'm not coming Saturday."

"Then I'll come there."

"Go ahead." She would leave. She wouldn't be bullied like this.

Sarah's voice became silky smooth. "NoraLeigh doesn't play hard to get."

"Good. Then see her." A persistent beat hammered in her head. She hung up and leaned against the counter for a moment, then poured herself a drink.

Gregg didn't ask about the call at supper. His jaw tensed when he spoke at all. Matt filled in the silences.

"How did you find Toni? Did she walk in off the street or what?"

"She answered an ad. Eddie and his wife are going to Arizona for a couple of months."

"You should pay me more if he can afford to be gone that long."

"He's on retirement. He worked for the post office for thirty years."

Gregg excused himself after one helping and put his plate and glass in the dishwasher. He headed for the living room, and she heard the TV come on.

"I'll clean up, Mom. Is Dad all right?"

"You'll have to ask him. That's okay, Matt. I'll finish up here."

Matt went to the living room, too. She heard him talking to his father.

On Saturday, Lindsey drove to the mall, someplace she always avoided on weekends because of the crowds. She was looking for Christmas presents that wouldn't take up much space and was standing at the jewelry counter in Younkers when Sarah appeared beside her.

"Aren't I lucky? Here you are, the needle in the haystack." Sarah looked pleased with herself.

Stunned to see her there, Lindsey said nothing.

"When you're through shopping, let's go to my place for a late lunch."

A heavily madeup sales clerk looked them over and asked, "Can I show you something?"

"Yes, that gold chain with the shamrock." Lindsey pointed.

The sales clerk took it out of the case. "Pretty, isn't it?"

"Yes. How much?"

"Well, it's fifty percent off today. That makes it seventy dollars."

"I'll take it." Natalie would love it.

She'd found a swimsuit and sandals for Gregg. Matt had dropped hints that he'd like a new portable CD player and carrier, small enough to carry around when he was working or exercising. She'd bought Gregg's parents gift certificates to Barnes and Noble, sure that there'd be a bookstore near their home.

The sales clerk offered to wrap the small package. While she waited, Sarah took the bag with her other packages from her. "Now you have to come with me."

Too embarrassed to put up a verbal battle in public, she said, "I will. Just give me the bag."

Sarah moved it out of reach. "When we get to the bookstore."

When faced with Sarah, she found herself unable to resist her. Sarah lifted her eyebrows and held the bag high when Lindsey lunged for it. Instead of the anger she'd felt on the phone at home, she laughed.

"Okay?" Sarah asked.

"Okay," she said, taking the wrapped package from the clerk and going with Sarah to the door. "Don't you have shopping to do?"

"I shop online."

At the bookstore, Sarah told Lorrie they were going upstairs. Sarah still held the bag.

Lorrie wasn't smiling. The store was busy. Lindsey thought Lorrie needed help, and said so.

"She'll be fine. That's her job, not mine. Come on." Sarah spoke to the customers as she headed toward the stairs. In the flat, she set the bag down and turned on the CD player.

Hands on hips, Sarah asked, "Why do you play hard to get?"

Instead of answering, she said, "Gregg followed me here the other day."

Sarah shrugged. "He would have found out sooner or later. It may as well be now."

Lindsey frowned. "You're compassionate."

"I'm not doing anything wrong."

Lindsey grabbed the bag and started toward the door, but Sarah blocked it with her body. "Get out of the way," she said, trying to ignore that now familiar thrill brought on when Sarah took charge.

Sarah stepped aside. Expecting to be stopped, Lindsey went down the stairs and out the door. No one followed her.

XV

They arrived at Phil and Darlene's condominium on Christmas Eve, having taken turns at the wheel and driven straight through. Gregg pulled up to the garage. The kids and dog slept in the back two seats, surrounded by luggage.

Gregg turned to Lindsey and covered her hand with his. "Let's have a good time."

"Of course we will," she said, closing her fingers over his.

His eyes were dark and unreadable, but he smiled and nodded as if he were answering some question he'd asked himself.

The heat rushed at them when they opened the windows and doors. "Wake up you two," Gregg called.

Natalie sat up, her eyes bleary with sleep, her hair matted on one side. "Hey, bro," she said, poking Matt.

The garage door opened and Phil and Darlene hurried out to greet them. "We were worried," Darlene said.

"Why?" Gregg hugged his mother.

"Because it's dangerous driving down here with all these seniors. They're either going thirty-five or ninety in a sixty-five-mile zone. Heaven forbid, they pay attention to the speed limit."

"I can't wait to put my swimsuit on," Natalie said.

Inside the condo, the cold air chilled Lindsey, who longed to throw open the windows. Instead, she helped her mother-in-law prepare hors d'oeuvres, which is what they ate on Christmas Eve. She urged Matt and Natalie to enjoy the sunshine by the pool. They would be flying back two days after Christmas. She and Gregg would stay on and start driving home New Year's Day.

Lindsey wondered what Sarah was doing for the holidays. She hadn't asked, hadn't seen or talked to her since she'd stormed out of the flat. It made her realize how little she knew about Sarah. Did she visit her parents, her brothers and sisters? Did she *have* parents and brothers and sisters? She and Sarah never talked. How could she miss so much someone she hardly knew?

"It's wonderful you came," Darlene said. She was putting the deviled egg mixture back in the whites.

"It's great to be here," Lindsey replied automatically. She was restless when she wasn't with Sarah, but she found no peace even then, only anxiety. It was as if she belonged neither with Sarah or Gregg.

They spent part of Christmas day at the National Seashore, stirring up all manner of birds in the backwaters where alligators lurked just under the surface, their snouts poking out.

Matt said he'd be happy working at a place like this. Lindsey preferred walking alongside the ocean, shoes in hand, waves washing her feet, sucking the sand out from under them.

After the kids left, Gregg played golf with his dad, while Lindsey read in the shade by the pool with Darlene. She found herself laying her book down often in order to remember behind hooded eyes her afternoons with Sarah. Mornings and evenings she drove to the beach to walk in the sand. At night, she and Gregg played bridge with Gregg's parents.

Before leaving, they spent one whole day by the ocean. Lindsey felt as if she'd been shrink-wrapped by the sun. She'd eaten too much, drunk too much and lazed around too much.

The drive home took close to three days, since they only had each other to spell. On the second day, Gregg asked her if she had made any plans that he should know about.

Startled into reality, she asked, "Like what?"

"Are you leaving?"

"No."

"Are you sleeping with that woman or what?" He threw a dark-eyed glance her way.

She cleared her throat, since nothing would pass through it. "I was."

"Have you been having affairs all along?" He sounded angry.

"No. Never. This is the first time."

"Maybe you should get it out of your system."

"What about our trip to the Dominican Republic? We've paid for it already."

They were speeding through the hills of southern Indiana. "We'll go. Then you can decide."

"Do you want me to leave?"

"No. God, no, but I can't live like this, sharing you with someone else. Why, Lindsey?"

"I don't know. I guess I was born this way."

"You could have fooled me," he said. "All these years . . ." His voice trailed away.

She patted her lap, and Willie jumped through the seats to sit on it. Burying her face in his coat, she hid the tears that were always so close to the surface these days.

An uncomfortable silence fell over them. Lindsey searched for a public radio station to break the tension. The Indiana country-side flattened after they passed through Indianapolis, and her spirits smothered under the brown and gray of the earth and sky.

They arrived home late at night. There were no messages on the machine, but there was a small package in the mail with the rainbow in the upper left-hand corner. The mail was stacked on the dining room table along with a note from Matt, saying he was stocking shelves at Kohl's.

Exhausted, Lindsey saved opening the mail for the next day. She would not open the package in front of Gregg, but it started a beat of excitement that kept her awake. She crept out of the bed after Gregg fell asleep and took the package to the kitchen.

Inside lay a small rainbow on a gold chain and a note that read: *Call me. I miss you.* She repackaged and readdressed the present and scribbled a reply: *I can't keep this.* She would mail it the next day.

Back in bed she stared at the shadows on the ceiling, Six weeks from now, they would leave for the Dominican Republic. She wished it were next week. She couldn't trust herself to stay away from Sarah.

The next day after work, she grocery shopped. When she was putting the groceries away, Hugh phoned. "You've been on my mind. How about an update?"

"We just got back from Florida, and next month we're going to the Dominican Republic."

"Tell me something interesting."

"Where are you?"

"Madison. I'm going to be in town tomorrow. Thought we could have lunch."

"I have lunch with Carol on Tuesdays."

"That's okay. I like Carol."

As soon as she hung up, the phone rang again. She grabbed it, knowing it would be either Carol or Sarah. It was Carol.

"Lunch tomorrow?" Carol asked. "It seems like you've been gone forever. Did you have a good time?"

"Yes, actually. How were your holidays?"

"Work. It always is when you have guests, but it was festive. We'll talk over lunch."

"Hugh is coming."

"Good. I look forward to seeing him."

The third ring she was sure would be from Sarah. Instead it was Natalie, wanting to know if they got home all right.

"We're here. We're safe. How's the job?"

"It's okay. I'm beginning to fit in. You know, I don't feel so much like the new kid on the block."

Gregg came into the room, and she put him on the line. When they sat down to eat, she told him she was having lunch with Hugh and Carol the next day. Did he want to come? He had just scooped up a fork full of fried rice.

"I can't. I'm going to the Landscaping and Nursery Conference in Stevens Point. I have to leave early."

"You never said anything about it."

"I didn't think you'd be interested."

"I've always gone in past years," she said.

"This year things are different," he pointed out. "Excuse me. I've got some things to do out in the workshop." He took his empty plate to the sink, rinsed it and put it in the dishwasher.

She finished her meal with only the radio for company, wondering if he felt as lonely as she did. When Gregg came in for the night, he stretched out on the couch in front of the TV. She sat in a chair and, after reading the newspaper, worked on the crossword puzzle.

"Are you staying overnight in Point?" she asked.

"Do you want me to?" He turned those dark eyes on her, and she saw only pain in them. She looked away.

"No, of course not. It's lonesome when you don't talk to me."

"What is there to say?"

"Is this the way it's going to be?" She felt tears crowding her eyes.

The business phone rang in the kitchen, and she froze.

"Aren't you going to answer it?" he asked.

"No." She fervently hoped it wasn't Sarah and if it was, that she wouldn't leave a message.

When it rang over and over, he got up and unhooked it from the wall.

The next morning she arose with Gregg at five thirty when the alarm went off. He said he was going to eat on the way, but she pulled on sweats anyway and saw him out. At the door, he turned and surprised her with a kiss. "I'll be late. Don't wait up."

Matt was sleeping upstairs, so she dressed as she would for work and left at the usual time. A cold north wind penetrated her jacket as she slid into the van. Gregg had taken the truck. Remembering she had a key to Hugh's apartment, she drove there, hurried inside, and turned up the heat.

Lying on the bed with a blanket over her, she read for about fifteen minutes before falling asleep. Her inner alarm awoke her at eleven thirty. She brushed her hair, put on lipstick and went out to meet Hugh and Carol for lunch.

They were already there when she arrived. She gave them both a hug and sat next to Carol, across from Hugh. The waitress brought coffee and they ordered.

"I guess we're all on the same page," Hugh said, jumping right in. "What is the status with Sarah, Lindsey?"

"No soft edges about you," she said.

Carol took Lindsey's hand. "If you don't want to talk, it's okay, sweetie."

She kept her eyes on her coffee. "There's nothing to talk about. I walked out on her before Christmas and haven't gone back, but now Gregg knows. He's quiet and unhappy and sort of surly. I'm having trouble living like this." She chanced a glance at Hugh. "I went to your apartment this morning. This is one of the two days I don't work, and there was no place else to go."

"I thought you cut your hours so that you could see Sarah," Carol said.

"I did."

"That is sneaky, sis," Hugh interjected.

"I'm not the one with a secret apartment." Sensing eyes on her, she looked up to see Sarah and NoraLeigh standing next to their booth. Her heart lurched painfully and slipped into an almost beatless slide that made breathing difficult. "What . . ."

"What are we doing here?" Sarah asked. "Same thing you are. Having lunch. Can we join you?"

Hugh shrugged. Carol glanced at Lindsey, who said nothing.

"That's okay. We won't stay long." Sarah slid in next to Hugh and fixed Lindsey with a look. "You're not working today, are you?"

She said defensively, "No."

"Are you coming to the bookstore?"

"I wasn't planning to."

Sarah turned to Carol. "I don't think I know you." She held out a hand and introduced herself.

Carol smiled and shook. "Carol Carollton, Lindsey's longtime friend. And who is your friend?" She nodded at NoraLeigh.

NoraLeigh had pulled a chair up at the end of the booth. She leaned forward, spilling her breasts across the tabletop, and shook hands. "NoraLeigh Stepanik. I'm a poet."

"How exciting. I write limericks for cards. You know, like 'the cat has a birthday gift for you, and it's a hairball'."

"Well, then we both write," NoraLeigh said.

"I guess you could say that, only mine are mostly one-liners."

Lindsey knew Carol made a lot of money for those one-liners. In comparison, NoraLeigh probably earned pennies.

The waitress brought more coffee and took orders. Lindsey's hands shook when she drank. She'd ordered soup, and when she spooned it to her mouth, it spilled. She pushed the bowl away and tore pieces off her bagel, eating it instead.

Sarah asked Carol about her funniest cards. Carol gave a few examples and they all laughed.

"I'll see you later," Sarah said to Lindsey when she and NoraLeigh left. Lindsey blushed like a child.

"What have you gotten yourself into, little sister?" Hugh admonished softly.

"Let it be," Carol said. "It's hard enough as it is."

"I hope you can ride out the storm," he remarked

A mixture of excitement tinged by sadness made Lindsey antsy. She wanted to dance and cry at the same time.

XVI

Sarah's Escort appeared in Lindsey's rearview mirror when she left the restaurant. Snow swept across the road. She headed toward the library to pass the hours between one and three when she would have gotten out of work. Sarah pulled up beside her as she parked in the lot.

She fought down the excitement, the desire Sarah brought out in her. It was lust, she told herself. Opening her door at the same time as Sarah did hers, she found her path blocked.

"Come over. I want you."

The wind swirled around them, and Lindsey shivered. "I have to take back these books and get more." She indicated the armload of novels she carried.

"Put them in the outside slot. I'll give you something to read. Anything you want. Come on, let me have the books."

She caved in and handed them over. She would go to the library later.

"I'll follow you," Sarah said, getting back into her vehicle.

Lindsey parked in the bookstore lot. She went inside with Sarah, said a few words to Lorrie, and climbed the stairs to the flat. Aroused and ashamed, she set her purse down on the floor and raised her gaze to Sarah's.

Sarah's hands rested on her hips. She cocked her head and smiled. "At last, you're here."

Lindsey looked around the room, taking in the stuffed animal decor, the Precious Moments collection. She had the odd feeling that this wasn't really Sarah's flat. The athletic looking woman in front of her didn't fit in.

"What do you do in your spare time? Do you bike or ski or swim?"

"All of the above. Come here. I'm going to have my way with you, and then we'll talk."

Talk, she thought. They never talked. That would be a good thing.

She went willingly, removing her own clothes, no longer a passive participant. Sarah was not the best lover, only the most persistent. Tender at first, their kisses became deeper, more demanding. They began a long, slow caress. Lindsey buried her face in Sarah's breasts and breathed in the odor of skin. She tasted and was tasted.

"Where did you learn this stuff?" Sarah asked afterward.

"From knowing myself."

Sarah put an arm around her. "You sly woman. You can make love to me anytime."

Was this making love? She wondered, pulling a sheet over their cooling bodies. Something had changed here, she realized. She wasn't backing off any longer. She'd made some sort of sexual commitment when she'd shortened her hours at work.

"Is this what you and Gregg do?"

She stiffened and pulled away. Gregg didn't belong in this room. She would not discuss her relationship with him. It was a separate, very different thing. "Leave Gregg out of this."

"Okay, okay." Sarah rolled out of bed. "You haven't glanced at your watch once. Would you like some coffee?"

"I'd love some decaf." There was no need to hurry home. Gregg wouldn't get back from Point till late. He'd said not to wait up.

When she finally left, she leaned into the wind. It caught the door of the van and whipped it open, and she tugged hard to close it. Stopping at the library, she took some books from the new fiction selection, picked out a few DVDs and drove home. Snow fell steadily. Maybe Gregg wouldn't come home that night.

Willie met her at the door. She picked him up and got a wet tongue on her lips. His breath was terrible, as usual. "Will you still love me, Willie?" He would, of course. He would probably be the only family member who did.

She awoke when Gregg came in the bedroom, and Willie barked. It was after eleven. She switched on the bed light and blinked. "Shush, Willie. How was the conference?"

"It was okay." He had snow in his hair.

"The drive home must have been bad."

"Terrible."

"Why didn't you stay?"

"I should have."

He slid in bed next to her, his skin cold. "How was your day?"

"Not too interesting," she lied.

January flew by in a flurry of cold, snowy days. Lindsey grew increasingly restive at work, although she was busier than she'd ever been, having less time to do the same amount of work. She couldn't imagine why she'd been satisfied with this job so long. Perhaps it was the in-charge feeling it gave her.

She spent her Tuesdays and Thursdays with Sarah, going there from home and leaving at three thirty. The flat felt cozy and welcoming compared to the bitter cold outside the windows. Some of those days they never got out of bed. As the month neared its end, she sensed restlessness in Sarah.

"Want to go cross-country skiing?" Sarah asked the last Thursday in January. Sarah had entered the Birkebeiner cross-country ski race from Cable to Hayward. She'd been training vigorously, except for the days Lindsey was there.

"I'm not a good skier," Lindsey admitted. She'd never been the athletic type. She stayed in shape only because of the nursery's physically demanding work in the growing season and the exercise machines and pool at the Y.

"Come with me. I'll teach you how to skate ski."

"I don't even ski diagonal," she protested.

They went anyway, driving to Standing Rock near Stevens Point. Sarah rented skate skis for Lindsey. "We'll only ski the trails once."

Terrified by Standing Rock's hilly terrain that would have challenged her on diagonal skis, she found skate skis physically beyond her. She fell and fell, until exhausted and soaked through, she became angry.

"I'm going inside to wait for you," she said when Sarah caught up with her on her second round. They were almost there anyway.

On the way home, she said, "I'm never doing that again."

"Well, maybe that wasn't a good place to start," Sarah admitted with a laugh. "Want to stop for pizza?"

Lindsey lay on Sarah's bed, trying to start the conversation they'd never begun, knowing she was going at it the wrong way. In less than a week she and Gregg were leaving for the Dominican Republic. Lindsey knew Sarah spent time with NoraLeigh on the days she wasn't with her.

"What do you do when you're together?" Lindsey attempted a light tone.

"Read poetry."

"How long can you read poetry?" she asked. "Anyway, her poetry isn't that good."

"You're a poetry expert?" Sarah lifted herself on an elbow and looked down at Lindsey. "I'm getting bedsores."

"From lying with me or with NoraLeigh?" Lindsey asked angrily.

Sarah said, "Hey, you sleep with Gregg."

110

"Leave Gregg out of it," she snapped, rolling out of bed and onto her feet. She would leave. She had enough to do to get ready for the trip. Forget this woman.

"Hey, babe, I didn't mean anything. I wish you never had to leave." Sarah hurried over and blocked her way.

Lindsey pushed her away and dressed. "I've got things to do."

"Give me a kiss good-bye. Will I see you before you leave?"

"No. It's only a week from now."

"I'm going up north for a few days. I have to practice for the Birkie."

"Is NoraLeigh going with you?"

"Is Gregg going with you?"

Lindsey's chest ached. She stopped to say good-bye to Lorrie. Lindsey had long ago sensed Lorrie's unspoken disapproval of her affair with Sarah. She wasn't sure why Lorrie objected or at whom the censure was aimed. Lorrie always seemed to have plenty to say to her before she went upstairs, but was short on words when she came down. Today was no different.

She drove home through the cold afternoon, feeling chilled inside and out. She would be glad for the diversion the Dominican Republic offered.

Only Willie waited inside the door. He followed her through the rooms, which were all empty. She put his leash on and shrugged into a warm jacket. They went to the workshop first. The lights were on, but the place was empty. Trudging along the snowy walkways, they opened the door to the winter shop, sending the bells jangling.

Gregg jumped. He had been standing close to Toni, who also took a step backward. The ache in Lindsey's chest deepened. She hadn't been aware that emotions carried so much physical pain.

"Don't let me interrupt," she said softly, and pulled Willie outside again before shutting the door.

Gregg caught up with her near the house. "I was giving her some tips."

"You have a lot to give," she said, knowing she had no right to be angry.

"She needed to know some things in case something came up while we were gone, like where to deposit the money and get change. Stuff like that." He walked at her side, both of them gaining on Willie.

She felt betrayed on both sides, by him and by Sarah. "Of course, she did."

"Are you ready to go?"

"Not yet."

"But you're going, right?"

She realized he wasn't sure. He had that little trust in her. "Of course, Gregg. I'm looking forward to it."

"Me, too. Let's have fun," he said as he had when they went to Florida.

She would guarantee him a good time, even if it ended up being their last vacation together.

XVII

They flew out of Milwaukee and landed in Porta Plata, stepping off the plane onto the tarmac in the intense heat of the afternoon. After going through customs, one of the waiting buses took them to the Sosua Bay Resort.

The poverty shamed her. A rural home was usually one room with an outside well and a few stick fences to keep in a cow or a donkey. The roads outside Porta Plata were unpaved and full of potholes, some the size of ditches. "I'm embarrassed to be an American."

"You're providing people with jobs and helping to boost the economy. Without tourists there would only be more poverty," Gregg pointed out. "Let's just enjoy the warmth."

Sosua Bay was the town, and as they bounced through its streets, she saw a grocery store, a few shops and several houses behind bars. She supposed if anyone had money here, they protected their assets by fencing themselves in. The resort stood in stark contrast to its surroundings. Made of tile and adobe, the walls were an earthen pink, the lobby open on all sides, the bay beyond the swimming pools and verandas dotted with sails. They checked in and were taken to their room along the outer hallways by one of the hotel employees. Maids, still cleaning rooms, nodded and smiled. Lindsey chatted to them in Spanish, bringing looks of surprise and more smiles.

The people were of a dark, handsome race, their features showing their Spanish ancestry. They struck her as shy and friendly, exhibiting no resentment to what must have seemed the almost obscene wealth of the visitors to their country.

In their room, Gregg threw back the drawn curtains and opened the doors to the balcony. They were at one end of the hotel with a view of the public beach and Sosua Bay. There was no sound of surf breaking, because there was no surf. The bay loomed flat and quiet.

They changed into swimsuits, smeared on sunblock, packed their books, T-shirts and hats, sunblock, a couple of bottles of water from the small refrigerator and headed toward the pools in their flip-flops. Wherever they went, they had to either climb or descend broad steps. Finding a couple of lounge chairs under a lone tree by the pool, they left their things on them and walked down to the bay. There was very little beach, and it was rocky.

Lindsey plunged off the long deck into the salty bay and floated toward deeper water. Water had always been a natural element for her, one that supported her just as well as land. She felt the swells under her, pushing her toward shore, and she back-pedaled against them. When she made her way back to the lounge chairs, she found Gregg stretched out, reading and drinking a pina colada.

"Hey, I want one of those," she said.

He pointed toward a small bar across the pool. "Go get one."

She did, going up and down steps. She came back the same way, plopping down beside him and taking out her book. She had brought with her *In The Time Of The Butterflies*, a fictionalized account of the Mirabal sisters who joined the resistance against Trujillo. Carol had suggested the book.

114

All around them were people speaking French and German and Spanish. She smiled to herself, eavesdropping on conversations, most of which were pretty boring. It made her feel very cosmopolitan.

At dinner in the open-air dining room overlooking the pools and bay, they sampled the rich display of food offered at the buffets. This was the first time they'd gone to an all-inclusive resort. Good food and drink were offered all hours of the day and night. A man played the saxophone on the lower deck as the sun set.

Later, a combo with a singer entertained them. She and Gregg drank coffee and listened. They talked little. When Lindsey looked in Gregg's eyes, she imagined hurt and anger. He tried to avoid hers.

"Want to dance?" he asked. He had always been a better dancer than she was.

When they went to bed, she was so tired from the heat, the trip, the sun, the dancing that she thought she would sleep through the night. The room was hot, and when they shut the balcony doors, the air conditioning was noisy. Lindsey lay on her side away from Gregg, but she knew he was awake. After a while, he moved to the other bed and she slept.

The days followed a routine. Breakfast, lunch and dinner where they sampled the wide ethnic variety of food in the dining room. In between, they swam, found shade from the unrelenting sun and read. They took a trip to a nature preserve, which included a boat ride to a dot of an island where they snorkeled with dozens of people among reefs and brightly colored fish. The drive to the preserve, the pounding boat ride, a not very good lunch at a restaurant along the shore, and the trip back were long, hot and tiring. They stayed at the resort after that, except for brief forays to the shops in town to buy gifts for Matt and Natalie.

Once they made love in a desultory fashion. It was too hot and each sensed the other's lack of enthusiasm. Afterward, as they lay on the sweaty sheets, Gregg asked if Lindsey would see a counselor with him.

She turned her head and met his eyes, which shone with what

115

might have been sweat or tears, and agreed. It would have to be someone other than Kate. Maybe she would have a recommendation.

They waited in long lines in the hot afternoon to pass through customs on the way home. Then they waited in the small airport to board the plane. Lindsey felt as if she'd lived in a silent world of her own for a long time. Her thoughts went unshared. She wasn't sure what she wished for anymore.

Pulling into the driveway late at night, they were greeted by an ecstatic Willie. Matt emerged from his bedroom in his briefs, shielding his eyes from the light.

"Hey, you two travelers. Did you have a good time?" He gave them each a hug. "You don't look terribly tan."

"We flitted from tree to tree. Couldn't take the sun," she said.

"We're pale people," Matt replied, and grinned widely. "I got a job. Guess with whom."

"It's too late for a guessing game," Gregg said with a forced smile.

"The Department of Natural Resources. I coordinate with the environmental coordinator from the Department of Transportation. Means I have to move, though."

"The kids are fleeing the burning barn," Gregg muttered.

"What was that, Dad?" Matt said.

"Congratulations." Gregg pulled himself out a kitchen chair. "Tell me about it."

Lindsey gave her son another hug. She made a pot of decaffeinated coffee, and Matt told his story. He'd gotten the job sort of by chance. The person who was going to take it had filled instead the one with the DOT, which was also being vacated. Matt had done some of his master's work with this person.

"Tell me what happened with you guys. What was the DR like?" Matt asked.

"Impoverished and hot. Good food. Good drink. Nice resort. That about sums it up." Gregg stood and stretched. "I'm going to bed. I'm happy for you, son."

116

"Something wrong with Dad?" Matt asked when his father left the room.

"He's tired," Lindsey said. "When do you start the job?"

"Next Monday. I'm going to see Natalie over the weekend. She said she'd phone tomorrow. That reminds me, your friend, Sarah, called. I told her you'd be back late."

Monday Lindsey called Kate and asked her to recommend a therapist, then set up an appointment on Friday of that week for herself and Gregg. When Gregg came in late that afternoon, she told him, and he nodded. He looked tired, as if he'd never been away at all.

The business phone rang during dinner. Lindsey stiffened and when Matt got up to answer, she said, "Let it go. They can leave a message or call back when we're open."

When their home phone rang, Matt eyed at Lindsey, who shook her head.

"I'll bet it's that Sarah," Matt said. "Toni said she called three times today. She phoned here, too."

Gregg got up, put his dishes in the dishwasher, and left the room.

"Did I say something wrong?" Matt looked at his Mom. "You should tell her not to call."

"I will." She already had. Sarah called when she felt like it. If it was meant to get Lindsey to call first, it usually worked. She hadn't phoned today, though. There hadn't been time at work, and it made her nervous to call from home. She would see her tomorrow.

She phoned Carol and changed their weekly lunch to Wednesday.

"How was the trip?"

"Hot, relaxing."

"Would you go back?"

"I don't know. Maybe. I prefer the Pacific."

"How's Gregg?"

117

"We'll talk on Wednesday. How's Teddy?"

"We'll talk on Wednesday."

She hung up and went into the living room where Gregg lay stretched out on the couch, watching a basketball game. Matt sat in a nearby chair.

"I'm going to unpack and wash clothes," she announced.

"Want to wash my stuff too, Mom?"

"Sure. Drop it down the chute."

As she sorted colors, she thought how limited her boundaries were and wondered if that was why she'd strayed. Was she searching for something more interesting?

She'd have to find the courage to be honest on Friday, to admit in front of Gregg that she had lesbian tendencies, or else why go to counseling?

When they sat in bed that night, the wind soughing in the trees, both reading, it seemed as if nothing had changed. This is what they'd done nearly every night of their marriage.

"Sounds like winter out there," she said to break the silence.

He grunted. "It is winter."

"In here, too," she whispered.

His dark gaze met hers, and she shrank from the anger in it. "Is there any point in counseling?"

"I don't know." She placed a hand on his, and his fingers closed around hers tightly as if she were a lifeline. She bit her lip, swearing she wouldn't cry even as she did.

He let go and went back to his book. "Let's not start anything tonight. We need to sleep."

She choked on silent tears. She didn't need sleep. She wasn't working tomorrow. The only way to make it right between them would be to ask his forgiveness and tell him she would stop seeing Sarah. It would be a cruel thing to do, though, knowing as she did that she might not be able to keep the promise.

XVIII

She pounded on the door of the bookstore at eight the next morning. It was a bitterly cold day, and she wasn't dressed for it. The wind penetrated her slacks and blew her hair into tangles. She shivered under its onslaught.

Dressed in sweats, her hair flattened by sleep, Sarah finally opened the door. "Why don't you get a cell phone?"

"We've got a cell phone. Remember? Gregg uses it most of the time." Lindsey pushed past her into the warmth and quiet of the store. The lights were off. No one roamed the stacks, nor was anyone at the computer. She'd never been there when the place was closed.

"There's no reason you can't get your own."

Lindsey turned on her. "So it would be ringing all the time? So there'd be two bills instead of one? A dead giveaway."

"Do you need an excuse to get your own phone?" Sarah ran strong fingers through her hair. "Come here and give me a hug. I missed you."

Lindsey closed her eyes as Sarah pulled her near and kissed her eyelids, her mouth. "Please don't phone anymore. Let me call you."

"Why didn't you when you got home? I wanted to hear your voice. A week is a long time."

"There was no time to call, and I knew I'd see you today."

Sarah held her at arms' length. "You don't look like you spent a week in the sun."

"I have to be careful. I burn easily. Look, Sarah, I've asked and asked you not call me."

"I know, but I get to missing you." Sarah put an arm around Lindsey and led her toward the stairs. "Let's go get some sleep."

But when they were in bed, Sarah leaned on her elbow and cradled her head in her hand. "Did you have sex with Gregg?"

"I don't talk about you with him. Why would I discuss him with you?"

"That means yes. Was it better than it is with me?"

She got up, wrapped herself in the old bathrobe Sarah had lent her, and went to the bathroom.

"Well?" Sarah asked when she came out and sat on the bed.

"I'll leave if you don't drop this."

Sarah pulled her down, opened the bathrobe, and looked at her. "You have a beautiful body."

Although she didn't think her body was beautiful, it was nice to hear it said. Goose bumps sprang up under Sarah's touch.

After, while they slept, Lindsey incorporated the knocks, the footsteps, the voice calling for Sarah into a dream. She awoke with a start when Sarah said in a startled tone, "What, what?"

Lorrie stood in the bedroom door, her eyes averted.

"For God's sake, you can look. We're all the same sex, and we're not doing anything except sleeping." Sarah fished the plugs out of her ears that had prevented her hearing.

Lindsey had no such excuse. She turned crimson.

"Look at you two." Sarah guffawed loudly. "You look like cooked lobsters."

"Did you place a five hundred dollar order for DVDs from GLBT Videos on the phone? I have no record of it, and apparently

120

payment's past due. They want to tack on interest. I thought we agreed you wouldn't order without talking to me."

Sarah sat upright. The sheet fell off her, revealing her breasts. "I'll talk to them." She grabbed the phone off the bed stand.

"Yes, this is Sarah Gilbert. Let me give you my credit card, but no interest. Okay?" She got out of bed, completely nude, and went to get her wallet.

Lorrie turned quickly to go downstairs. Sarah pointed at her back and stifled a laugh, then gave the person on the phone her VISA number and hung up. "I always order in bulk. It's more economical." She convulsed with laughter. "Lorrie's such an innocent."

"Doesn't she have anyone?" Lindsey asked.

"Not that I know of. She's a lesbian in name only. Maybe I should seduce her." Sarah looked at Lindsey and laughed. "Just kidding."

"Like you did NoraLeigh?"

"NoraLeigh doesn't need seducing. She'd jump in your bed if you asked her to."

"If you're going to sleep around, you can do it without me."

"You're sleeping around. What about Gregg?" Sarah's blue eyes glittered.

"He's my husband."

"You can move in with me and be my wife."

"You don't want that." Nor did she want to be someone else's wife.

"What will you do when you leave Gregg?" Sarah straddled her.

"Who said I was going to leave him?"

Sarah pinned her arms to the bed and leaned over to kiss her.

Lindsey turned her face to the side. "Let me go."

"You like being held down. Admit it." She took both wrists in one hand and used her other hand and mouth to tease Lindsey into response.

Afterward, Sarah fixed sandwiches and coffee. They sat in bathrobes at the counter in the kitchen nook and ate hungrily.

When Lindsey left, she avoided Lorrie and slipped out the door unnoticed.

Friday afternoon she met Gregg in the new counselor's office. Her name was Peg McLaughlin, and she looked to be around their age. She was a plain woman with shapeless hair, inquisitive brown eyes, a slight overbite and a soft voice. Lindsey liked her immediately.

"Give me a summary of what's going on." She smiled warmly, mouth shut.

Lindsey looked at Gregg and he at her. She gave a slight nod for him to begin.

He cleared his throat, clearly embarrassed. "I think my wife is having an affair with a woman."

Peg never flinched. She nodded as if for him to continue.

"That's about it. I mean isn't that enough? We've been married twenty-four years, have two grown kids, a family business." He paused and finished with saying, "I don't know what to do with this."

"Is it true?" Peg asked Lindsey.

She felt herself color and took a deep breath. "Yes."

"So what do you want to do with this?" she asked Gregg.

"Do with it? I want it to go away. How do I compete with another woman?"

"Why are you here?"

Lindsey was startled by the question.

"I don't want a divorce," Gregg said. "I don't know what I thought you could do about it."

"Some people stay married, knowing one or the other is actively gay. Is that what you want?"

Gregg shifted in his chair. "I don't know what I want anymore."

"Do the children know?"

"No," Lindsey said quickly, "and they must not find out."

"And how are you going to prevent that?"

"If we're together, why do they need to know? Why does anyone?" she said.

"We're living a lie," Gregg pointed out.

"We're not. I love you. I always have."

He smiled thinly. "Not the way I love you."

"Perhaps I should meet alone with Gregg a couple of times. That might prove more fruitful. You're already seeing someone else, Lindsey?"

Lindsey nodded, trying to put away the feeling of being left out of the loop. She felt as if whatever control she had was spinning away from her. She left the room and sat in the reception area, waiting for Gregg. They had come in one vehicle.

The weekend lay in front of her, a wasteland with the kids gone and Gregg going about in a quiet fog. She phoned Carol and Theo and asked them over Saturday night when she could no longer stand the silence.

"I don't want them to know," Gregg said. When she didn't reply right away, he asked, "Carol knows already, doesn't she?"

She nodded, looking at the floor.

"Why don't you tell the world?" He stomped out of the kitchen.

"I'm not like you, Gregg. I can't keep everything bottled up," she called after him.

The four of them played bridge, which limited the conversation. When they stopped to get dinner on the table, Carol followed Lindsey into the kitchen.

"What's going on here?"

"We went to counseling. I'm sorry to drag you into it, but I couldn't spend another night like last night. He's so quiet. I can't live like this."

Carol took her hands and searched her face, but said nothing.

When Lindsey went to bed, Gregg stayed on the couch, watching TV. She fell asleep over her book and awoke in the night, her reading glasses and the bed lamp still on, the book lying on her chest. Gregg was not next to her.

The following day was much the same. She longed to escape to the Y, but knew Gregg would think she was seeing Sarah. The business phone rang a number of times, but they were still closed on Sundays, so no one answered and no messages were left. No one called on the private line.

When Matt came home that evening, he threw an arm around his mother and asked what was for dinner. "Next week I'll be gone. You won't have to feed me anymore."

"You mean you're never coming home to visit?" she asked with a forced smile. "How's your sister?"

"She's going to call tonight and tell you all."

"All what?"

"My lips are sealed."

"She got a boyfriend or a promotion. Which is it?" She tried to tickle him, but he held her tight till she said, "Okay. Let me go. I'll wait for Natalie's call."

When Natalie phoned, she told them she was dating a man who lived in the same building, an attorney. She'd already been given a slight promotion at work and a raise. She sounded very happy.

Thursday when Lindsey came home, she found Gregg sitting in the kitchen with a drink in hand. "Want one?" he asked.

She shook her head, feeling sick inside. Something had happened. "Did you see Peg today?"

He looked up at her, his eyes nearly black. "Yes, after I called you at work and found out about your new hours."

"That," she said.

"Yes. That. How long have you been off Tuesdays and Thursdays?"

She felt as she had when she'd been caught in a childhood lie. "Since after Christmas."

"Where do you go? To see Sarah at that bookstore?"

She took a deep breath, knowing it was over. "Yes."

"I can't do this anymore." He stood up and slammed his chair into the table.

XIX

She found a one-bedroom apartment. It wasn't as nice as Natalie's or Hugh's, nor was it near Hugh's. It was in among several apartment complexes. They allowed dogs, though, and it was important to her that Willie be permitted to visit. She put down the last and first month's rent.

Then she went home and walked through the house. It felt as if she'd already left it. Matt and Natalie would both be home over the weekend. She would have to tell them she was leaving at the end of the month. Whenever she thought of how she would say this to them, her mind went blank with panic. It would be different if she was moving back to her childhood home, but she was staying in town. So why would she go anywhere? She had to give them a reason.

"What am I going to say to them, Gregg?" she asked in desperation. Her voice sounded loud. It broke the silence of their meal as they pushed the food around their plates, neither of them hungry.

He gave her such a look of despair that she ached for him. "I don't want you to go."

"I put money down on an apartment. You said you couldn't live this way anymore, and I don't blame you." She didn't. It was unfair to ask for such understanding.

He nodded and looked down at his still full plate.

"Are you going to be all right, Gregg?" she asked, worrying more about him than her.

His temper snapped. "Does it matter?" He pushed away from the table and went into the living room. Work and watching TV had become his refuges. Hers were reading and Sarah.

Willie's ears went up. He sensed the discord between them and began to whimper.

She bent over to soothe the dog before following Gregg. "I can't tell them the truth." She still couldn't say the L word. "You won't tell them, will you?"

"They already know the truth, Lindsey. They're not stupid."

She went back in the kitchen and began putting away the leftovers, emptying the uneaten food off their plates into the disposal. Willie nearly trod on her heels, looking for reassurance.

Should she take him with her? Matt and Natalie were gone. Gregg spent his time in the shop or on the grounds or in front of the tube. Who would pay attention to Willie? Yet he'd never been confined indoors. He'd always been able to run free. The customers thought he was cute.

She would take her clothes, of course, and the things that had been her mother's. That left her needing a bed, a dresser, a TV and video recorder and living room furniture. She couldn't denude the house. Gregg probably wouldn't care, but the kids would resent it.

The week flew by much faster than she anticipated. Matt and Natalie were due to arrive before seven on Friday, in time for supper. She fixed creamy rigatoni, having to consult the recipe often, even though she knew it well. Bread baked in the breadmaker. The salad was made. She'd bought ice cream for dessert.

Gregg was watching the news in the living room when Matt and Natalie drove in the driveway, one behind the other. Willie barked at the door, his tail whipping back and forth. Although it felt like winter, the days were longer. It was still light out, and the birds were singing. They knew it was spring, despite the cold.

The door flew open, letting in a rush of chilly air, and her son and daughter spilled into the kitchen—laughing and talking.

Natalie snatched Willie up. "Hello, stranger. Phew, what horrid breath you have." She leaned out of reach as Willie tried to lick her face. "Did you miss me?"

She put her cool cheek against her mother's. "Did you, Mom?"

Matt gave Lindsey a hug and a kiss. "How's it going? Where's Dad?"

Lindsey dipped her head toward the living room. "Watching the news."

Her two children looked at each other over her head and went to find their father.

She stayed in the kitchen in a state of mindless panic. After supper, she'd tell them then, she thought. Why spoil everyone's appetite?

When Gregg sat glumly at the head of the table, his lack of interest in everything obvious, Lindsey wondered why the kids weren't more alarmed. They chatted on, talking about their jobs, new friends, apartments.

"I want you two to meet Paul," Natalie said to Lindsey and Gregg. "He's the attorney who lives in my apartment building."

Lindsey doubted Natalie would want her to meet him once she found out she was leaving.

"Oh, yeah?" Gregg said, making an apparent effort to show he cared.

"Oh, yeah, Dad. Where are you anyway? In Neverland?"

"Sorry. It's ordering time. You know how that goes. Tell me about this Paul."

The orders had already been sent, Lindsey knew.

A slow smile lit up Natalie's face, and she stabbed pasta with her fork. "His name is Paul Williams. He's tall and cute and he's an assistant DA."

"How did you meet?" Lindsey asked.

"On the stairs in the building."

"I've already met him. He's a pretty good guy," Matt said.

Natalie socked him on the arm.

"Okay. He's a really great guy."

Lindsey put the food away after dinner, while the kids filled the dishwasher and washed the pots and pans. She felt sick with dread, her heart hammering with anxiety.

"What's with Dad, Mom?" Natalie asked. "Matt said something was going on between you two."

"I'm moving out," she blurted, feeling as if she was backed against a wall.

The silence that followed terrified Lindsey with its unasked questions. Then it spilled over into words.

"Matt said a Sarah was calling all the time and coming over. Is she your lover, Mom?" Natalie asked.

"Come on, Natalie. Mom wouldn't do that," Matt intervened.

She lied. "No, of course not."

"Then why are you moving out?"

"I need some space." It was the only reason that came to mind.

"There's lot of space now that we're gone," Matt said.

They looked at her, their dark blue eyes accusing, waiting for her to tell them something that made sense of her leaving.

"Dad will be all alone," Natalie said and choked on tears.

Lindsey took a step toward her, as she always had when one of her children needed comfort. How could she tell them it was leave now or never go, that staying was unfair to their father, and it was he who had told her to go? Explanations would be seen as excuses.

"Why don't you go to counseling, you and Dad?" Natalie asked.

"We have," she said.

Natalie backed away from her. "Come on, Matt, let's finish the dishes."

The rest of the weekend was clothed in denial. It was as if they all decided to make the best of it. They ate out and went to a movie Saturday night. Matt and Natalie showered Willie with attention.

Lindsey overheard Natalie ask, "Will you be all right, Dad? I could move back home and get a job on the local paper."

"No," Gregg said flatly. "I'll be fine. Me and Willie."

Lindsey fled to her bedroom and cried.

On Sunday afternoon when Natalie and Matt were ready to leave, Lindsey held her emotions together with difficulty. She wrapped her arms around herself to stop shaking as they stood by the door, saying good-byes. If she let go, she thought she might spring apart in all directions.

Cool and distant, Natalie spoke to her only when necessary. Her daughter's slender frame remained rigid in her arms, and she recalled with sadness the daughter who melted against her when something or someone broke her heart.

Matt hugged her carefully. "You're shaking, Mom. You must be cold." He grabbed a jacket from the hook by the door and put it around her shoulders.

Her lips trembled when she said thanks. She pulled the jacket's lapels tightly together, but the shaking continued. She and Gregg stepped outside to wave as their children drove away.

Exhausted, Lindsey went to her room to lie down. Willie lay on the rug next to the bed. The sun shone through the windows, covering her with warmth, but still she shook. It was done, she told herself over and over. Nothing would ever be the same again because of this. She had split the family.

She rolled onto her side, one thin arm hanging over to stroke Willie. She'd lost twenty pounds in a matter of weeks. Gregg ate little, and when he dumped his leftovers in the garbage, she did, too. The skin on her arms and legs hung loose.

She fell asleep with one hand on Willie's head. She'd told Kate she'd been sleeping a lot and at odd times. Sleep was an escape, she knew. The phone rang into her dreams. She tried to answer it but couldn't move fast enough.

Awaking with a start, she realized it was probably Sarah calling.

129

No matter how many times she told her not to call, she continued to do so. Gregg no longer answered either phone when he was in the house.

She knew she should start taking her things over to the new apartment, but she couldn't bear to move anything today. She climbed under the bedspread and fell asleep. When she awoke again, night was falling.

Putting together a meal of leftovers, she waited for Gregg to come inside. When he hadn't by seven o'clock, she went looking for him. It was the second week in March and the nights remained bitterly cold. She and Willie headed toward the lights in the workshop.

Through the glass in the door she saw Gregg sitting on a lawn chair, his back to her. For several minutes she watched him, and he didn't move. She opened the door and Willie ran to greet him. Automatically, he patted the dog.

"Aren't you hungry?" she asked.

"I had a bite earlier," he said without turning. "I'm not hungry. You can leave Willie with me."

She left Gregg sitting as she'd found him. A fist closed around her heart, squeezing it until she squirmed from the hurt of it.

She started putting clothes in the van the next day. She would move out little by little, but she had to find someone to transport the bigger things. There were the bed and dresser in the guest room, the Hoosier cupboard and the desk that had been her mother's, the older TV/video set and sofa/sleeper in the basement. She would have to leave the computer and printer. They belonged to the nursery.

She couldn't ask Theo or Hugh or Matt. Maybe Hugh's friend, Jimmy, would move her. Perhaps he knew someone who would agree to help. She'd gladly pay for their services. Gregg had offered to give her two hundred a week in maintenance, and when she'd demurred, he'd said gruffly that she was entitled to it. If they divorced, she'd get a settlement, he pointed out. She also had a small inheritance from her mother's estate. If necessary, she could work five days a week at the brass factory, but she didn't want to.

When she started to fill the apartment with her things, she thought it would make her feel less desolate. Gregg was obviously reluctant to see her go. When the kids left, it had been as if they were leaving her for good. Carol was there for her, though. They met for lunch Monday. Lindsey hadn't been able to wait longer. She had to talk to someone.

When Carol asked how her weekend went, she said, "Awful," and found she couldn't talk about it without crying.

"You need to move as soon as possible now that you've decided to do so. Honey, stop crying. Your eyes look almost loon-like. Do you know why loons have red eyes?"

She laughed and blew her nose. "So they can see underwater?"

"That's not a priority of yours, and it's not an appealing eye color. Don't you have to go back to work?" Carol put a warm hand on her arm. "And aren't you a little skinny, kiddo?"

She nodded. "I have no appetite. Neither does Gregg."

"That's not attractive either. You better eat."

Lindsey began to talk in a shaking voice. "You're right. I need to go. Having a foot in both worlds is like being in some kind of hell. I'm worried about Gregg."

"Theo says he's been letting go. He'll be busy soon, and that will be good. We'll keep an eye on him, or at least Theo will. I'll have my eye on you." She smiled.

"How's Teddy?"

"He broke up with his girlfriend, so much for that crisis. I guess there were lots of other more interesting chicks." Carol leaned on her forearms, her eyes serious. "I'm worried about you."

"Me too. I almost wish I hadn't started all this. This probably sounds stupid, but one of the saddest things for me is leaving Willie. I can't explain anything to him."

"Can you have dogs at the apartment?"

"Little ones, but he'd be too lonesome during the day, and

131

Gregg would be too lonely at night. I can't take him." Large tears teetered on her lids.

"You can have him on weekends."

"Imagine having almost your entire family go away and not know why."

"Stop it, Lindsey. You're going to make me cry. Let's get out of here."

XX

She called Hugh on his cell phone to ask for Jimmy's number. "I hope you're not making a mistake, sis."

"Don't tell me that, Hugh. I can't handle any more guilt or misgivings. I've done it. If I go back now, I'll never leave."

"Would that be so awful?"

"Yes. For Gregg and me it's a form of torture. He knows about Sarah, and I know he knows. It's worse than unkind to stay."

"Maybe you'll get over her before she does you."

"Now what the hell does that mean?"

"She's not a sticker. I told you that."

"Well, I'm not moving in with her."

"I suppose Gregg would take you back."

"This has been agony. If I'd known, I probably would have stayed." But she doubted that. There was a kernel of excitement buried inside all the grief. She had pretty much gone from her parents to college and from college to Gregg. She was finally going to be on her own.

She called Jimmy as soon as a phone line was hooked up in the apartment. Sitting on the carpet next to the patio doors, she asked him if he and a friend would move her. "I'll pay."

"Through the nose, honey," he said, and laughed. "Just kidding. You rent the truck, and I'll find the friend. He'll want to be paid. You don't have to pay me."

"I want to, Jimmy."

"When are we going to do this?"

"When can you?"

They decided on the following Saturday. She knew neither Natalie nor Matt would be around. It was mid-month, so there should be plenty of trucks available.

She had taken the smaller things—her mother's good dishes and silverware, a few pots and pans, a portable radio/CD player the kids had given her for Christmas a year ago, a bookcase and books, the pictures that had been her mother's, some of the family photos, a couple of end tables and two lamps. Gregg had said it would be better if she took the van rather than the pickup.

Gregg was nowhere around Saturday morning. She met Jimmy and his friend, Patrick, at the U-Haul place where she filled out the paperwork. She drove the van to the nursery with the two men following in the rental truck.

Eddie had just got out of his vehicle in the parking lot when she drove in with Jimmy and Patrick behind her. "I thought the kids already moved out," he said as she stepped out.

"I'm moving, Eddie." She realized that Gregg hadn't told him.

The shock on his face registered somewhere deep inside her. She'd known Eddie for years. He had seemed like a surrogate father at times.

"Why?" he asked and then probably guessing that was an inappropriate question, he waved. "See you."

She wanted to give him a hug but hesitated, wondering how he would react. "I'll miss you," she said instead.

Then he was gone, slipping into the workshop, as Toni Fields drove in and parked in front of the winter shop. Lindsey experienced a spurt of misplaced territorial jealousy to which she had no right. She had given up her place willingly. No one had told her to go. Well, yes, Gregg had in a fit of pique, but she thought he would have taken it back if it weren't too late.

Jimmy and Patrick carried out the furniture and loaded it into the small moving van. They called themselves two queers and a van, and grunted and made quiet jokes. She felt a tugging sadness and at the same time a desperate need to hurry. Willie must have been with Gregg, for which she was overwhelmingly grateful. Where the Hoosier cupboard, the desk, the bedroom set had been were empty spaces she felt a need to fill, but, of course, she couldn't. Instead, she vacuumed in their wake. In the end, she felt guilty about taking anything.

Carol had said women too often leave behind most of their belongings out of guilt and warned she must not do that. She knew what she forgot to take she would never come back for. So she checked all the closets, under the beds and the basement for things she might have missed. The sadness grew until it threatened to consume her, and she fled the house and drove away. She would come back, she told herself, but it wouldn't be her house then.

She'd given Jimmy the key to the apartment, and he and Patrick had nearly emptied the truck when she arrived. They were waiting for her to decide where to put the furniture. The two men were patient and not hesitant about suggesting how they thought things should be arranged. They moved pieces around until they all were satisfied with their placement.

The three of them were sitting on the sleeper/sofa in the living room, drinking coffee Lindsey had made. If a little on the empty side, the apartment looked livable. The sofa, TV, desk and bookcase stood in the living room. The Hoosier cupboard and table and chairs took up the small dining area space next to the kitchen. The bed and dresser occupied the bedroom. The pictures were stacked against an empty wall.

"Should we put them up? These walls need some help," Patrick said.

"You've already helped so much," she demurred.

"This is free of charge," Jimmy said. "We're decorators at heart."

He and Patrick jumped to their feet and began holding the paintings up. Lindsey had brought picture hangers and a few tools, including a hammer. The pictures brightened the place up.

"You saved me," she said, writing out checks for fifty dollars each. That was all they would take. They went with her to drop off the truck and took her back to the apartment.

"You get lonesome, give a call," Jimmy said before they drove away.

In the apartment she was already lonely. She called Sarah. "Come over and see the place."

"I'm on my way."

She buzzed Sarah in and stood in the hall to greet her. Closing the door, she watched as Sarah walked around the few rooms. "A little empty, but it looks good."

Compared to Sarah's stuffed flat, it would look that way to her, she thought. "It's okay." That's all it was.

"Let's try out the bed."

"I have to make it first."

When the bottom sheet was on and the pillows covered, Sarah pulled her down on it. "You left your home for me. That blows my mind."

Had she? Was Sarah more important than her children and Gregg? Something rebelled inside her. "I did it for myself. It was unfair to Gregg and to me to stay together."

She and Sarah rolled back and forth across the bed, caught up in desire, each trying to overwhelm the other. Where did this come from? It was unseemly, shameful, this lust between them. Lindsey wondered if she'd ever get enough.

Afterward, they finished making the bed and lay on it. "Tell me about yourself, Sarah. I don't know anything about your family." There never had been much time to talk before.

Sarah spoke in spurts. "I have four brothers. I was raised a

Catholic. My dad and I don't get along. He says I spoiled his basketball team, but I play basketball better than my brothers."

"What about your mother?"

"She never disagrees with my dad. What he says goes. Even my brothers toe the line when he expects them to. They all had cars when they turned sixteen. They worked for them, but he wouldn't let me have a car till I was eighteen when he couldn't stop me."

"Maybe he just didn't want anything to happen to you." Lindsey turned her head and flinched at the bright anger in Sarah's eyes. It flickered like a blue flame.

"I'm a girl, which is dead weight as far as he's concerned. The boys all worked construction with him. I wanted to, but he wouldn't let me. Instead, I was the only one to go to college."

"That should have made them both proud," Lindsey murmured.

"It didn't, and now that they know I'm a dyke, they say I'm unnatural. You'll have to go home with me next time. Meet the family."

She shrank from the thought. "Why would you go there if he wants nothing to do with you?"

"He calls and orders me home when he wants us to look like we're a normal family. Like to celebrate his and my mom's fiftieth wedding anniversary next month. I never go alone."

Lindsey wasn't about to be Sarah's shield against her family. She had enough emotional baggage of her own. "Didn't he help you pay for college?"

"Nope."

"You worked your way through?"

"That and loans. I've got a degree in recreation. My brothers have zip. I teach spinning and aerobics classes at the Y, and I'm involved in the summer parks program."

"I never saw you at the Y." How many times had she said she was going to the Y and gone to the bookstore instead, but there were also those times she'd exercised at the Y with Natalie and Matt. "Why didn't you ever tell me?"

"I work there weekday mornings. You're never there when I am. I'm in the pool or up on the second level in the Lifestyle room during the spinning classes."

No wonder Sarah was so fit. "Spinning is the bike thing, right? I thought you worked at the bookstore."

"I do. I set up most of the after-hours and weekend programs at the store."

"Didn't your grandfather leave you the house? He must have cared about you."

"My mother's father. He left her the cottage and the boys some land. He was a wealthy man. I think he wanted my dad to get as little as possible."

"I can't imagine your dad not wanting you. Most dads cherish their daughters."

"Mine doesn't. Believe me." The fiery glow in Sarah's eyes flickered and went out. "Are you hungry? Let's go get a pizza and some wine and bring it back here to celebrate your move."

"Is it okay if I stay here and empty some boxes while you go?" Lindsey asked, putting on her clothes. She pulled ten dollars out of her purse.

"My treat," Sarah said, going out the door.

Lindsey thought how different their backgrounds were. They'd both gone to college, yes, but that's where the similarities began and ended. Lindsey had been raised Presbyterian. She had never felt undervalued. Her dad had gone to his job dressed in a suit. Both of her parents had been college educated, just as both of her siblings were. They all read voraciously. Although Sarah lived above a bookstore, Lindsey had never seen a book in Sarah's flat.

She set the table with her mother's best dishes and silverware. Tomorrow she would get some plain china and tableware. She'd taken one set of glasses. They would have to use them for the wine. She was searching for a corkscrew when Sarah returned with one along with the pizza and wine.

In her absence, Lindsey had turned on public radio. Garrison Keillor was doing his Guy Noir skit.

"What's this?" Sarah asked, her head tilted toward the radio. "How about some music or a video. We can eat on the sofa and watch a movie. I rented one. Hope you haven't seen it."

She hadn't, but she wanted to sit at the table and talk, not watch a movie during their first meal alone.

"All right," Sarah said, "but let's have some music." She tuned the radio to a pop station, and Lindsey felt her hackles rise.

"Let's just turn it off. It's a distraction."

"Okay." Sarah poured the wine, took a piece of pizza and put it on her plate, and asked Lindsey about her family.

"You met my family, all except my sister, Suzy, who's an attorney."

"What's your degree in?" Sarah wiped her chin with a paper napkin.

"Languages."

"What kind of a job do you get with that?"

"The kind I have."

"Does your husband have a degree?"

"Yes. In business." At this moment, she missed him.

"Everybody but the dog, huh?"

Lindsey realized how she sounded—snobby. "It's a family thing."

Sarah changed the subject. "It'll be our first night together."

"Yes," she said, no longer annoyed, grateful that she wouldn't be alone.

Lindsey had never thought of sleeping together as intimate. She'd always kept a few inches between herself and Gregg. Someone touching her while she slept woke her up. She needed the insulation of space around her.

Sarah cuddled against her when they went to bed after the wine and the movie. Street lights backlit the blinds. The headlights of passing cars crossed the walls and ceiling, their tires and engines noisy. Every once in a while the bass from some kid's car radio beat its way into her consciousness. She lay awake a long time before easing her body away from Sarah's so that she could sleep.

XXI

In the morning she awoke early and lay there wondering if Gregg had let Willie out. Sarah slept soundly beside her. She rose on an elbow and stroked her into wakefulness.

Sarah growled and grabbed her.

"Wait," she said, suddenly remembering. "I haven't brushed my teeth."

"Who cares?"

She laughed as Sarah pulled her down every time she tried to get up. "Okay. Okay. I give up." She let herself be drawn against the warm, firm, sweetness of Sarah's body still heavy with sleep.

Sarah's cell phone rang. She lifted her head before burying her face in Lindsey's neck and murmuring, "Okay, okay." Rolling over, she snatched the phone from amidst her pile of clothing on the floor and flipped it open.

"It's Sunday," she growled and mouthed Lorrie's name to Lindsey. After listening, she said, "Oh, I forgot. Tell them I'll be there at ten."

Sarah shut the phone and turned to Lindsey. "It'll have to be a quickie. I promised to give spinning demos at the Y today. It's open house." At Lindsey's blank look, she explained, "The bike kind of spinning we were talking about last night."

She hadn't known about the open house. "I just thought we'd spend the day together." Lindsey noticed an unpleasant whine in her voice.

Sarah glanced at her watch. "Let's time ourselves."

Lindsey reluctantly relented.

"Five minutes. That's a record for us," Sarah said afterward as if proud. "Got to go, babe. Why don't you come see me at the Y today? We would have met there sooner or later, you know. I'll grab a piece of toast."

Lindsey got out of bed and pulled a robe on. Already she felt lonely. "Are you going to demonstrate in jeans?"

"I've got a locker." The toast popped. "Come on over."

"Are you coming back tonight?"

"There's a book review at the store tonight. I'm in charge. Why don't you come? Can't remember the name of the book and author. Call Lorrie. She'll know." Sarah shrugged into her jacket and left.

Lindsey turned on public radio, started a pot of coffee and sat down with the Sunday paper. She'd arranged for its delivery starting that day.

After breakfast, she went out to buy the everyday china and tableware. She bought wine glasses, too. Then she grocery shopped for staples and next week's meals. Carrying the stuff inside, she put it away and made her lunch before calling Lorrie.

"What's happening tonight? Sarah said there's a book review."

"A book discussion of *The Magician's Assistant*," Lorrie told her, "by Ann Patchett. It's a pretty good book. She wrote *Bel Canto*."

"I read them both."

"Well, maybe you can help Sarah lead the discussion, because I know for a fact she hasn't read either," Lorrie said, voice tart with disapproval.

"I hope I won't have to."

After lunch, she put on her workout clothes and drove to the Y. Sure enough, Sarah was on the second level in the Lifestyle room on a spinning bike, talking. She climbed the steps and sat on an empty bike in the back row.

"Good, another participant." Sarah turned on the speed, then slowed it down, then speeded up again.

Lindsey was covered with sweat in a matter of minutes, but she kept up the pace for a half an hour. It was as if Sarah was teasing her, trying to break her down. She'd brought her gym bag with her, so she put on her swimsuit and sat in the hot tub before getting under the shower and going back to the apartment.

Before seven she drove to the bookstore. The parking lot was full, and she parked down the street. Mostly women clustered in groups. She knew none of them and looked for Lorrie and Sarah.

She had picked up *The Magician's Assistant* at the library. Now she sat in an end chair with a cup of decaf and flipped through the pages, trying to remember the parts she thought worth talking about. She had loved the book and had read the rest of Patchett's books afterward, but, except for *Bel Canto*, she didn't think they measured up.

Hearing Sarah's voice, she snapped to attention. "We have someone here who's much more able to lead the discussion than I am. Isn't that right, Lorrie?"

Lindsey thought she meant Lorrie and relaxed, eager to hear what Lorrie would say.

"Let me introduce Lindsey Stuart Brown. Come on up here, Lindsey."

She broke into a sweat. Her eyes felt like live coals. She started to shake her head no. When the others clapped, she got reluctantly to her feet and walked in a panic to stand next to Sarah. It occurred to her that if she experienced many more of these moments of extreme angst, she'd probably have a heart attack. Would Natalie talk to her then? Would Matt forgive her? And Gregg?

The audience blurred into colors. She turned to Sarah. "Isn't this your job?"

"I'm not proud," Sarah said with a grin. "Let the best person do the job. Here, sit on a stool." She pulled one close to Lindsey.

Lindsey's mind worked at a frantic pace. She hadn't talked in front of a group since she'd been president of the PTA, but she knew from experience that whatever she had to say would soon be forgotten.

"Tell me. What did *you* think of the book?" she asked those in front of her, stalling for time.

And sure enough, as she'd noticed in nearly every crowd, there was someone who loved to hold forth. Anyone else, including herself, had trouble getting a word in. She had to interrupt several times to snatch back the monologue and turn it into a discussion.

Like bats zeroing in on mosquitoes, the audience closed in on the lesbian scene near the end of the book between the protagonist and the magician's sister. They looked for meaning in it. When time was up, the group scattered.

Lorrie patted her on the back. "Good job, girl."

"I suppose my leading the discussion was your idea."

"You read the book." Lorrie smiled, her blue-gray eyes bright. "Didn't you?" Lorrie looked like a reader to her.

"I haven't quite finished it. I will, though."

"What shampoo do you use?" Lindsey asked on impulse. She wanted her hair to look like Lorrie's always did. "Your hair shines."

"Whatever's cheapest," Lorrie admitted, blushing and looking away. "Thanks."

Sarah came over and put an arm around Lindsey. "Didn't she do a great job?"

"I just told her she did." Lorrie's smile lost some of its glow. "I knew she would."

Then others gathered around Lindsey to talk books. Lindsey could hold her own on that subject.

"Are you coming next month?" one of the women asked her. Lindsey had been trying to place her and her friend. Then she remembered. Barb had the crew cut. Jody wore her hair long.

"What are you discussing?"

"Ellen Hart's latest book."

Maybe she could find it at the library. "Sure. Why not?"

"You're good at this," Jody leaned over and whispered. "Better than Renata."

"Which one is Renata?"

"She's the one who talks so much. Renata Fisher." Barb spoke in a normal voice and Jody shushed her. "Well, maybe someone should give her a clue."

Lindsey stayed over, spending the night in Sarah's bed for the first time. They linked ankles, lying on their backs, talking before sleep. Hyped up, Lindsey realized after a while that she was talking to herself. Sarah had fallen asleep.

Picking up the book she was reading, she immersed herself in it. Reading kept her from thinking about Gregg and Natalie and Matt. And Willie. She decided to ask for custody of the dog every other weekend. He, at least, still loved her.

Monday she went to work, knowing she'd have to tell John that she had moved, and dreading it. She arrived before he did and was booting up her computer when he walked in.

"How do you always get here before I do?" he asked.

"I leave before you do. I have a new address and phone number, John." She handed him a piece of paper with the changes on it as he paused by her desk.

"Is everything all right, Lindsey?" He looked uncomfortable.

"It's different is all, John."

"How are Gregg and the kids?"

She surprised herself by saying, "We're all a little upset."

He asked no more questions. "I'll be in my office if you need me. We have a French client who refuses to write in English nor, apparently, will he ask anyone else to do it. He's all yours." He handed her the file.

She relished the few translations that came her way. At times she'd wished she lived in New York and worked for the United Nations. Every once in a while, she wondered how her life would be if she had been more adventurous.

Would people think she was being adventurous now? She was sure they would consider her selfish, tearing apart her family after all these years.

She asked Kate that question when she saw her on Wednesday.

"You had a catalyst in Sarah. My guess is she gave you the incentive to make such a difficult choice. It's nearly always easier to stay."

"I phoned Natalie on Monday. She said she couldn't talk. I called Matt next and he spoke a few words before saying he had to go. Then I called Gregg and he said what did I expect. I'm taking Willie on the weekend. At least he'll be happy to see me." She was crying now, her words hard to understand through the sobs.

Kate pushed the tissue box toward her, and she jerked one out and blew her nose.

"Give them time. You just left. They have to absorb this. Children, even grown children, don't always see their parents as individuals with lives of their own. They certainly don't want to think of their parents as sexual beings."

She heaved a sigh that ended in a sob. "Nor do they want their home to change. Gregg and I are supposed to be there, waiting for them to return, just as they left us. I expected my mother to keep the home fires burning even after my dad died."

"Did she?"

"Yes. She never remarried. We all returned year after year, but she surely wanted a life of her own. She had a lot of friends, but she must have been lonely. Kids are selfish, aren't they?"

"We all are. Maybe thoughtless is a better word."

XXII

Wednesday Sarah called to say she wouldn't be over as planned.

"But I've already started dinner." She had picked up a salmon fillet and made a glaze for it. The bread she had started in the breadmaker was nearly done. She had the red potatoes ready to steam and the salad made.

"Put it in the freezer."

"What's come up?"

"An old friend just broke up with her lover. She needs to talk."

"I wish I'd known earlier."

"I didn't know earlier. Sorry, babe. Tomorrow night."

She hung up, wondering what she was going to do with herself all evening. She told herself she didn't need Sarah to entertain her. She'd eat a sandwich and go for a walk. It was warm out at last, and there were hours of light left.

People coming home from work parked in the lots behind the apartment buildings in her neighborhood. No one was on the sidewalks. She walked until tired, not really noticing what was around her. On her return, she bumped into Jody and Barb, who were walking their dog. The huge, ill-mannered shepherd type animal was dragging Barb along behind it.

"Do you live around here?" Jody asked, stopping.

The dog pulled Barb to a tree, where it lifted its leg.

"Yes. Do you?"

"In this apartment here. Want to come up for a drink or coffee?"

"Don't mind us," Barb said, hanging onto the dog with both hands. "This is Tarzan."

Just then Tarzan decided that Lindsey was a friend. He left the tree and lunged toward her. Standing on his hind legs, he put his paws on her chest.

"Off. Down," Barb yelled.

Lindsey nearly fell over backward.

"I guess he likes you," Jody said, as the dog dropped to all fours.

She followed the two women to their second floor apartment, three buildings down from hers. The dog sounded as if it was strangling as it pulled Barb up the stairs.

"He must have a strong neck," Lindsey said of the dog. Barb was no lightweight herself, yet she couldn't manage Tarzan.

"He's a mass of muscle," Barb announced proudly. "We've been going to dog obedience, but he really needs a place where he can run."

The inside of the apartment smelled strongly of dog, and looked very much like her own. "Have you been to the dog park?"

"We just got back and decided to go for a little walk. It's such a nice day."

"Finally," Lindsey said.

"Sit down. Would you like a drink or coffee?" Jody asked, while Barb took off the dog's leash.

Lindsey braced herself as the animal made a beeline toward her and plunged its muzzle between her legs. She held him off with one hand and patted him with the other.

"Give her a drink," Barb said, laughing. "Vodka or gin or beer?"

"Vodka's good." Lindsey managed to make Tarzan sit. The dog placed its head in her knees.

"He really likes you," Jody remarked.

Lucky me, Lindsey thought. "I have a little dog." She explained that Willie lived elsewhere but she would have him over the weekend.

"We can go to the dog park together," Jody said.

The other two women drank beer and sat on the couch, close together. A small silence followed while Lindsey tried to think of something to say.

"Have you been together long?" she asked finally.

They smiled at each other. "Three years," Jody said. "We met at the bookstore."

"Seems like it's a good meeting place." She thought of Hugh. If she needed to talk to someone, she could call him.

After hurriedly finishing her drink, she invited them over for one at her place tomorrow, hoping they would leave the dog home. She wouldn't allow herself to be lonely.

Curling up on the sleeper/sofa in her apartment, she watched public television for a while, then opened her book and read until she fell asleep. She awoke disoriented in the night. Nothing anchored her here, she realized, once she placed herself. She needed some other reason besides Sarah for being here.

She picked up Willie after work on Friday. Gregg had left a note fastened to the door. *Willie's inside, ready to go.* When she went to look for Gregg, he was neither in the workshop or the winter shop. Toni told her he was gone for the afternoon.

Willie jumped up and down, panting and emitting excited little groaning sounds when she put his leash on. His food and water bowls along with his dog chow and treats were in a paper bag by the door. She grabbed the bag in one hand, the lead in the other. She could hardly stand being in the house alone like this, knowing that Gregg had left in order to avoid seeing her.

After changing clothes, she took Willie for a walk around the neighborhood. Sarah was coming over for the evening, and she had some prep work to do on dinner. Forsythia bloomed near the buildings; pale blue clusters formed on lilacs; trees sported new leaves, and the birds sang their heads off. The new smells drove Willie crazy. He stopped every few minutes to sniff the ground or a bush or tree. She practically dragged him back to the apartment building.

He barked when Sarah stepped inside the apartment. "Whoa, little dog. You're a fearsome sight, all twenty pounds of you."

"He weighs more like thirty," Lindsey said.

"Whatever you're fixing smells great." Sarah threw her light jacket over the sofa arm.

"It's creamy rigatoni, fresh bread, and salad," Lindsey said, one of her kids' favorite meals. "Hope you're hungry."

"It's open mike night at the store. I have to go back after we eat."

"Can we come?"

Sarah looked doubtfully at the dog. "We'll sneak him in. He's so little maybe nobody will notice."

"I can't leave him. He's mine for the weekend."

"We have to do doggy things, huh?"

"I do," Lindsey said. "Come on, let's eat."

Willie stuck close to Lindsey's leg at the bookstore, bumping into her, dodging the hands eager to pat him. Lindsey took a chair in the back, and he lay on her feet.

Barb and Jody saw her there and came over. "We've been on the lookout for you and your dog," Barb said. "No wonder we didn't see him. He's tiny."

Lindsey laughed. "He's not that little. Anyway, he doesn't think he's small."

"He sure is cute," Jody crooned, letting Willie sniff her hand.

Sarah's voice cut through the noisy talk and laughter. "Time for the open mike. Who wants to go first?"

Renata Fisher stood up, the one who had so much to say during the book discussion group. She'd written a short story, she said.

It was about two women whose signs were crossed. Actually, Lindsey thought it quite funny, although she wasn't sure it was supposed to be. She said she found it entertaining during the comment period afterward.

"Sad, though, too. Here are these two people who are star-crossed from the get-go. No wonder they can't get their lives lined up," Renata explained.

Lindsey couldn't think of an answer to that, so she kept her mouth shut.

NoraLeigh got up and read two new poems, both so erotic that Lindsey squirmed. Again she pictured NoraLeigh doing the things she wrote about with Sarah. She wanted to ask if NoraLeigh wrote about anything other than sex, but, of course, she didn't.

So far only women had taken the mike. Now Jimmy came forward with his friend Patrick. Patrick carried a guitar. Jimmy took the microphone off its stand while Patrick played a few chords. Then Jimmy sang some song she had never heard before. His voice twanged, slightly off-key. Lindsey was embarrassed for him, but neither Jimmy nor Patrick showed any sign of being uncomfortable. When they sat down, everyone clapped.

Lorrie walked over from her seat in the front row with a piece of paper in hand. "I want to share with you a few sentences from the book, *Five Smooth Stones*, which I reread a few days ago. The book is a fictionalized account of a black man during the civil rights struggle. We are now in our own battle for civil rights, not so unlike that other one. I think these sentences describe what drove David in this book to stay with his people when he could have walked away, married the white woman he loved and taken a state department job overseas."

Lindsey leaned forward to hear over the hum of whispers.

Lorrie read in a soft voice. It was something about God not being a crutch, but a force that moves within us, and once it is recognized, it can't be ignored.

A hush fell over the place, and people looked uneasy. Lindsey wondered if that was what really drove those involved in their

150

struggle for equal rights. It seemed a little weighty for the audience and the occasion, but she, nevertheless, asked Lorrie to read the passage again.

Sarah threw an arm over Lorrie's shoulders. "Heavy stuff, woman. Maybe a little too philosophical for this crowd."

Lorrie turned a bright red.

"That's a great quote," Lindsey said, flushing as crimson as Lorrie. "Something moves us to work for what we think is right. Call it God or conscience or whatever. For some of us it is an inner drive."

Lorrie scurried back to her seat and the blush slowly faded.

Several other people got up to sing or read something. By nine-thirty everyone milled around, talking, putting away chairs, making dates. Lorrie sidled up to Lindsey.

"Thanks for the support," she said.

"I read that book years ago. I think I'll read it again."

"I'll lend it to you." Lorrie went to get the novel.

"Hugh's coming next weekend," Jimmy said as he and Lindsey put away chairs. "Maybe we can double date. You and Sarah, me and Hugh."

"Sounds like fun," she said, but she wondered why he and Hugh wouldn't want to be alone. They saw so little of each other.

She left with Willie before Sarah did. "I have to take him out before bedtime."

Sarah waved absently. She was talking to her old friend, Nancy Ferguson, known as Fergie, who had been dumped by her lover.

Willie gave Lindsey a reason to be outside on this warm night. She ran into Barb and Jody, walking Tarzan. There wasn't room for them to walk together on the sidewalk, so they took to the street. Willie and Tarzan lunged toward the small Japanese maples in the grassy areas between sidewalk and road. Tarzan sniffed Willie's behind while Willie snuffled the trees. Once the big dog attempted to wrap his legs around Willie's midriff and mount him. Willie snarled, whirled and snapped, and Barb pulled Tarzan off.

"Horny bastard for not having any balls," Barb remarked. "Sorry about that, Willie."

"How'd you like the open mike?" Jody asked. "I thought you'd have something to read."

"I didn't know there was an open mike till suppertime. Besides, I had Willie. Actually, though, I didn't have anything to say. I liked what Lorrie read."

"I wish I was a writer," Jody said wistfully.

"Me too," Lindsey agreed, thinking of Natalie laboring away on short stories.

She and Willie came back to an empty apartment. The answering machine light flashed. When Lindsey pushed the button, Sarah's voice filled the room. "I'm staying here tonight, Lindsey. Fergie needs to talk. I'll call you in the morning."

Lindsey's hands trembled when she took Willie's leash off. He showed her all his tricks—rolling over, standing on his hind legs, offering his paw to shake. Only when he barked did she remember to give him his treat.

Had she left her home and family to be alone? Stretching out on the couch, she opened *Five Smooth Stones* and started reading. At first, concentration eluded her, but before she went to bed, she was caught up in the story. Some books never lose their timeliness.

XXIII

She read late and awoke when Willie put his paws on her bed and licked her arm. Throwing on sweats, she took him outside. The morning greeted her warmly. Birds defined their territories with song. She'd always loved spring, but this one made her sad.

She started to make the bed once they were inside, then climbed into it instead and fell asleep. Willie's barks became incorporated into a dream. Natalie and Matt were outside the house, but she couldn't get the door open. She called for Gregg to help, and realized he wasn't there. She was locked inside alone.

When she felt someone pressing against her, she opened her eyes. "Sarah!"

"Don't talk." Sarah's kisses traveled down her body. When she tried to move, to respond, Sarah said, "Don't move. This one's on me."

Lindsey wasn't good at being the only one on the receiving end. Lying like a limp weed didn't turn her on. "Let me . . ."

"What's the matter, woman?" Sarah asked.

"I have to be part of it," she explained, getting up on her elbows, and pulling Sarah to where she could nestle against her. "Want to start over?"

Afterward, they lay separate on the bed, arms and legs spread, windows open. Still, the apartment remained hot. Lindsey thought she'd have to open the windows if it was below zero.

"This is a hot place," Sarah said.

"I know. I should move, but I signed a six-month lease."

"What do you want to do today?"

"Take Willie to the dog park. What do you want to do?"

"I have no plans. I'm all yours."

"We have to call Barb and Jody. They want to meet us there."

"Let's eat breakfast first," Sarah said.

"How's Fergie?" Lindsey asked as she fried bacon and eggs to put in toasted muffins with tomato slices.

"Devastated."

"How long have you known her?"

"Years. I used to be with her when I was very young. She was my first."

Lindsey felt the heat of jealousy. "She must be special then."

"She is." Sarah sat at the table, drinking coffee, her feet up on a chair.

"How special?"

"Special enough that I'd drop everything to go to her when she needs support."

"I see." Lindsey stood with one hand on her hip. She was barefoot and wore a T-shirt and shorts.

Barb and Jody were on their way over. Sarah had invited them to breakfast. They knocked on the door, and Sarah let them in.

"Where's Tarzan?" she asked.

"We'll get him when we go to the dog park. He's so big he practically takes the food off our plates."

Lindsey pictured Tarzan eating off the table. She breathed

easier when they left the dog at home. She liked the two women. They were good-natured, if a little boring.

She felt like a short-order cook—taking the bacon out of the pan, putting the eggs in, frying hash browns and making toast. "Sarah," she said, "would you mind slicing the tomatoes?"

"I don't like tomatoes," Sarah replied. "Want some more coffee, you two?"

"I like tomatoes, and I'll have some coffee, too."

"Her highness speaks. I better make another pot."

"I'll slice the tomatoes," Jody offered.

"Thanks," Sarah said. "I thought this was going to be a relaxing meal." She refilled Lindsey's cup, winked at her and lightly slapped her on the fanny.

"Cut it out," Lindsey said, peeved.

When Barb and Jody left to get Tarzan and their truck, Lindsey washed the dishes and put away leftovers. "How about some help? You invited them over."

"Sure, boss." Sarah saluted.

Furious, Lindsey swallowed her anger for fear she'd say something unforgivable.

"You remind me of my mother," Sarah remarked. "Her lips sometimes looked like they were sewn together."

"Yeah, well, maybe she had a reason."

"I was annoying." Sarah set the dried dishes on the table. "Can't we put these in the dishwasher?"

"You're being annoying now."

"Want me to go home?"

"No. But I'm not cooking for a bunch of people unless I ask them over. Next time we'll go out to eat."

The already trampled ground at the dog park was more mud than grass. The two dogs loved it and ran with ears pinned and bodies flattened. In a short time, Willie looked like a mud-ball.

Tarzan kept cutting him off in attempts to play. Once Willie ran right under the large dog. Lindsey imagined him laughing.

The four of them trailed along behind. The hazy sun warmed Lindsey and made her sleepy. Her hiking boots sported an inch of mud, making them heavy.

"So, what are you two doing this weekend?" Jody asked.

"Doggy stuff," Lindsey said. "It's my weekend with Willie. We'll do things he likes."

"Like what?" Sarah asked. "Watch doggy movies? Eat doggy food? Have a doggy friend over?"

"Ha, ha," she said. "I can't go off and leave him alone."

"Then take him. He can wait in the car if he has to." Sarah paused and looked back at the vehicles in the lot. "Why don't I go to the bookstore till five and come over then. I've got things to do."

"So that's why you drove your own car," Lindsey said, disliking the accusation in her tone.

"I promised to help Lorrie. She wanted some time off."

Lindsey couldn't object to that. She thought Lorrie worked way too many hours. "See you tonight then?"

"Sure. Let's go out for dinner. You two want to come?"

"Love to," Jody replied at the same time Barb said, "Sounds good."

Why hadn't Sarah asked her if she wanted anyone along, Lindsey thought, thinking she sounded way too possessive. She didn't want to leave Willie alone, though, and said, "Why don't we get takeout?"

"We'll decide later." Sarah turned and headed toward the parking lot. "See you. Keep an eye on those dogs. Wouldn't want to lose them."

At five, Lindsey turned on the news. She'd come home from the dog park and given Willie a bath. Now she sat on the couch with Willie at her feet. When the phone rang, she jumped for it.

"Hi, babe. I'm not going to make it tonight. Fergie's taken a turn for the worse."

"Are you going to be home?"

"Nope. I'm going to her place."

"Want me to come along and add my two cents?"

"You don't have to be sarcastic," Sarah said. "She needs me."

"I need you."

"You've got Willie."

"And Jody and Barb. What should I tell them?"

"What I just told you. I'll come over later. Don't wait up, though."

It crossed Lindsey's mind to tell her to not bother, but then she recalled how lonely it was without Sarah.

She took Willie home late Sunday afternoon. The nursery was closed, no one on the grounds. Willie streaked around the exterior of the house three times, his tail straight out behind him. She had to laugh.

Gregg stepped outside. The evening was cool. She stood with her arms wrapped around herself, wondering if he'd ask her in. It hurt to look at him, even when he too laughed at Willie.

"What did the two of you do?" he asked. He wore an old button up sweater she'd given him years ago over a plaid shirt and jeans.

"Went to the dog park, walked, watched videos and ate popcorn."

"Sounds like a great weekend escape for Willie. He gets little enough attention around here when I'm working."

She didn't ask what he'd done those two days and nights. She didn't want to know.

He gestured at the door with his head. "Want to come in. It's cooling off. I can put on some decaf."

"Sure. Thanks."

He made the coffee, while she sat at the kitchen table. That was weird by itself, their positions reversed. Setting a full cup in front of her, he settled across the table.

"What do you hear from the kids?" she asked.

157

"They call all the time, especially Natalie, like they think I can't get along on my own."

She found his eyes unfathomable, his smile wry. "They don't call me," she said, her voice small.

"They will. Give them time."

She blinked and looked away.

"What did you expect?" he asked, his eyes on her.

"This. Have you met Natalie's boyfriend?"

"Yes. Last weekend they came over on Sunday."

"Did you like him?"

"Yeah. He's a nice guy."

"What was he like?"

He shrugged. "Tall and dark, looks like he exercises a lot."

"Did he have a sense of humor? Did he treat Natalie well?"

"They stayed an hour. That's not enough time to get to know someone."

What had she been doing last Sunday? She couldn't remember. "Do you think she'll marry him?" Would she be invited to the wedding?

"Not soon anyway. Want something to eat? I made Chinese stew. Found your recipe."

"I love Chinese stew." The smells registered only now, she'd been so distraught. "I thought I took my recipes."

He tossed the card at her with a piece of paper and pen. "Copy it for me."

Her hand shook a little as she wrote. He stood at the stove, dishing the stew into large soup bowls. He put plates, forks and napkins on the table along with some bread and two glasses of water and began to eat. "Tastes just like yours."

"Want me to copy more recipes for you?" she asked, slipping the card in her pocket.

"That'd be helpful. You can bring them over next time you come to get Willie."

At the sound of his name, Willie sat up, ears perked, tongue lolling.

"He's thinking food," Gregg said. "You can almost see the balloon over his little head."

"It says, *Please, please*."

They laughed and, for a moment, it seemed as if they were still a couple.

When she left, clouds covered the sunset. Gregg had asked how she and Willie had spent the weekend. He hadn't spoken about himself or the business. There were adjectives for her life right now, she thought—empty, lonely, purposeless. Or were empty and purposeless the same thing?

When she unlocked the apartment door, Sarah was sitting on the sofa watching TV. She was so glad not to be alone that she forgave her for not coming back Saturday, for being gone till now.

"Where you been, woman?"

"I should ask you that. I took Willie back and had dinner with Gregg."

"Do you miss him?"

"Yes." She turned down the TV. "What program are you watching?"

"*America's Funniest Home Videos*," Sarah said.

She sat down and watched a few minutes before getting up and going into the bedroom. "I'm going to read. I can't watch that." It was too insipid.

"I was just passing time, waiting for you to come back." Sarah switched off the TV, followed her into the bedroom, and grabbed her from behind. "How about a little nookie?"

Lindsey's leap from depression to desire in a split second surprised and appalled her. She suspected she'd jump into bed with Sarah, even if she knew Sarah was cheating on her or lying to her.

Sex connected them, she thought before she stopped thinking and began acting. It was the lubricant that made their relationship work.

XXIV

It was a long week for Lindsey. She called Natalie every evening and always got her answering machine. She talked to Matt twice. Their conversations were short and unsatisfying. She asked him why she was getting Natalie's answering machine. He admitted that Natalie was screening her calls. "Did you leave a message?" he asked.

"Yes, and she hasn't called me back."

Wednesday she told Kate her kids were blowing her off, and she hated it.

"I suspect they'll warm up after a while. That's been my observation over the years, after parents separate for some reason."

"God, it hurts. Everything hurts."

"Tell me what hurts."

She told her Sarah had spent most of the weekend elsewhere, probably with Fergie. She talked about her conversation with Gregg when she took Willie home. How she'd felt like a shit when she left him. How her chats with Matt on the phone were just that, a few sentences with little information. And then she said, "I'm afraid Natalie will marry without telling me, without even introducing me to her boyfriend, that's how shut out of her life I feel."

Kate shifted in her chair as if she were going to say something.

"My life is without meaning," Lindsey whispered.

"Maybe that's what we should talk about, how to put meaning into your days. There are a lot of people out there who need help. There are organizations looking for people to provide that help."

"I know. I'm just not ready for that. I feel like I need help."

Kate nodded. "What did you think it would be like after you moved out?"

"I didn't give it enough thought, I guess. I think I left for the wrong reasons. I was so anxious to be with Sarah. But I would have gone sooner or later." She looked away. "I think Sarah's cheating on me already."

"Why do you think that?"

"She spends a lot of time with her old lover, Fergie." Lindsey slumped in the chair. What a fool she'd been. Did she think she'd have a relationship like the one she'd had with Gregg? "But, of course, we don't have a commitment. I'm not sure I want one. I know this will sound terrible, but she's sort of a surface person."

"A surface person?"

"She has no depth."

Sarah and Lindsey met Hugh and Jimmy at Gourmet Dining, one of the pricier restaurants in town. The host took the two women to the table, pulled out their chairs and put their napkins on their laps. The men stood.

"I've always wanted to come here," Sarah said as the host handed them menus, filled their water glasses and asked for their drink orders.

Lindsey peeked at the menu and stifled a gasp. The cheapest dinner was twenty-nine dollars and everything that came with the it was a la carte.

Hugh grinned at her. "Don't have a heart attack, sis. I'm treating."

161

"Why don't we just have a drink and go someplace else to eat?" she suggested.

"If I were paying, I'd go along with that, but Hugh's a big spender," Jimmy said.

"Let's not talk money. How are you? I haven't seen you in weeks." Hugh's eyes were on her.

She smiled, trying to look as if everything were all right, even though she and Sarah had fought fiercely on their way over. Sarah had spent Friday night with Fergie.

"What's going on?" Lindsey had asked. "Are you sleeping with her?"

"She can't bear to be alone so much."

"Yeah, well, neither can I," Lindsey said, "and I don't want to sleep with someone who's sleeping with someone else."

"Did I promise to spend every night with you?" Sarah asked.

"No. I guess I made a wrong assumption. Since Fergie came back, you've spent more time with her than with me."

"Did I ask you to move? I don't want the responsibility for that."

"You were insistent on seeing me. You called the house when I asked you not to. You made it impossible to stay."

"Hah. All you had to do was tell me to take a hike."

Lindsey didn't believe that, but she hadn't asked, so she couldn't say. She shifted in her chair.

Hugh looked intently at her as if trying to read her thoughts. "We'll talk more later. I'm going to be around till Monday."

"Good. Why don't you come over for breakfast?"

"You bet I will," he said.

"What's new?" Hugh asked when their drinks came.

Lindsey shrugged. "Time is dragging. I'm thinking about going back to working five days a week." She needed the money anyway.

"Not yet," he said. "I want to take you on a trip."

Sarah jumped in. "Can I go, too?"

"Where?" she asked.

"No, you can't go, Sarah, nor can Jimmy. Just my sister and I are going. Think you can get some time off, Linds?"

"Not in April. Maybe May or June."

"It'll be warmer then," Hugh said.

Hugh ordered for her, knowing she would probably ask for the least expensive thing on the menu. He had no such qualms about Sarah or Jimmy, he said, and they proved him right. Portabella mushrooms stuffed with seafood for starters. Beet soup next and fresh baked bread. Tenderloin tips with garlic mashed potatoes and asparagus tips, washed down with an excellent merlot.

She ate and drank it all and then was sorry. "Thanks so much, Hugh. It was too good. Excuse me a minute."

"Me too," Sarah said.

Being able to go to the ladies' room with your lover should be considered a plus. Right now was not the time, though. "I'll wait till you're back." She sat down again.

Jimmy glanced at Hugh and grinned. "I gotta go, too. Man, I don't know how you digest this rich food and get away with it at your age."

"I'm not that old," Hugh protested.

Sarah went off chatting with Jimmy.

"What do you do in these situations?" Lindsey asked.

"Well, you admit you're human," Hugh said with a shrug. "It's always difficult when you're new to each other."

"Where are we going, Hugh?"

"Home. I have a little place on the big lake. You need some time off from all this."

She told him that she thought Sarah was cheating on her with Fergie. He lifted his eyebrows and spread his arms, palms up, in a helpless gesture. "I warned you."

"I hate it when someone says I told you so."

"Me, too. Sorry." He glanced in the direction of the restrooms. "I'll come over in the morning, and we'll talk.

"Okay." Jimmy and Sarah were on their way back, still chatting. She grabbed her purse and got up.

When she got back, there was a Riesling waiting for her.

"I'm really too full," she demurred, and drank it anyway.

❖

"Something wrong?" Lindsey asked. She had hardly been aware of the silence till they got into the car. There it blossomed into something very large.

"Where are you and Hugh going?" Sarah's profile stood out. Her hands clutched the wheel, her chin jutted, her full-lipped mouth appeared sullen.

"Home, where we grew up."

"Why?"

"He wants to." She didn't say he thought she needed to get away.

"Then you won't care if Fergie and I take a little trip at the same time, will you?"

More silence. Did she care? Yes, but how could she object?

At the apartment, she changed clothes. "I'm going for a walk. I feel like there's a pound of lead in my gut."

Sarah turned on the TV and plunked herself on the sofa. "I'll be here."

It was after midnight and the empty sidewalks lit by streetlights spooked her. She had never been afraid at the nursery when out walking the grounds. Here, she expected someone to jump out at her from the hidden corners or doorways of the buildings or from behind the parked cars. She hadn't felt that way when she was walking Willie, as if Willie could protect her.

She returned to the apartment after a short time. Sarah was still watching the tube. "I'm going to bed," she said.

"Okay."

She dozed, her physical discomfort just under the surface of slumber. When Sarah came to bed, the mattress shifted under her weight. Sarah rolled away from her and fell into a noisy sleep.

Lindsey awoke tired at six, closed the bedroom door behind her, and made coffee. She sat on the sofa and read *Five Smooth Stones*. She had forgotten more about the book than she remembered. She doubted that two people could still love each other after years of separation like the couple in the story. She hoped Gregg didn't love her like that. She knew Sarah never would.

Sarah was still sleeping when Hugh rang the buzzer and galloped up the stairs. Lindsey poured him a cup of coffee and smiled tiredly.

"You okay, little sis?" He looked around. "I thought I saw Sarah's car out there."

"You did. She's still asleep."

Hugh's gray hair fell over his forehead, and he brushed it back. She handed him a hot cup of coffee. They sat at the table, talking about Hugh's home on the lake. "I think you'll love it there. It's a good getaway."

"God knows, I need one," she responded.

"What's with all the noise?" Sarah said.

"Just your normal everyday conversation at eleven in the morning," Hugh remarked. "Put some clothes on, will you?"

Sarah wore an undershirt and panties. "It's hot in here." She returned to the bedroom and came out in a T-shirt and shorts. "What's for breakfast?"

"Eggs and bacon and tomatoes on toasted muffins," Lindsey said. "I'll start the bacon."

Hugh left after they ate. As she listened to him bound down the steps, Lindsey realized she'd miss him. He was the link to family she was missing.

Sarah sat on the couch, drinking coffee and watching TV.

"I can't stand having the television on all the time," Lindsey said.

"Maybe you can't stand having me around," Sarah shot back. "I'm going to take a shower."

When she squeezed her eyes shut to put shampoo in her hair, the shower curtain moved and Sarah stepped inside the tub.

"Let me do that," Sarah said, taking over the washing. Her wet lips touched Lindsey's as water streamed down their faces.

It was the first time they'd done it in the shower, and it wasn't so easy. The hard, smooth walls and tub were confining. When Lindsey's legs shook, Sarah lowered them both to their knees. The water turned cool before they were done.

XXV

Lindsey phoned her daughter and son twice a week, trying to keep communications open. She left short messages on Natalie's answer machine, keeping her tone light, never saying anything about Sarah or asking about Natalie's personal life. Her attempts at conversation with Matt were awkward and short. Again, she said nothing about Sarah or her personal life, knowing such comments would put off Matt and alienate Natalie even further.

Natalie never replied. Matt sometimes called his mother. Lindsey drove to Madison every couple of weeks to have lunch with him. When he could, Hugh joined them.

She asked Gregg or Matt for news of Natalie. Matt said his sister had told him she missed her mother, but she just wasn't able to talk to her right now. Gregg told her he couldn't make Natalie call her. They both said Natalie was more than a little involved with the attorney who lived in her apartment building.

"Have they moved in together yet?" Lindsey asked Matt.

"Confidential info, Mom."

She was cut out of the loop. This threw her into such a depression she hardly noticed the progression of spring into summer. When she took Willie home on Sunday after a weekend visit toward the middle of May, she was amazed at the number of people at the nursery. A teenage boy asked her if she needed help as she stood outside the van, staring out over the greenery.

"You're new here," she said.

"Yes." He looked uncertain.

Eddie hurried toward her, his homely face lit with a smile. He shooed the boy away. "You're looking good, Lindsey."

Was she? She didn't feel good. "Thanks. How was your winter?" Somehow she had missed seeing him other times when picking up and leaving Willie.

"Okay. It feels good to be working again. How about you?"

"I'm all right. I brought Willie back."

"Should I find Gregg?"

"Don't bother him, I'll just put Willie in the house."

"It's not the same without you, Lindsey," Eddie said, toeing the ground.

"I miss the place, too." She longed for the fresh air, the sun, the smell of growing things and the sounds and sight of birds. The brass factory was confining. The grounds around the apartment buildings spawned sterile environments with little bird life, fewer flowers, identical trees and trampled grass littered with dog poop. People were supposed to pick up after their dogs, but there were plenty who let the stuff lie where it fell for others to step on.

"How's Toni working out?"

He blushed and looked away, which meant Toni was probably cozy with Gregg. Well, more power to him and her, she thought. She couldn't even hang onto Sarah, who spent as much time with Fergie as she did with Lindsey.

"I better let you get back to work." She turned toward the house.

"Nice to see you," Eddie said, also turning away.

"Same here, Eddie."

She patted Willie, cooing into his ear before leaving, "I'll be back soon." She had nothing to bring back with him. She had bought a leash, food, treats and bowls for his visits. She'd even purchased a doggy bed. Her apartment was his home away from home, and he seemed to love going there.

It was like having weekend custody of a child. She did what he liked to do, which meant long walks and trips to the dog park. She blinked back tears and wiped her nose with the back of her hand when she left and he tried to follow.

Someone from out-of-town named Reba Mackenzie was reading her novel at the bookstore that night. Lindsey had bought her book, entitled *A Matter of the Heart*, and had read it over the weekend. It wasn't a long book, but her attention span was often short.

Sarah had told her she was coming over Friday night. Around five o'clock she'd phoned and said she couldn't come.

"I'm making enchiladas with Spanish rice and beans," Lindsey said. It was one of Sarah's favorite meals. "The margaritas are made, the chips are out. You said you were coming over."

"I forgot Fergie had tickets to the PAC. Can't turn that down, can I? We could come and eat first."

Sometimes Sarah's callousness left her wordless, but this hadn't been one of the times. "Never mind," she snapped. She didn't like Fergie. Fergie's moods switched from dark to light with a rapidity that frightened Lindsey. Sarah just ignored the quick changes. She would invite Jimmy and Patrick or Jody and Barb instead. But everyone else had made other plans, so she ate and drank alone. And started the book.

Sarah called her Saturday morning, when Lindsey was out walking with Willie, and left a message. "We're going to the flower and patio show. Want to come?"

She phoned back. "Who are we?"

"Fergie and me. I don't care much about flowers or patios. Why don't you come?"

"No, thanks. Am I going to see you tonight?"

"Maybe later. You have Willie, right? We're going to a movie. I don't suppose you want to leave him behind."

She wondered if Gregg had experienced the same physical pain at her infidelity that she experienced with Sarah's. What goes around really does come around, she thought. She had no proof, but she'd have to be a fool not to believe Sarah and Fergie were intimate.

She passed Barb walking Tarzan and beeped the horn. Pulling in behind the apartment, she bounded up the stairs. Slathering peanut butter on two pieces of bread, she ate the sandwich on the way to the bookstore Sunday night.

She was running late, and the rooms were crowded with those who came as much to see each other as to take part in whatever was going on. The anger she harbored toward Sarah flared and ebbed. What was the point unless she was willing to give her up? Her chest hurt behind her ribs, but she couldn't stay away.

A woman stood at the front of the room with Sarah and Lorrie. Lindsey took a seat in the back row next to no one she knew, slouching down in the chair, hiding from those in the front.

Jimmy called to her, "Come sit with us, Lindsey." He patted a chair next to him near the front of the room, then stood up and gestured at her.

"Okay, okay," she said more to herself than to him.

Sarah looked out over the crowd as Lindsey slunk next to Jimmy.

"Are you hiding or something?" he asked. "Where's Willie?"

"Yes, and I took him home. I only have custody every other weekend."

"You're trying to avoid Sarah, aren't you?" His eyes pierced hers for information about this.

She nodded.

"You look like you haven't slept all weekend."

"I didn't," she muttered.

"She's cheating on you, isn't she?" He sympathetically nodded his head, which she found annoying.

169

Sarah tapped the microphone and cleared her throat. "Okay, guys, listen up. Reba Mackenzie is here from Madison. She's going to read from her book. We'll have copies for sale after the reading."

Reba stepped up to the mike, and the room hushed. "Hi. I wrote this book at the end of a devastating love affair. It got me over the hump. Writing is good therapy. I'm going to start at the beginning of the book," she said, and began to read.

I last saw Joan on New Year's Eve a year ago. She was leaning into a stiff breeze outside the house where Tim and Mike were giving a party. I thought at the time that she needed something to keep her on her feet, and wind was as good a prop as any. She was drunk and nasty. The two went hand in hand with her. We'd had a terrible fight. One of those quiet, intense battles that happen in the midst of other people. I walked away from her into the stinging snow, not caring if she fell face first onto the sidewalk, which I heard later she did.

She would have died of hypothermia had not a couple come across her wandering the semi-deserted streets and took her to the hospital. I should have done that instead of striding away, but she wouldn't have gone with me. Still, I should have tried. I was too angry at the time, and I knew others would see her there. For some reason it never occurred to me that she would wander off.

I spied her across the room at the art gallery, standing in front of Tim's paintings with Tim and Mike, the two men whose party she had left that New Year's Eve. Tim's art took up an entire wall. He'd told me that when he'd called earlier, begging me to come see his work.

I wanted to leave, but my friend, Evelyn, grabbed me by the arm and marched me toward the threesome. She whispered encouragement in my ear, "She's just a woman. Get over it, honey. She can't hurt you anymore."

There was no use digging in my heels, we were moving too fast, narrowly avoiding clusters of people, some of whom we knew, who spoke to us in passing. Then we were there, and I stared at Joan, my former lover of ten years.

She gave me a twisted smile. "I wondered when I'd see you again. You look terrified. Do I do that to you?"

170

Did she? Yes. So much so that I'd left most of my belongings in the apartment we'd shared. Twice I'd snuck back during a weekday to get some things. The third time the locks had been changed.

"I still have some of your most prized possessions." She arched an eyebrow and took a sip of wine.

A server stopped with a tray of wine-filled glasses and a plate of cheeses. Evelyn put a glass in my hand. I forced myself to look at the wall, at Tim's art brightly splashed across the watercolor papers, framed in metal and glass.

"Brilliant, Tim," I said. "I love the colors."

"Thanks," he replied, looking from me to Joan. "You should give them back."

"She should come and get them," Joan shot back.

"You changed the locks."

"Maybe Tim and Mike will move them to your place. Say next Saturday?"

She stopped reading and smiled.

Lindsey was fascinated and shuffled in a line to the table where the author sat, signing books. "I wish I could write."

Reba Mckenzie smiled at her. "Anybody can write. Give it a try." She wasn't a good-looking woman. Her nose and mouth were slashes in a long face, but she had luxurious black hair just beginning to gray, and her eyes behind wire-rimmed glasses looked kind.

"I loved the reading," she said, giving Reba her copy to sign.

"Thanks."

A woman crowded up behind Lindsey, and she moved toward Sarah, who took her arm.

"Stay the night," she said.

"I can't. I don't have any clothes for work tomorrow."

"You can go home early. I'm not letting go till you say yes." A slow, promising smile curved her lips. "I'll make it worth your while."

The physical effect was actually debilitating. Her legs turned into the proverbial wet noodles, her pulse became rapid, and her skin turned a deep red. "No," she said.

Sarah laughed. "Your body says yes."

She ended up hanging around and going upstairs with Sarah, but she went without the enthrallment that had accompanied their first days and weeks together and with no illusions about Sarah. She just wasn't ready to let go yet.

They'd gotten better and better at sex. Their bodies slid in a layer of sweat, their moans deepening with the achingly exquisite climb toward climax.

Afterward, they lay on their backs, a cooling space between them, their breathing slowing to normal. It was then that Lindsey felt someone watching.

She looked toward the bedroom door. Fergie stood there, an expression of wondering disgust on her face. Lindsey pulled the sheet over her body.

"You told me you weren't doing it with her anymore," Fergie said. "Liar."

"You have no right to be here." Sarah jumped up, totally naked as she had been when Lorrie had surprised them. Lorrie had fled in embarrassment. Fergie stood her ground.

While they yelled at each other, Lindsey wrapped herself in the sheet off the bed and carried her clothes into the bathroom. She dressed and tried to slip around them and down the stairs, thinking once she was out of there, Fergie would calm down. Fergie caught her by the hair and jerked it hard. She wrenched her head sideways, leaning into the pressure, trying to escape the pain. Her eyes watered, and she grabbed Fergie's wrist, but Fergie was stronger and angrier than she was.

"Tramp. You're fucking a married woman."

Sarah wrestled Lindsey's hair out of Fergie's hands and Lindsey shot out the door and down the stairs. Not until she was in her van, heading toward the apartment, did she feel safe. She stopped trembling when she climbed in bed under the sheet.

XXVI

Sarah called her at work the next day. "I'm sorry about Fergie. She's got a temper."

"I can't talk about this here. I don't have time. Just keep her away from me."

"The thing is, Lindsey, I don't know if I can."

Chills spread across her body. "What do you mean?"

"I don't think she'll hurt you, but she may show up at your apartment or work. Just tell her to fuck off."

"You tell her to stay away from me."

"I did. I'll come over to your place nights."

"That'll be sure to anger her."

"I can't leave you alone."

Because Lindsey didn't want Sarah to leave her alone, she didn't respond, but asked, "What does Fergie drive?"

"A dark green Explorer. There are a hundred million of them around. Hers has a diversity bumper sticker."

"I'll call you if I see it. Now I've got to go."

Frightened, she looked around like a startled animal when she went outside. She figured she knew what a deer felt like during hunting season. Her heart leaped painfully whenever she saw a dark green Explorer.

Sarah kept her word and spent the nights at Lindsey's apartment. After a week, Lindsey began to relax. Maybe Sarah was wrong in her assessment of Fergie. Or perhaps Fergie hadn't found out where Lindsey lived.

Then one Saturday night around midnight someone pounded on the apartment door. Sarah sat up sleepily. "Should I go see who it is?"

"No, wait." Lindsey pulled on sweats. "I'll ask. Then I'll call the police."

She could see no one through the peephole. "Who is it?" she called.

"Open up. There are a couple of lesbians in here," Fergie shouted.

Lindsey punched in 911. Before the police got there, Fergie left, pounding on doors, announcing that the women in 211 were lesbians.

When the officers arrived, the policeman asked with pad of paper and pencil in hand, "Do you know who this person is?"

"No," Sarah said.

"Yes, we do," Lindsey countered.

"We never saw her. She was very homophobic, though, yelling stuff about us." Sarah gave Lindsey a look that said *shut-up*.

Lindsey met Sarah's eyes. "Her name is Nancy Ferguson."

"What did she do besides yell?" the woman cop asked. Lindsey thought she was a handsome thing, tall and lithesome with short reddishm curly hair, gray eyes and freckles. She glowed with health. In contrast, her overweight partner's ruddy face lined with broken blood vessels warned of a heart attack waiting to happen.

Lindsey felt a flush coming on. "She yelled for us to open up, and on the way out she pounded on doors."

A smirk crossed the chubby man's face, but disappeared when his partner glared at him. "Sounds like disturbing the peace and trespassing. How did she get in the building?"

"She must have buzzed some other apartment or followed someone in."

"What other history is there on this person?" the woman officer asked. "Has she threatened either of you?"

"She grabbed me by the hair when I was visiting Sarah."

"Do you want to press charges?"

"I don't want her coming here again," Lindsey said.

"We'll pay a call on her. Do you know where she lives?"

"Sarah does."

Lindsey knew Sarah was silently fuming, but so was she. Sarah said she'd forgotten Fergie's address, and Lindsey challenged her. "You go over there often enough. You must know the street."

"Do you know her telephone number?" the woman asked.

Sarah reluctantly gave them the number.

"We'll be in touch," the woman cop said.

Several tenants were standing in the hallway when the officers left.

Sarah stomped into the bedroom and turned on Lindsey. "That was just great. Do you realize what you've done?" she hissed.

"No, what have I done except report someone who attacked me and tried to break into my apartment?"

"You turned on a fellow lesbian."

"One who goes around assaulting other lesbians and outing them."

"She's my ex-lover and friend," Sarah said.

"After what she did the other day and now? Some friend."

Sarah picked up her backpack and headed toward the door.

"Where are you going?"

"Home." She turned with one hand on the doorknob.

"You weren't going to leave me alone? Remember? What if she comes back?"

"Call the police. You had eyes for that lady cop."

"Yeah, sure."

Sarah shut the door behind her, and Lindsey heard her feet on the stairs. Looking out the window, she saw Sarah's Escort zip out of the parking lot and accelerate on the street.

Her head pounded in time to her heart. She knew she wouldn't sleep. She read until after three in the morning, when she finally slipped into a dream.

She awoke to sunshine and the ringing phone. Rolling over in bed, she picked up the receiver.

"Hi. It's Paula Nelson. I'm the police person who was at your apartment last night."

"You're still working?"

"I'd just gone on duty when we were sent to your apartment."

Lindsey looked at the clock. Eight o'clock. She felt limp with fatigue and fell back on the pillows.

"We paid that call on Nancy Ferguson. She denied being there, and since you didn't actually see her, there isn't much to go on."

"Sarah knows her well," she said. "It was Fergie all right."

"I'm sorry I can't do more. You could try to get a restraining order."

"I'll think about it. Thanks for taking this seriously."

"That's my job. If you have any more trouble, call and ask for me."

"Right. Paula Nelson."

She spent Sunday alone, only going to the store for groceries. While walking around the back of her van, she noticed glass on the blacktop. Her right taillight was smashed.

"Shit." She'd have to have another one put on, and she couldn't do that till Tuesday. If she'd been at the nursery, she'd have had the tools to replace it herself. "Damn her."

Fleet Farm's garage was open. She stopped, paid them to replace the light, and went on to the grocery store, where she ran into Paula Nelson.

176

"I do my shopping before I go home to bed. Otherwise I won't do it at all."

Lindsey almost blurted that she looked great for not having had any sleep. "I was up most of the night myself. So, I guess we're both a little bushed."

"Did you have any more trouble?"

"My taillight was broken. I didn't know that when I talked to you on the phone. Other than that, no." She was ashamed to say how frightened she was of Fergie.

"There are some scary people out there," Paula said, as if reading Lindsey's mind.

"I guess so. Well, thanks again for coming to my rescue last night."

"I'll rescue you anytime. Just let me know." Paula pushed her cart toward the checkout counters.

Lindsey wondered if Paula's remark was meant to show a personal interest in her and decided probably not. The woman was into saving people. That was her job. She finished her shopping and drove to the apartment.

It was a gorgeous day. A week from Monday was Memorial Day. She threw open all the windows in the apartment, put the groceries away, and sat on the balcony with Reba's book open in her lap. Sunshine covered her. She knew she should be doing something outdoorsy, like hiking in a park, but she had no energy. She was struggling not to fall into a funk.

The phone rang several times, but she stayed put. Her chin sagged to her chest, and she slipped in and out of sleep. When the sun was positioned on the west side of the building, she grew cold. Grabbing an afghan that her grandmother had made, she wrapped herself in it. People sprawled on blankets on the grassy strips between buildings. The buzzer buzzed loud and long. She ignored it.

"Hey, sis, open the door," Hugh called, pounding on it.

She jumped up from the lawn chair, her butt sore from so much sitting, and unlocked the latch. "How did you get into the building?"

"Someone let me in. Why aren't you answering the phone?" He peered closer at her. His eyes mirrored hers, hazel and darkly lashed. A lock of gray hair fell over his forehead. "What happened?"

She told him, while he poured them each a drink. She pushed hers away. "I don't want it."

"Drink it." He shoved it toward her. "I'm taking you away from here. It's time for that vacation I talked about. I'd planned to go later in the summer, but it looks like you could use a break."

"I've got a job. Remember?" she said gloomily.

"So do I. Take a week off."

"When?"

"Friday we leave. That'll give you plenty of time to talk to your boss and do everything else needs doing. We'll come back the following Sunday. You'll need your swimsuit, sunblock, jeans, shorts, T-shirts, sweatshirts and pants. Nothing fancy. Better throw in a jacket."

She stood transfixed, thinking about logistics—telling her boss and Gregg in case anything happened, communicating with her children, not telling Sarah, washing clothes and packing, going to the bank, getting library books, rescheduling any appointments. She was lunching with Carol on Tuesday and seeing Kate on Wednesday. Of course, she had to work Monday, Wednesday and maybe Thursday if she wasn't going to be there Friday.

"It's my weekend with Willie."

"Ah, the custody thing," he said. "Bring him along. There's room for one small dog."

"Really? You don't mind?"

"I like Willie."

"What time are we going?"

"Between eight and nine. I'll leave you alone to get ready. You can tell me what happened on Friday on the way."

XXVII

After Hugh clambered down the stairs, she sat on the sofa. A mistake. She wanted to lie down and sleep, and there were all these things she had to do to get ready to leave Friday.

The phone rang. She stared at it as if it were an explosive device. Perhaps it was Paula, or Carol, or Matt, or, more likely, Sarah. Whoever it was could leave a message.

Forcing herself to get up, she gathered her dirty clothes and carried them downstairs to the laundry room. No one washed clothes on Sunday, so she had the washer and dryer to herself. She started the wash and went back up to her apartment.

Just deciding what to pack became a problem. She looked into her dresser drawers at the assortment of T-shirts, turtlenecks and sweaters. After a while, she started putting things that matched into the suitcase next to her on the bed.

When she finally felt pangs of hunger, the laundry and packing were done. She slid the suitcase under the bed just in case Sarah showed up and let herself in. She had hooked the chain on the apartment door, but no one had come other than Hugh.

Making herself a peanut butter sandwich, she turned on public television. The phone continued to ring intermittently with no one leaving a message. In one of the pauses, she called Gregg.

"Have you got a minute?" She heard his television in the background.

"Sure. I have something to tell you anyway."

Sure it was about Natalie, she asked, "What?"

"You first," he said.

"I'm going out of town with Hugh Friday. I'll be gone a week, at least." She wasn't sure why she added the 'at least.' "It's my weekend to have Willie. Do you mind if he comes with us. I'd have to pick him up Thursday afternoon."

"He'll be waiting on the porch. Where are you going?"

"Home. Hugh has a place on the lake there." She gave him Hugh's cell phone number. "Just in case . . ." She paused before asking, "How are the kids?"

"Natalie's engaged to Paul."

The pain of being excluded left her a little breathless. Not even Matt had told her. She struggled to keep her composure. "Don't you think it's kind of soon?"

"That's not my decision to make," he said, anger creeping into his voice.

She ignored it. "Have they set a date?"

"Not yet."

When she hung up, she unhooked the phone from the wall receptacle. In the night, the buzzer woke her. She'd fallen asleep on the sofa. Getting up, she turned off the television and all the lights and went to bed. After a while, the buzzing stopped. Curled in a knot, she waited tensely for someone to pound on the door. Sarah still had a key, so why would she buzz? When no one knocked, she wondered if it had been Fergie. At last, she fell asleep.

♋

Tuesday at noon she met Carol at a different downtown restaurant. As yet, she hadn't talked to or seen Sarah. She embraced her friend more warmly than usual.

"Are you all right, Lindsey?" Carol swung her purse off her shoulder and threw it and her jacket onto her side of the booth. "You look kind of peaked."

"I'm just glad to see you." She was lonely.

The waitress brought them coffee and they ordered sandwiches and chips.

"I'm always glad to see you." Carol gave her a small, questioning smile. "What's going on, girl?"

Lindsey told her of Natalie's engagement, about Fergie's scene at the apartment and the smashed taillight, how Sarah tried to cover up for Fergie when the police showed up.

"I haven't called either Natalie or Matt since I talked to Gregg. I don't know what to say to them, not that Natalie answers the phone." She hadn't had a conversation with Natalie since she'd left Gregg.

"You need a computer, sweetie. Do you want me to e-mail or call Natalie?"

It wasn't what Lindsey expected to hear, nor was it what she wanted. "What? To put in a good word for *me*?"

"Sorry, sweetie. Kids can be brats. I know mine can, anyway. Congratulate her. Give her time. She'll come around."

Without warning, Lindsey began to cry. She swiped angrily at the tears. "My life sucks. I feel as if I made a terrible mistake. I must have been nuts to leave Gregg for someone like Sarah. Please don't say you warned me."

"I know some very nice lesbians, including yourself. Sarah is not a poster woman for dykes. There are others out there."

"I can think of one, but she works at the bookstore." Lorrie failed to set off any sparks in her, but maybe if she knew her better, that would change.

"I think you need to stay away from the bookstore."

"I'm going on vacation with Hugh Friday. We'll be gone a week."

"Sounds like an idea that came just in time. Where are you heading?"

"Home," she said.

"Come back. I'd miss you terribly."

"And I you. How's your life?" Lindsey asked, surprised at the plea.

"Better than yours, kiddo."

She phoned Natalie that night and left a message congratulating her on her engagement. Steering clear of giving any unsolicited advice, she said she hoped to meet Paul someday soon.

Matt came next. She told his answering machine that she was going out of town with Hugh, and that Gregg had Hugh's cell phone number if he needed to get in touch.

She'd informed everyone who needed to know. John, her boss, had told her to take as much time off as she wanted, but to let him know if she planned to stay longer. He would hire a temporary worker.

Because he'd been good to her, she wished she liked the job better. If she walked out of the office at the end of the week and never went back, she knew she'd not miss the place. She had told him that she'd work Thursday in lieu of Friday.

After work on Wednesday, she drove to Kate's office. As soon as she stepped into the reception room, a calm settled over her. Here she could tell all and be safe from censure.

Letting out a sigh as her shoulder and neck muscles relaxed, she sank into a chair in Kate's office. Carol had been right when she said the vacation had come just in time. Experiencing a moment of panic, she wondered if Hugh would change his mind. Surely he would have let her know before now if he had.

"I'm going away for a while." She brought Kate up to speed. "It's such a struggle to get ready, though. I want to lie down and sleep in the worst way. I have to force myself to do anything."

"Sounds like depression," Kate said.

"I wonder if Gregg felt this same physical ache when I left him. There are no meds for it, and it doesn't let you alone. I never knew till now. All that talk about heartache I thought was the stuff of songs."

Kate nodded, and Lindsey wondered if she'd experienced it, too. She didn't ask. Her own was as much as she could bear. If she dwelled on how she'd hurt Gregg and the kids, she'd collapse under the weight of guilt.

"I haven't seen Sarah since the weekend, nor have I answered the phone or door. I don't respect her or even like her a lot of the time, but I know I won't be able to resist her." She chewed on her lip. What did this say about her? Did she have no will? "The only escape is to run away."

"Are you not coming back?"

"You're the third person to suggest I might not."

"What do you say to that?"

"I can't just walk away and leave everyone and everything behind."

"People have," Kate told her.

"I suppose." She pictured Carol's face when she'd asked her to come back. "Are you suggesting I should?"

"Certainly not. I think you should consider staying longer if you feel the need, though."

At the apartment, she left her car in the parking lot and climbed the stairs. She had only to get through tomorrow, and she wanted desperately to be gone. The door was unlocked, meaning Sarah was there. She possessed the only other key.

Sarah sprawled on the sofa, her arms outstretched across the back of it. "So you're going home with Hugh," she said.

Guessing Sarah didn't know where home was, she kept an even tone, "I want my key back." She wiggled her fingers, but kept her distance.

Sarah tossed the key on the floor between them. "I could take you right now if I wanted to. You're not worth it, though."

"Leave then." Lindsey bent over to retrieve the key, and Sarah threw her to the floor. She landed with a thud that knocked the breath out of her. She hadn't the strength to throw Sarah off.

Turning her head sideways when Sarah tried to kiss her neck and face, she felt herself responding. The helpless anger of that moment should have shielded her from any desire, but there it was.

Sarah held her down with the weight of her body and one hand. "You're ready." She laughed as she slipped her hand in Lindsey's pants. She pulled her fingers away and jumped to her feet.

"You can finish the job yourself," she said, going out the door, leaving it open.

Well, that's it, Lindsey thought, still flat on her back. It's over, and on Sarah's terms. Instead of relief, she felt an almost unbearable loneliness. Getting up, she closed and locked the door, putting the chain on for good measure.

She'd trashed her life for this woman. What a fool she'd been. The need to get out of the apartment overwhelmed her. It was warm and fine outside. She emerged into the same bright sunlight she'd left and drove to the nearest park. There should be plenty of people on trails that meandered through acres of woods. Her imagination made her a little hesitant. If she met up with Fergie when she was alone, she could neither outrun her nor was she a match in a physical struggle.

Lindsey started into the greenery, watching her feet so as not to trip over the roots on the path. When she looked up, she saw Paula coming toward her. "I thought you worked nights and slept days," she blurted in pleased surprise. Here was someone who could protect her if needed.

"Sometimes I work days and sleep nights." Paula wore jeans and a T-shirt with the words *Off Duty* across the front. A small smile grew steadily stronger. "It's odd that we keep meeting."

"If we'd run into each other before last weekend, I wouldn't have known who you were." Lindsey didn't believe fate threw people together. It just happened.

"Want to walk a ways?" Paula asked.

"Sure, but aren't you headed back?"

"I don't have anything to go back to, and it's too nice to be inside."

They went further into the woods. The leaves were the pale, nearly translucent color of spring. A carpet of white and blue flowers covered the ground in the open places. Dust and tiny insects danced in the sun that glinted through the branches. Breathing deeply the odors of earth and new growth, Lindsey tried to expunge the scene with Sarah from her mind.

"How did you happen to become a policewoman?" she asked.

"On the career test, I scored high in that category." Paula laughed. "Everybody always said I was bossy, that I like to be in charge."

Lindsey couldn't remember taking a test to determine what career might best suit her. "Are you? Do you?" She wondered what her test results might have been. Perhaps they would have given her some direction.

"Doesn't everybody want to control their environment?"

Lindsey nodded. "I suppose. The only control we really have is over how we react to things."

Paula stopped and turned toward her, forcing Lindsey to halt, too. "We have control over what we do."

"Not always."

"And when is that?" Paula's eyebrows arched in question.

Lindsey searched for examples. "Suppose someone took your gun from you and forced you to rob a store. Or a car ran yours off the road."

"Those are extreme situations."

"True, but they show that you're not always in control of everything except how you react."

Paula moved on, and Lindsey picked up the pace. She hadn't been to the Y to exercise for at least a week. Now she stayed away for fear she'd run into Sarah.

"You walk fast for someone so short," Paula said.

"I could say for a tall person, you sort of poke along."

Paula laughed. "I thought we were having a conversation."

185

"No reason we can't walk and talk at the same time, is there?"
And then she tripped and fell headlong onto the dirt-worn path.
"Goddamn!"

"Are you all right?" Paula asked, helping Lindsey to her feet
and brushing her off.

Her shirt was smeared and her right arm ached, but she tried to
hide her embarrassment and limped on a few steps. "I'm okay."

"Hold on. You hurt your ankle." Paula stopped her with a hand
on her shoulder. "Sit down for a minute." She pointed at a fallen
tree by the side of the path. "Let me check you out."

"What? Now you're a nurse, too? And bossy." Lindsey was sure
the ankle was okay. Her arm hurt more.

"And you're a feisty little thing." Paula made her sit and knelt
on one knee. She held Lindsey's ankle gently in her hands.

"I'm annoyed at being so clumsy, is all. I can walk the ankle
out." Paula's probing fingers hurt only a little.

"Why are you holding your arm?"

Lindsey carefully moved the arm around. It wasn't broken. "It's
fine. Let's go on."

"Let's go back. We can get a cup of coffee. There's a place down
the road."

Over coffee, Lindsey apologized. "Sorry if I snapped at you. I
do that when I hurt myself."

"I'm used to it. People snap at me all the time," Paula said,
"even when I'm trying to help."

"It's the control thing again."

"Can I call you sometime?" Paula asked.

"Sure, but I'm leaving for a week's vacation tomorrow."

"After you get back, I'll give you a buzz."

The phone rang two different times that night. When the
answering machine kicked in, whoever it was hung up. Shortly
after the last call, someone hit the buzzer. Lindsey turned off the
lights and radio and went to bed. Apparently, Sarah wasn't through

with her, or maybe it was Fergie. She listened intently. The door was locked and chained. When the phone rang after midnight, she disconnected it.

After work on Thursday, she drove to the nursery to pick up Willie. These trips to the house were awkward for her. She always felt anxious beforehand, and both relieved and disappointed when she saw no one she knew, except Willie. Gregg arranged to be gone at such times, she was sure.

Always glad to see her, Willie waited inside the porch door. She clipped his leash on before taking him outside. He jumped in the front seat of the van and sat there looking out the windshield, panting expectantly.

XXVIII

Lindsey awoke just after six. She hadn't slept well, waiting as she had for the buzzer or a knock on the door. Light filled the apartment. Mourning doves cooed in the bushes below. A robin sang repetitively from a nearby tree. Relief that they were leaving today flooded her with excitement.

Willie stood and stretched. She took him out for a quick pee and poop, and fed him a little food, while she made a pot of coffee and took a shower.

After eating a couple of pieces of toast and dressing, she dragged her suitcase out from under the bed. She was sitting on the sofa, reading when Hugh called on his cell phone. She picked up the phone when he started to leave a message.

"I'm in the parking lot."

She buzzed him in and stood in the hall while he galloped up the stairs.

"Ready?" he asked. "Looks like Willie's got baggage, too."

"Yep." She slung over one shoulder her backpack with books in it, picked up the bag with Willie's bowls, and grabbed the dog's sleeping pad and leash.

Hugh carried the heavier suitcase and Willie's bag of dog food out to his Sebring, and stowed them in the trunk. Willie jumped into the backseat.

"Going in style," Lindsey said. Although she'd seen the car before, she hadn't ridden in it.

"Get in. Let's hit the road."

They zipped up U.S. 43 to Milwaukee where they picked up U.S. 41 North. The scenery north of the Kettle Moraine district was pretty boring, much as she remembered it. Hugh opened the moon roof and Lindsey fell asleep with her hair tickling her face.

When she woke up hungry, Hugh handed her a peanut butter sandwich. They turned off onto the 441 bypass, crossed Little Lake Butte des Morts and picked up state highways 10 and 114.

"Almost there," Hugh said, turning off onto one of the fire lanes that led to Lake Winnebago.

Almost every waking mile came back to her as if she'd made the trip only a week ago, except for the last stretch to the lake. She had never been to Hugh's new home. The lake lay in full view as they approached the road that accessed the backyards of the homes fronting the water.

Willie panted in her ear as if he knew the trip was almost over.

Hugh pulled into a wooded lot with a smaller house than its surrounding neighbors. He opened the garage and drove inside. "Here we are, sis."

From the garage they entered a mudroom with hooks on the walls and boot trays lining the floor. This small room led to a kitchen and dining area, which were adjacent to a great room with windows facing the lake. The water glinted in the sunlight as it washed steadily against the shore. An open stairway at the east end of the big room climbed to a sleeping loft with two bedrooms separated by a bathroom. The door to the master bedroom with its own bath was under the stairs. A fieldstone fireplace with bookshelves on either side occupied the entire west wall.

"It's wonderful, Hugh," she said, turning in a circle. The floors were oak, the furniture comfortable, the photographs on the walls were mostly of the sailboats racing across the waves.

He smiled. "Come on. I'll show you the lake."

He took her down wide stone steps to the beach, a small stretch of sand flanked by rocks. The water, widening away from the shore, stretched for miles to the south. A greenish tinge hid the lake bottom. Willie took a drink, then waded in up to his belly.

Hugh sat in one of the Adirondack chairs near the beach and motioned to the other. "Sit, sis. You haven't told me anything."

She realized with surprise that she hadn't even thought about the things in her life that distressed her—not Sarah, not Natalie, Matt nor Gregg. She hated bringing them front and center by talking about them.

A soft breeze blew their way, carrying the smell of the lake and lifting Willie's ears. Offshore a sailboat race was in progress, the sails dipping in the wind.

"I thought you'd have a sailboat after seeing all those photographs on your walls. Is it in there?" She pointed at a small building on the beach.

"No. It's at the marina." He stood up. "Tell you what. I'll make us drinks. You can fill me in on what happened last weekend when I return."

She leaned back in the chair, her eyes on the water. Too restless to sit long, she took off her sandals and walked across the cool grass into the cold water. She waded out until the water lapped at her shorts. Willie followed till he started to float, and backed off. The sun beat down, creating a shimmering, watery pathway. Her legs turned numb from cold, contrasting with the heat radiating off her upper body.

"Come on back, Linds," Hugh called. "It's happy hour."

What a joke, she thought, but for the first time since she left Gregg, she felt almost carefree. She turned and waded back, the sand squeezing between her toes. Wiping her feet on the grass, she sat down in the Adirondack chair and lifted her glass. "Thanks for the drink and for bringing me here, Hugh. I feel like I've been rescued."

"That bad, huh?" he said. He made no further comments till she finished telling him all that had happened, when he asked, "That's it?"

"Isn't that enough?" All the worries had swooped down on her with the retelling.

He sighed. "You've got yourself in a conundrum, sweetie. You could chase your tail all day, every day, trying to please these people and never succeed. Forget about trying to resolve things with Natalie and Matt. That'll come with time. My advice is to steer clear of Fergie, which you can only do by avoiding Sarah. Are you able and willing to do that?" He looked at her over his sunglasses.

"Carol asked if I knew any nice lesbians, and I thought of Lorrie."

"Lorrie's always at the bookstore. You have to stay away from the bookstore."

"I'll be lonely." Where else would she meet any lesbians? She decided she sounded pathetic. The dog sat down next to her, and she stroked him.

"What about this Paula?"

"What about her? Being a policewoman doesn't make her a lesbian. But she did ask if she could call me when I got back." Her friends didn't have to be lesbians. Carol wasn't.

"See. There's a possibility." He wagged a finger at her.

"Paula's bossy and controlling. She told me that. Is Jimmy coming up?"

"A little bossy gets things done. And no. This is just family. Jimmy's got a big mouth. He might tell someone you're here. We don't want Sarah showing up."

"Oh, she's given me up. She threw the key on the floor and walked out."

"Then who made all the phone calls and never left a message?"

A chill rolled in over the lake, forcing them to move inside, which wasn't much different than being outside. The views from the house were only slightly muted by the glass. Hugh cranked a couple of windows open enough to let in the smells and sounds. Gulls screamed, fighting over a fish one of them had caught.

191

"Do you like salmon?" he asked, "fresh green beans, a baked potato?"

She hadn't seen him bring in any food, but an empty cooler sat on the kitchen floor. "Sounds great." She put food and water into the dog's bowls and climbed onto a stool at the counter. "Anything I can do?"

"Talk to me."

"Do you ever see Suzy?" She hadn't seen her sister since their mother died.

"About once a week we have lunch together. I keep her up to date on you and the kinder. She's coming Sunday and Monday, just to see you."

"Why didn't you tell me?"

He shrugged. "I thought it would be a nice surprise."

"What did she say when I left Gregg?"

"She said she always knew."

Astounded, Lindsey asked, "How could she know when I didn't?"

"There were never any boys around when you were growing up, only girlfriends." He puttered around the kitchen, getting out the salmon, washing the potatoes.

Lindsey took the beans and began breaking them in the sink. The window over the sink looked out on the backyard and access road. It felt almost as if she had begun life anew. She could stay, find a job and an apartment. Maybe Carol hadn't been so far off the mark.

"How much does one of these places along the lake cost?"

"Half a million or more," Hugh said idly. "This is a cheap one. I owned the lot twenty years before I built anything on it."

"Can we drive past Mom's house and go to the cemetery while we're here?"

"I always do." He poured them both a glass of Shiraz and lifted his. "Here's to you and your new life."

"Right," she said sarcastically. "Don't remind me."

❧

She and Willie slept in one of the loft bedrooms with the door and windows open, so that she could smell the water and listen to the waves slapping the shore. Falling asleep immediately, she only woke once and briefly wondered where she was.

Willie softly woofed from his bed, waking her again toward morning, but she was too lazy to get up. "Shush, doggy." He quieted, and she thought she heard someone outside the house. Tiptoeing to the open window fronting the road, she saw a figure standing in the driveway, looking at the house. Heart pounding, she crept down the stairs to Hugh's bedroom, knocked lightly on the door and went in.

"Someone's in the driveway," she said, quieting the dog who kept emitting little woofs.

He rolled out of bed, dressed only in briefs. "Who? Where?" he said groggily.

When they looked out the kitchen window, they saw no one. Hugh threw on shorts and a sweatshirt. Lindsey did the same and put the dog on his leash.

The night was incredibly beautiful. The restless lake reflected the stars strewn across the black sky. She breathed in the redolence of earth and water, and forgot all about the reason they were out there. Besides, they found no one.

Hugh carried a flashlight and played it on the dew-dampened ground near the paved driveway. "See the footprints in the grass. Someone was here. Did it look like Sarah?" He straightened and stared at her.

"I couldn't tell. Why would she bother to come? It's over." She looked around, suddenly afraid again.

Willie snuffled at the ground, straining at the leash, letting out occasional woofs.

"Well, whoever it was is gone. Let's go back inside," Hugh said. "It's a lovely night."

"Want to sit by the lake for a while? I'll get some blankets."

They wiped the dew off the Adirondack chairs, wrapped themselves in afghans and curled up. Willie settled on the small blanket that Hugh brought outside for him. A warm breeze blew away mosquitoes and lake flies. Bats swooped overhead, gobbling up the bugs. The sky and lake seemed as one. When the sky began to lighten, the wind died and the biting insects drove them inside.

She was happy and sleepy. Hugh put on the coffee, and she fed Willie, although it was barely five.

"What do you want to do today, Lindsey?" Hugh asked.

"See your sailboat, go past the old house and visit the cemetery."

"Let's wait for Suzy to do the family stuff. Is Willie seaworthy?"

"Well, he can swim."

XXIX

They left the marina powered by the small outboard motor, the sails furled against the masts. Once past the breakwaters, they followed the channel till they cleared the last sandbar and reached deep enough water to unfurl the sails.

Willie stood at the prow of the boat, looking over the great expanse of water. Hugh had hooked his leash to a life cushion that would keep him afloat if he went overboard or at least mark his location should he go under. Hugh insisted Lindsey wear a life jacket. He wore one himself.

What had seemed a light breeze on the shore turned into a wind that grabbed the open sails and tipped the boat toward the green waves. Lindsey hung onto the railing and the dog. She thought it a wild ride, although later Hugh would say they were never in danger of capsizing. Looking up at the taut white sails against the blue sky, she thought she would remember all of it— the colors, the speed they traveled, the sound of the boom coming round and the sails snapping, water spraying over the sides when the craft dipped dangerously close to the lake. She loved it. It reminded her of sailing with Pete Stafford years ago when she was young. Willie's ears and hair floated above him. His tongue hung out, and Lindsey swore there was a smile on his little face.

Matt would love this, too, she thought, wishing he were here. So would Natalie, but thinking about Natalie hurt too much, so she put those thoughts away. She would live in the moment today and all the days she was here.

Late in the afternoon, Hugh motored back to the marina. As he docked at his berth, Lindsey looked up to see Sarah standing on the pier. Hands in pockets, legs slightly spread, a cocky grin plastered on her face, she looked sure of her welcome.

"Fasten the rope to that cleat, Lindsey. Hurry," Hugh yelled as the bow drifted away from the pier. Hugh jumped in front of her and threw the heavy rope around the cleat and pulled the boat tight. Then he saw Sarah.

"What the hell . . ." he said angrily. "What are you doing here?"

She lifted her brows innocently, her smile intact. "What kind of a welcome is that?"

"It's a warning. We don't want you here."

"Nice boat," she said as if he'd not spoken.

"Go home, Sarah," Hugh said tiredly. "If you trespass on my property again, I'll call the cops."

Lindsey stood quietly, holding Willie by his collar, unable to understand why Sarah was there.

"I just want to talk to Lindsey for a few minutes." She reached out a hand for Lindsey to grab.

Lindsey shook her head, ignoring the hand. For the first time, she realized that Sarah might not let her go easily. Perhaps she had needlessly worried about driving Sarah away, when she should have been concerned about not being able to get rid of her. Even though she knew this was harassment, she also realized if she were alone with Sarah, it would be difficult to say no. She could hide, but not quell the desire.

"Can I come down and see the boat? You've even got a cabin. I've always wanted a sailboat." Sarah put a foot on the ladder.

Hugh grabbed her leg. "What don't you understand about *go away?*"

Sarah kicked, her toe connecting with his chin. "Don't touch me, Hugh. That's assault."

Hugh lay on his back on the floor of the craft. Willie barked in distress. Lindsey knelt by her brother.

"Get my cell phone," Hugh said, massaging his chin. "It's in my duffel bag in the cabin."

Lindsey stumbled down the steps into the cabin, looked wildly around, and came back with the phone in hand.

By now, Sarah was in the boat, and Hugh was on his feet. He took the phone from Lindsey and punched in 911. When he did, Sarah climbed back to the pier.

"I'll be around," she said, strolling toward the Escort parked in the lot.

"Jot down her license number," Hugh said.

This time Lindsey went looking for paper and something to write with. She found it in the drawer of an attached table inside the cabin.

Hugh wrote the number down from memory and told it to the dispatcher. He told Lindsey he didn't expect much action, but it added to the verbal record of harassment.

Lindsey tried to silence the dog. Willie never had warmed up to Sarah. She should have paid more attention.

After gathering their gear, Hugh locked the cabin, and they took off for home. "We'll stop for groceries in Sherwood. I thought we'd go to the supper club out here for dinner, but maybe we better hang around the house. Who knows what she'll do next?"

"I'm sorry. I should have listened to you, Hugh."

"Forget it. I didn't know she was this bad." His chin had begun to swell and discolor.

"Maybe you should have that X-rayed," she said.

"Nah. A couple of drinks will take care of the pain."

It was over those drinks that she confessed she still felt desire for Sarah. "I don't like her. I certainly don't love her. I don't get it."

"It's called lust," he said flatly. "Is she that good?"

They were locked inside the house, watching the waves crash against the shore. The wind had picked up, crowding the sky with clouds.

"No. She's overwhelming, domineering."

"That excites you?" He looked at her with interest.

"I guess. Does it you?"

"Quite the opposite. I like to be in control. You should try it."

"She makes me feel desirable. Of course, I know it's just pretense, but let her corner me and . . ." She shrugged.

"Then we'll just have to keep her at bay." He leaned over Willie, who lay asleep on the rug between them. "Hear that, Willie. That's a dog's job."

Lindsey laughed. "He's good at barking, but he's never bitten anyone."

They ate while the rain sluiced down the windows and the wind whipped the water into giant waves. "This is a dangerous lake in a storm. Huge waves, sandbars and fishing nets that snag boats."

"I know. I got caught out on it in a storm once while crossing in a small boat."

"Yeah? What happened?"

"We were lucky. We ended up on shore instead of at the bottom."

"Whose boat?"

"Steve Randolph. A guy I dated between college years. Did you ever date girls?"

"Sure. I even slept with a few before I got my head on straight and realized what I wanted."

Before going to bed, Lindsey stood in the open garage door, urging Willie to leave shelter and do his business. She ended up getting an umbrella and dragging him outside, where he quickly got the idea.

In the morning water dripped from everything, but the sun hanging over the cliffs on the eastern shore promised to dry things up. The temperature had dropped from the seventies to the fifties. Lindsey again stood inside the open garage door, waiting for Willie to stop wandering around the yard and do what he was there to do.

"Dogs are a pain that way, aren't they? Why can't they learn to use the toilet?"

Lindsey froze for a moment. She called the dog, but he was in pursuit of just the right spot to drop his load and paid no attention, even though she used her dog obedience tone. "Come, Willie."

Sarah walked toward Willie slowly and grabbed him from behind. He let out a surprised yelp, and she put a hand around his muzzle. "I'll take him somewhere where he can run," she said, "unless you want to come with me instead. I'm sure he'd be happier with Hugh. Where is your annoying brother, anyway?

She'd been asking herself that, willing him to appear. "Hugh," she yelled.

Sarah tossed the dog in the back of the Escort and walked around to the driver's side. "Are you coming?"

"Tie the dog up, and I'll come."

"Get in the car first." When Lindsey slid into the Escort, Sarah opened the back door, pushed the dog out, and took off. Willie chased the Escort, barking.

Lindsey opened her door and glanced down at the road moving under them, hesitating long enough for Sarah to reach over and grab her arm. She wrenched free and jumped. The door banged against her as she tumbled from the seat, pushing her against the rear fender of the car. She bounced off it and landed on someone's yard.

Sarah slammed on the brakes, skidding on the asphalt, and leaped out of the car. Hugh was running toward them, yelling something, his cell phone in his hand. The dog landed in Lindsey's lap. Skinned and bruised, she could hardly believe she was in one piece.

"What a stupid thing to do," Sarah said as Hugh reached them.

He bent over, hands on knees, gasping for breath, before kneeling next to Lindsey. "Are you all right, Lindsey? I'll call the police." He sat on the grass and punched in 911.

"She should be X-rayed," Sarah said.

"I can't believe you're still here," Hugh remarked.

"I'm worried about Lindsey."

"You should be worried about being arrested." He began talking to the dispatcher.

Sarah got into her car. "Okay. I'm going. I didn't force her to get into the car. She got in willingly."

"You had the dog," Lindsey said indignantly.

"Last I saw the dog he was chasing my car down the road." Sarah slammed the door and drove off.

"Is she always going to be lurking around wherever I go?"

"Are you cured of her yet?" Hugh asked.

Lindsey struggled to her feet. Everything hurt, especially her right side. She moved her limbs carefully. "I think I'm okay."

"We need to get you X-rayed," Hugh said.

"No. You didn't bother with your chin. Let's wait and see how I am tomorrow. It's too nice a day to spend in a clinic. Besides, I'm not sure I'm covered anymore." A convenient lie. Gregg would tell her before dropping her name from the policy.

"I'll go get the car," he said.

"No, let me walk it out." She thought of her ankle and arm, hurt when she'd fallen while hiking with Paula. She wished Paula would be the cop who came to investigate.

They spent the day sitting in the Adirondack chairs, soaking up sun, reading and occasionally wading into the now calm lake. Willie stuck close as if he'd learned a valuable lesson.

"Think she's gone?" Lindsey asked after the police had appeared and left. "Too bad they couldn't arrest her."

"She didn't break any laws."

"Dognapping."

"Can't be proven. It's our word against hers. You should have gone to the hospital. We'd have a better case against her if your injuries were substantiated."

"I don't understand why she won't leave me alone."

Hugh's cell phone rang. "Lorrie!" he said with surprise. "You're looking for Sarah? She was here, harassing my sister." He told her the details, while Lindsey listened, then handed Lindsey the phone. "She wants to talk to you."

"Sorry about Sarah. I should have warned you. She has a problem letting go. A Paula Nelson came in asking about you. Are you in hiding, or can I give her your number."

She gave the phone back to Hugh for him to decide.

"Yeah, give her the number. Maybe she can scoot up here and scare Sarah off. You're welcome if you want to come, by the way. We like your company, don't we, sis?"

Lindsey pulled her sunglasses down and eyed him. "Of course."

Lorrie told Hugh she couldn't leave the store unless Sarah was there to run things, and if Sarah found out she was going to see Lindsey, she would soon put a stop to it.

Later, Hugh called Matt and Natalie without her knowledge and told them their mother had fallen out of a car and was badly bruised.

First Matt, then Natalie phoned and asked to speak to Lindsey.

"Are you all right, Mom?" Matt asked, worry in his voice. "Uncle Hugh said you fell out of a car. How did that happen?"

His call was so unexpected that Lindsey couldn't think what to tell him, other than, "The door opened. I didn't have my seat belt fastened." She didn't want him to know it was Sarah's car.

"Why?"

"We'd just started out."

"Maybe I should drive up there and check you out," he said.

It was the hesitancy in his voice that made her reply, "I'm okay, Matt. You just started that job."

"I was thinking about the weekend."

201

"Well, if you want. We'll be back next weekend."

"Don't take any more flying leaps, Mom," he warned.

Natalie called next, sounding a little sullen despite her words, "I miss you, Mom. I'm sorry I didn't tell you about my engagement. We think maybe we jumped the gun anyway. We've decided to wait at least a year before setting a date."

She ended up comforting Natalie.

After, she turned on Hugh. "You didn't have to call the kids and drag them into this. If they find out Sarah was involved, they'll be furious, and I'll look like the fool I am."

"I thought they'd want to come and see you."

"That's nice, Hugh, but I want them to come when they want to, not because they think I'm hurt. And don't play matchmaker with Lorrie or Paula. All I need is another woman hanging around."

"Okay. Calm down. It's been a stressful day."

XXX

Suzy and her lover arrived in a Mustang convertible Sunday morning. Her short, windblown, dyed blond hair framed her tan face and accentuated her dramatic brown eyes.

"This is Martin," she said.

Hugh told Lindsey later that Martin's last name was Stein. He said they'd never married because his parents threatened to disinherit him because she wasn't Jewish. It was as much Suzy's choice as his to wait till he'd inherited.

It made them sound a little avaricious, even though she understood the importance of money. It was an issue for her now that she'd left Gregg.

"Isn't this the greatest little place, Lindsey?" her sister said.

"Yes, but I don't think it's little."

Martin had gone out in the front yard to smoke while Hugh took their baggage to the other bedroom in the loft. Suzy and Lindsey stood alone in the living room.

"This is Willie? Right?" Suzy sat on the floor and cooed, "See, I remembered his name." She stretched out a hand for Willie to sniff, and he allowed her to pat him. "Every time I see this dog, I want one of my own. He is so cute."

"Why don't you get one?"

"Are there any little Willies?"

"No. He's neutered. You look really good, Suzy."

"For my age?"

"I didn't say that," Lindsey protested.

Suzy jumped to her feet from a cross-legged position as if she were nineteen, instead of forty-nine. "That's because I exercise, drink every night, eat good food and don't get too much sleep."

"Really? That sounds like a recipe for a heart attack, except for the exercise."

"How's it going for you? Hugh filled me in on the changes in your life. Major stuff. It can't be easy. Why are you all black-and-blue, and what happened to Hugh's chin? Did you have a fight?"

"I fell out of a car that Willie was chasing, and Hugh got kicked in the chin."

"Are you all right, Willie?" And then she was on the floor again, cooing to the dog. Willie climbed in her lap.

"I'm okay. How are you? I haven't seen you in over a year."

"I know. My life would sound boring compared to yours."

"I could stand a little boring," Lindsey admitted.

Suzy asked more questions about her fall from the car and who kicked Hugh in the chin.

"No seat belt and a loose boom," she said, misleading her sister.

"Dangerous things," Suzy replied, looking at her askance but asking no more.

They spent the day on Hugh's sailboat, dropping the sails and rocking on the waves while they swam and ate lunch. Martin and Hugh handled the boat. The women lay on the hatch and deck and talked and read.

Suzy was deep into defending the poor, guilty or innocent, but they had to shout at each other to be heard over the wind in the sails and the distance between them. Suzy was preaching to the choir when she talked about white-collar crime and the unfairness of the system. "A rich CEO wastes his employees' pensions and gets off with a few months in a fancy prison, if that, while a poor guy caught with a bit of marijuana on him gets years in the slammer. It's an unjust world."

"I know," she said. She did, but she didn't know what to do about it.

"Have you got enough money, Lindsey?" Suzy lifted her head from the beach towel she was lying on and peered at Lindsey from the depths of a hooded sweatshirt. "I can help you out any time."

They were all dressed in shorts and wearing windbreakers over the sweatshirts. The wind on the lake blew cool, and the sun played hide and seek among the clouds piling up overhead.

"Yes, but thanks." Because she then felt a need to defend him, she said, "Gregg would never be unfair."

"Good," Suzy said. "Just remember you've got a sister as well as a brother."

When they tied up around four o'clock, Suzy said she felt like a broiled lobster and asked if they wanted to go out for dinner. "Martin and I'll buy."

Monday morning, leaving Martin at Hugh's home, the brother and two sisters drove past their childhood home and stopped at the cemetery to stand by their parents' graves in silent communication. After lunch, Suzy and Martin left. It seemed to Lindsey that they'd been there a lot longer. Suzy liked to talk about her work and politics. She was a pro bono attorney for civil rights. She and Martin and Hugh had intense discussions. When Lindsey tried to join in, they all looked at her, listened, commented on her views, and went on talking to each other. The fervor of their discussions tired her.

Enough time passed that she began to believe Sarah had gone home. One day merged into another, all spent either on or near the huge lake, and the following weekend arrived almost unnoticed.

"I have to go to Madison Sunday, but you're welcome to stay as long as you like. I'll return next weekend. Think about it."

"What if . . ."

"I called Jimmy, and he said Sarah's back."

"I don't have a car."

"We'll grocery shop before I leave. If you need to go somewhere, you can always call a taxi or ask the neighbors. They're very nice people, even though we don't talk a lot. We respect each other's privacy."

"I'll have to call Gregg and my boss." The thought of staying longer filled her with excitement.

"I've got a present for you." Hugh handed her a black briefcase-sized bag. "Open it."

Surprised at how heavy it was, she unzipped it and pulled out a small computer.

"It's my old laptop, so don't get all grateful. It's not worth selling. I thought maybe you could keep a journal or something while you're here. You'll need a break from reading once in a while. I'll show you how to use it."

She blinked back her gratitude. "Thanks. This is so . . . so nice of you."

"Maybe you'll turn into a writer. Set it down on the table and open it up."

"It's kind of late in life for that."

"Hell, no. Lots of writers started late—as you should know. Frank McCourt, the guy who wrote *Angela's Ashes*, for instance. Anyway, you can send e-mail. Just hook it up to the phone outlet. It's a Mac. It's easy."

Instead of Sunday night, Hugh left Monday morning before Lindsey woke up. Willie barked once when the garage door opened, and Hugh's car pulled out.

Lindsey ran downstairs and out onto the lawn in Hugh's old bathrobe, but he was already gone. She stood outside while Willie did his business, then they both went back in the house.

After making coffee, she sat in front of the windows facing the lake while she drank it, idly stroking the dog and talking to him. "What should we do with this day, Willie?" The sun spread a sheen of gold across the water. Fishing boats dotted its surface. Tiny wavelets rapped the shore.

After feeding herself and the dog, she sat at the dining room table, facing the front windows. Opening the laptop, she began writing.

Beth's best friend, Arlene, told her she was pregnant, that she was marrying the rat-like, high school dropout boy she was dating. That way she wouldn't have to finish school or live with her dad and stepmother any longer. Arlene talked as if it were an exciting thing that had happened. When they were married, she would live with her husband in his parents' house, sleeping in the bedroom where he'd impregnated her.

The day of the wedding in the courthouse, Beth squirmed with shame as she finally told her mother.

"We'll go, Beth. Why didn't you let me know before now? Poor Arlene. She's so young." Her mother looked worriedly at her.

They sat in the third row, behind Arlene's dad and stepsister. Arlene's stepmom wasn't there. As the judge married her and Tommy, Arlene turned and looked at Beth, covering her mouth, giggling.

No return laughter welled up in Beth. She felt only a heavy sadness. Arlene had been her first best friend, and she had a fierce love for her. She hated the boy she was marrying. Arlene had told her about doing it with him, and it filled her with disgust. Her mom didn't need to give her worried looks. She hadn't liked kissing Tommy's friend, even though she and Arlene had kept a tally of their kisses. The boy's mouth had been wet and sloppy.

They drove home in silence, her mother emitting small sighs that made Beth clench her hands. She stared out the window when her mother asked her where Arlene was going to live, and her mother sighed again when she told her.

"I don't suppose she'll be able to go back to school," her mother said, more to herself than to her daughter. Pregnant girls were always expelled. The guys who got them pregnant might not be able to play sports, but they didn't have to leave school. Even then, Beth recognized the unfairness of the double standard.

The coffee was drunk. Lindsey still sat in Hugh's bathrobe at ten thirty in the morning, wondering why it had taken four hours to write a few paragraphs. She closed the laptop and went to get dressed.

The ringing phone startled her, and she waited for the answering machine to click on with Hugh's message.

Sarah's voice, impatient and angry, said, "Come on. Pick up the phone, Lindsey. I'll drive up there again if you don't."

The urge to answer drew her close to the phone, but she knew she would never break away if she picked up the receiver. Reluctantly, she backed away and continued upstairs to dress.

Taking her book, she went outside with the dog. She'd finished reading Reba McKenzie's book. Reba had said that writing was therapeutic. When Hugh gave her the computer, she felt she should try, but what she was writing was a story her mother had told her, only she had put herself in her mother's place.

She was partway through *The Time Traveler's Wife*. The way the future husband kept time traveling into his wife's childhood and youth bothered her. She thought he interfered with the girl's growing up. She was on her last book. She'd figured Hugh would have something to her liking, but it appeared from his bookshelves that he only read science fiction.

The day turned colder as the sky became completely overcast and a wind kicked up. She was forced to go inside mid-afternoon and turn on the gas fireplace. For supper, she made tuna fish salad and slathered it on bread. As she ate the sandwich, the phone rang again and once more she waited tensely for a message.

"It's only me, kiddo. You can answer," Hugh said.

She picked up. "Sarah called earlier and left a message."

"What did she say?" After she told him, he asked, "What was the name of that woman cop?"

"Paula Nelson. Why?"

"I'm going to call her. Maybe she can ward off Sarah. Do you know her number?"

"She gave it to me. I think it's in my wallet. Hang on." She found it buried among the other cards in her billfold

"I'll call you tomorrow night. Got to go now. Keep the doors locked."

XXXI

The next morning, she opened the laptop around eight thirty and reread what she'd written the previous day. Finally, she began typing.

Arlene taught her about sex shortly after Beth's family moved into the house next door. They lay on Arlene's bed and kissed when no one was home. Arlene touched her in places that Beth knew were private. The sensation was so intensely exciting that she was unable to resist.

Beth thought Arlene must love her as much as she loved Arlene, but as soon as Arlene's boyfriend started coming around, Arlene told Beth that those games they played had to stop. They were things that should be done with a boy.

As she drove home with her mother, Beth's heart curled up like the yellowing leaves of the elm trees lining the blocks of their small town. The winter stretched ahead of her, and she wasn't sure how she'd fill the days.

The sudden ringing made Lindsey jump. She waited tensely to hear who was on the other end.

"Hi, Lindsey. Paula Nelson here. Your brother called . . ."

Lindsey reached for the receiver. "Hi."

"I left a message on your machine before Hugh told me you weren't coming home. I did go over to the bookstore, because Hugh asked me to. I tried to talk to Sarah. Are you sure you don't want her to come up there?"

"Did Hugh tell you what happened?"

"He said you jumped out of a moving car to get away from her."

"She took my dog to get me in the car, and then pushed him out. He was chasing the car, and I thought he was going to be hurt." It hadn't been that she was afraid of Sarah. "What did she say when you talked to her?"

"That, um, you were together and Hugh wanted to pull you apart."

"Not true." Had they ever been together, even when they were intimate, when she couldn't stay away from Sarah?

"I wish I could do more than convey messages. I can't stop her from coming, but I tried to discourage her."

"Thanks. I appreciate it."

"What's it like there?"

"Why don't you come see?" The words came unbidden, a surprise even to Lindsey.

"Hugh suggested that, but I didn't want to show up without an invitation from you."

"Consider yourself invited."

"I have Wednesday and Thursday off."

"I'll see you tomorrow then?" It was a question.

"Yes, if you really want me to come."

"I do." It would be a friendly visit, she told herself. If Sarah showed up, Paula could handle her.

She turned back to the laptop. She doubted her mother had fooled around with her best friend, but Lindsey had—not with her mother's friend but her own.

After a peanut butter sandwich lunch, she went out on the lawn and read in the Adirondack chair. She was beginning to have mixed feelings about Paula coming. She wouldn't be able to write, nor would she have alone time like this. As soon as she knew she wouldn't be alone, she wanted to be. How was that for being indecisive?

Willie wandered over to the boathouse and began barking and digging. She went to investigate, found a groundhog hole, and dragged him away. Peering in the small boathouse windows on either side, she saw a kayak and rowboat. The two big doors that fronted the lake were padlocked. Inside the house, she found the key on a ring of keys that Hugh had left with her.

She carried the small kayak outside to the sandy beach and went back in the boathouse for the paddle and a life jacket. There was no room for the dog, so she locked him in the house and set off across the small waves, going out onto the lake at an angle, crossing the sandbars until she reached a depth where she couldn't see the bottom.

Paddling was more work than she thought it would be. The craft waddled like a duck with each thrust, the waves rocked it back and forth, and the water dripped down the paddles and onto her legs. This wasn't a fancy kayak for experts, but a fat, stable one for amateur recreation.

She traveled down the beach for half an hour and turned to return home. Facing the wind, she found the trip back much more difficult. Her shoulders ached as she dug the paddle into the water. After what seemed a long time, she started crossing the sandbars and beached the kayak on the sandy shore. Stepping out, she turned the kayak over on the grass. Perhaps Paula would want to use it.

The next day dawned hot and muggy. Sitting in the Adirondack chair, she drank coffee and waved away lake flies. Willie snapped at the bugs flying around his head. She'd forgotten about lake flies, how they hatched by the thousands in the spring and early summer, but there weren't as many as she remembered as a child.

They were bearable. Nevertheless, she hoped the wind would pick up during the day.

Inside, she continued her story.

When Arlene came over to visit during Christmas break, Beth's mother brought them cookies and orange pop on a tray and sat with them in the living room for a while.

Once, Beth would have been annoyed by her mother's presence, but now she was grateful because she had nothing much to say to Arlene. Their lives had taken different turns.

When Beth's mother left the room, Arlene talked about how she hated being married to Tommy. She said he seldom bathed, and his mother expected her to cook and clean. It was lonely, she said, and she didn't like the changes to her body. She looked forward to having a baby, though. A baby would love her, she told Beth.

Beth yawned, bored with the talk about marriage and babies. She realized that she didn't know this Arlene and didn't want to. She'd lost her best friend.

She closed the laptop around eleven and put on her swimsuit. She and Willie went out the front door and ran to the lake, where she plunged into its green waters. Dead lake flies floated on the surface and buzzed above it. She walked across the sandbars and swam between them until she reached deeper water, where the lake flies were less active.

Willie barked from the shallows. When Lindsey turned to see why, Paula Nelson was balancing on one foot at the edge of the water, taking off her sandals. Her legs looked longer and leaner in shorts. She waved away the lake flies and waded into the water.

"Hey, I'm coming in," Lindsey shouted and started toward shore.

Reaching Paula, she said, "Sorry about the lake flies. It's that time of year. I'd forgotten all about them. Maybe there'll be a break after this hatch. They only live a few hours."

"They're good fish food," Paula pointed out.

The two women faced each other, smiling and swaying with the rhythm of the waves. Willie splashed into the water.

"Want to go inside where there are less bugs?" Lindsey asked.

"Wherever you want to go."

Lindsey grabbed her towel off the chair, shook the lake flies off it, and wrapped it around herself. "You must have gotten an early start."

"I did. I hate to waste a vacation day in travel."

Lindsey slid open the glass door. "I'll just go put on some clothes." She gestured toward the stairs. "I can show you your room at the same time."

Paula threw her backpack across one shoulder and followed Lindsey up the stairs.

"Nice place."

"Did you have any trouble finding it?"

"Nope. Your brother gives good directions."

"Did you meet Hugh?"

"No, I only talked to him on the phone. He was worried about you. You are bruised pretty badly."

"It looks worse than it is." Lindsey's side, especially her shoulder and thigh, had turned a dark purple.

"You don't seem to be very stiff."

"When I first get up, I am. The water helps keep me limber." Lindsey showed Paula the other guest room. It was identical to the one she was using. "The bathroom is between your bedroom and mine."

Opening the door, she caught a glimpse of her face in the mirror over the sink. Her hair was plastered to her skull. She ran her fingers through it.

"Do you want to use the bathroom first? I think I'll take a quick shower."

"Sure," Paula said.

Lindsey grabbed clean clothes from her bedroom.

They spent the afternoon outside. Paula kayaked, and Lindsey read. The lake flies dissipated as the day wore on.

Toward evening, Lindsey grilled chicken, sliced red potatoes, and asparagus over the gas grill on the stone patio out front. The sun hung low over the western shore, casting long fingers of light on the water. A slight breeze blew away the bugs.

Lindsey felt as if she'd been roasted on a spit, her skin pulled taut by a day in the hot sun. Sleepy from sun and water, she sipped a vodka and tonic.

"I don't know much about you?" Paula said.

"Nor I you," she replied.

"Who goes first?"

"You do," Lindsey said, wary that her story might scare Paula away.

"Well, I'm single. I have two brothers, who are also cops. One has a couple of boys. The other has two girls. My mom and my dad dote on the grandchildren, but then so do I. Your turn."

"I'm separated from my husband, and I have two grown children who don't want to talk to me."

"How does Sarah fit in?"

Lindsey's feeling of harmony deserted her. "I had an affair with her." She thought back to the beginning, knowing she'd ignored all the warning signs about Sarah.

"Tell me about your children."

"Natalie works for the *Centralia News*. Matt has a job with the DNR. They're good friends." Should she say something about Gregg? "My husband owns Second Nature Nursery."

"I've been there. Nice place. Who lives in the house?"

"We did, all of us. Now Gregg and Willie live there."

"It must have been hard to leave," she said.

"Yes and no." She didn't want to talk about her recent past.

They ate inside. The setting sun blanketed the quiet lake with shades of purple. Sitting in the half dark, they lingered over a bottle of wine after dinner.

The talk gravitated to the Administration's disastrous war in Iraq, its gutting of environmental laws and regulations, its energy policy that favored the oil and gas companies, its chipping away at civil rights, its secrecy and lies. "I don't understand why the whole country isn't up in arms," Lindsey said.

"I don't either."

They took their nearly empty wine glasses to more comfortable chairs, facing the nearly dark lake. Lindsey wondered what they would do now. "Hugh has some DVDs. Want to watch one?"

"I'd rather talk a while. I don't meet up with someone who shares my views every day."

"What do you like to read?"

"Mysteries and suspense," Paula said with a grin.

"Figures," Lindsey replied. "Have you read *Other Women*?"

Paula smiled. "I loved it. Did you?"

"Very much." She knew then that they were on the same page, or thought she did.

The next day was much the same as the one before—hot and muggy. The lake flies disappeared, though. Lindsey smeared herself with sunblock and offered it to Paula. Willie lay under Lindsey's chair. When they swam, he went with them.

"I have to leave tonight," Paula said at some point in the middle of the afternoon.

"You can't get up early in the morning? That's what Hugh did."

"Afraid not. I have to be at work at seven in the morning. I've had a great time. Thanks for asking me."

"Thanks for coming."

"When are you going home?" Paula asked.

"Sunday, I suppose. I have to go back to work." She looked out at the water. A tug of war waged inside her. She wanted to stay on, yet it would mean leaving everyone she knew.

Paula gave Lindsey a hug when she said good-bye. "Call me when you get back. We'll get together."

She took the kayak out after Paula left, even though the sky had turned dark. Beyond the sandbars the waves rolled two feet high. The kayak rocked, taking in water over the sides. The wind picked up as the clouds turned a sickly yellowish green. She realized she was in trouble.

Turning to go back, a wave caught the side of the boat and

tipped it over. Water flooded her nose and mouth and eyes. Panicking, she wiggled herself free of the small craft. She'd put on her life jacket but hadn't fastened it, and it floated away from her. Grabbing the belt, she pulled it back.

"Never leave the boat if you overturn," she heard Pete say those twenty-some years ago as if he were beside her.

But there was little to hang on to. The kayak was perfectly rounded on the bottom with no keel to grab. She worked her way to the front where she thought she'd seen a handle. Feeling around, she grabbed the rubbery piece and hung on. With her other hand she maneuvered into the jacket and fastened it as the first bolt of lightning shot through the clouds.

She doubted anyone could see her, lost in the troughs of water. Everyone would be scrambling to get off the lake. Thunder boomed alarmingly close, followed by more lightning. A cold downpour followed. She knew she was being pushed toward shore, but the rain and waves made it difficult to see.

When her feet touched sand, she knew she'd make it. She had to swim to the next sandbar, but after that she could wade, dragging the kayak behind her. As she pulled the craft up on someone's lawn, a whirlwind danced above the grass and out onto the water. It looked like a miniature tornado and became immediately lost in the storm.

She was shaking with cold when she knocked on the door of the house and limp with relief when it opened. Wrapped in a beach towel, she waited out the storm with an older couple. After it was over, they put the kayak on top of their van and drove her back to Hugh's place.

"Watch the sky before you go out again," the man said as he helped her unload the kayak and carry it around the house.

"I'm not going out again." She walked back to their vehicle and thanked the couple profusely. As far as she was concerned, they'd saved her life.

When Hugh arrived the next evening, she was reading in the Adirondack chair. The sky was cloudless, the lake becalmed.

XXXII

Her apartment was an empty, sterile, lonely place. The answering machine flashed in the dark room. She switched on a light and dumped her suitcase on the bed. Pressing the playback button, she listened to Sarah asking her to call, and erased the message before it ended. Paula spoke next, saying she had to work Sunday night and would call Monday afternoon.

She sank onto the sofa, missing Willie and Hugh and the lake. Switching on the television, she watched *Nature* and *Mystery* on public TV. The lake with its myriad of moods had been her television while at Hugh's place. Her world was reduced to these few walls.

At work the next day, she gave John notice and offered to train someone to take her place.

"I'd appreciate that," he said. "I was surprised you came back at all."

It wasn't in her to abandon everything and everyone without at least telling them, she said. She worked the rest of the week to catch up. She would train her replacement the following week.

She'd have to find some other occupation. Nothing in the classifieds fit her education or interests.

Paula came over the first weekend she was back. She'd been working nights, but she'd called every day before she went on duty. She knew Lindsey would be training her replacement that next week.

Except for grocery shopping, Lindsey had gone from the apartment to work and back again. She hadn't even seen Carol, although she'd talked to her on the phone. She'd been too busy to go out for lunch. After she trained her replacement, there would be time for lunch every day.

A little desperate at not having a job, on having to live on her small inheritance and the two hundred dollars Gregg sent weekly, she had trouble concentrating on other things.

When Paula smiled, Lindsey realized that she'd forgotten little things about the way she looked, like the freckles that marched across her nose. It seemed as if there were many more. The summer sun brought them out.

"Want a cup of coffee?" Lindsey asked. "There's some left."

"Sure. I wanted to show you something anyway. Are you looking for another job?"

"You know I am." Lindsey sat at the table and took the sheet of paper Paula handed her.

It was notice of a position being created within the police department for a cultural relations coordinator. A grasp of languages, ability to network, knowledge and tolerance of minorities were considerations.

Lindsey met Paula's earnest gray gaze.

"Interested?" Paula asked.

"The question is am I qualified?" Yes, she was interested. She was also frightened by such a challenge.

"You speak other languages."

"Spanish would probably be the only useful one."

"That's a start." Paula spread her arms, hands palms up. "What's to lose?"

"I didn't see this in the newspaper."

"It'll be in this Sunday's paper. Why don't you apply?"

She would, she decided in a moment of self-assurance that quickly disappeared. She'd read a book about a Hmong child who had epilepsy. It had been a revelation on how the Hmong regard Americans. "Why is this position part of the police department?"

"We need someone who is trusted and knowledgeable to step in during disputes, and we have a grant for the position."

"I don't exactly fit the description."

"You could. It would mean a lot of networking. You have to hook up with the various communities. I think you'd be great, and I want to keep you here."

Lindsey said, "You do?"

"I'd like to know you better."

"We'd be working in the same place. Besides, I'm a lesbian." She felt as if she'd made a great confession.

"They don't ask that on the application," Paula said, looking very serious. "At least, it wasn't on mine."

"It could be a problem if it was found out."

"It could be, but you can't be fired for being homosexual in this state."

"There are other ways to get rid of people. The Hispanic and Hmong communities are pretty male dominated."

"You're looking at this wrong. You have to be positive and put away all this internalized homophobia shit."

"Have you put it away?"

"No, of course not. Does that mean you're not going to apply?"

"Of course I'm going to apply. Right now. Let's drive to the police department."

"Let's go back to my apartment. I want to change clothes," Lindsey said when they left the police department. She'd worn a skirt and blouse and low heels.

220

"You look terrific," Paula said. "How did it go?"

"I feel like a wet noodle. My pits are soaked. And all I did was fill out the application. If I get an interview, I'll be a sopping wreck."

"Let's go celebrate at a good Mexican restaurant."

"Celebrate what? Nothing's happened."

"It will."

"Let me ask you something. What does the police department have to say about dating co-workers?"

"You won't be a cop."

Popping a chip in her mouth at the Mexican restaurant, Lindsey nearly choked when Gregg walked in with Toni Fields. She touched his arm as he and Toni started to pass their booth.

"Lindsey!" he said in surprise.

"Paula, Gregg and Toni."

Gregg grunted. Toni shook hands.

She smiled at Gregg, at a loss for words. It bothered her to think she'd been intimate with this man for over twenty years, and now they maintained a distant polite facade."Nice to meet you, Paula," Toni said.

Gregg nodded curtly.

"Everything okay?" Lindsey blurted.

"Why wouldn't it be?" Gregg asked, his jaw set.

"Have you talked to the kids lately?" she pushed.

"They're fine, busy." His smile looked more like a grimace. Touching Toni's arm, he steered her after the hostess, who had stopped at a booth further down the aisle and stood waiting for them to catch up.

She watched them go, not sure how she felt about anything. It all hurt. When she became so angry with her children for patently avoiding her, she'd count the reasons for their behavior. She'd lied to them. She'd cheated on their dad. She'd left the family home. One of those three would be enough to exact their ire. All three amounted to an indictment only time or a crisis would overcome.

Hugh had said give them time, don't chase after them, and let them come to her. Now that she had e-mail, she'd stopped phoning them and sent short messages at least once a week.

Paula said, "I recognize Gregg from the nursery."

Lost in her thoughts, Lindsey had nearly forgotten Paula. "Toni started working for him before I left." She wondered how long before he filed for divorce. She would give him that option.

"Nice looking man." Paula's eyes were unreadable.

Lindsey nodded absently.

Paula put a warm hand on her arm. "What are you thinking?"

"That you can't go back to what was and reconstruct it."

"Do you want to?"

Did she? She hated the estrangement between herself and Gregg and the kids, the awkwardness of it when they met or talked. It was as if she'd turned into a stranger.

"I'd like their trust back, the easiness we had with each other." Feeling her throat close, she studied her hands until her composure returned.

The waiter put margaritas in front of them, and Lindsey took a deep swallow. An instant headache made her wince. "I know better than that," she said.

"Me too." Paula touched her forehead.

"Some celebration," Lindsey remarked with a laugh. She began to devour chips. "Let's liven things up."

They left before Gregg and Toni. Lindsey glanced at them as she exited the booth. Gregg was talking, pointing a chip at Toni for emphasis, she guessed discussing the business. She turned away before she wished she was the one he was confiding in.

Paula invited her into her home, a small ranch on a narrow tree-lined street. She made coffee, while Lindsey sat in the living room looking at the magazines on the coffee table and the books in a bookcase. Somehow that reassured her. She felt suddenly very tired and leaned her head back on the couch.

She wakened when Paula sat next to her. "I should have taken you home."

"I'm okay." Seeing Gregg had stirred up emotional ballast. "This will revive me." She picked up the coffee cup.

"It's decaf," Paula pointed out.

When Paula took her home, she wanted to ask her to stay, but she knew that would be a mistake. She wasn't ready for another relationship.

The next week flew by. She walked out of the brass factory on Friday, and experienced a wonderful sense of freedom. When she took her mail out of its little box in the entryway of the apartment building, there were envelopes from the police department and from an attorney.

She opened the police department envelope with apprehension, not sure what she wanted to find—a date for an interview or a rejection. She had hoped for some time off. Instead, she was offered an interview on Monday.

Still thinking about the interview, she opened the envelope from the attorney. In it was a petition for divorce. She sat on the sofa, absorbing the implications of the two mailings. The job, so unlike any she'd ever had, frightened her. The petition for divorce pulled the safety net out from under her. She'd have to get an attorney of her own.

The light on her answering machine was flashing, and after a while, she pushed the play button, hoping it would be one of her children. Instead, it was Hugh, asking if she wanted to go to the lake over the Fourth of July. The second message was from Lorrie, canceling a dinner date they'd made for that night. Lorrie said Sarah was suspicious.

Lindsey hadn't thought about Sarah since she came home from Hugh's. She phoned the bookstore, knowing Lorrie would answer. "I got your message. Maybe we can have lunch one of these days. Give me a call if you can get away."

"Thanks. Sorry for the late notice."

"It's okay. I don't want to make things difficult for you." Actually, she didn't want Sarah intruding in her life, not even if it meant not seeing Lorrie.

She phoned Paula and left a message about the interview.

Dressed in her uniform, Paula showed up at Lindsey's door around seven. Lindsey had ordered a pizza and was watching a DVD she'd picked up at the library about the Hmong. "I called home for my messages and got yours. I should have phoned you before coming. I was excited for you."

Glad that she was at home and not out with Lorrie, Lindsey opened the door wide. "Come on in. This pizza is way too big for me to eat alone. You're the good news of the day. Are you off-duty?"

"Yes. Am I interrupting anything?"

"Just a boring DVD. I'll turn it off."

Lindsey opened a bottle of Shiraz and told Paula that she'd been served divorce papers.

"I'm sorry," Paula said.

Shrugging, Lindsey said, "It was coming sooner or later. I'm more worried about the interview and the job, if I get it."

"No guts, no glory." Paula smiled, raising her eyebrows for emphasis.

"I guess." Lindsey hadn't thought of it that way. The job presented a challenge. The divorce represented an ending. Her life had been easy till now. She thought of the saying about one door closing and another opening, but the doors were opening and closing a little fast for her. "I don't have the job yet. I'm not even sure I want it."

"You will."

When the pizza was gone, they put their feet up on the coffee table and finished off the wine bottle, while the DVD droned on. Lindsey felt herself dozing off.

She awakened with her head on Paula's shoulder and Paula's head resting on hers. The DVD was over. She was looking through several strands of Paula's hair. Not wanting to jar Paula, she closed her eyes and drifted off.

XXXIII

The day she drove to the lake dawned hot and sunny. She got up early with Willie, taking him out for a quick walk. It was July first. Her new job at the police department started on the sixth. She'd told Hugh she felt she should stay home and hone her intercultural skills.

How was she going to do that, he'd asked. She could learn on the job. Besides, it might be the last vacation she took in a while.

She'd caved in easily. Paula was on duty over the weekend. Carol and Theo had invited her to their Fourth of July barbecue, but Gregg would be there with Toni.

She had talked twice to Lorrie since she'd cancelled out on their Friday night dinner. Lorrie sent Lindsey lists of activities going on at the bookstore, but Lindsey stayed away.

She wanted to leave early to avoid traffic, but found the highways already crowded. Police cars were parked in the median strips and off the shoulders, poised to catch speeders. Willie stood precariously perched on the front seat, head sticking out the narrowly open window, tongue lolling, ears floating in the wind.

Lindsey set the cruise control at sixty-eight and worried about her first day on the job. She had been given lists of the various minority groups to contact. They were on her desk in the small windowless office that was hers. She would attend their meetings and get-togethers, which meant working some weekends and nights. Paula often worked weekends and nights too. She hoped their schedules would mesh once in a while.

The scenery zoomed past her, unseen. She nearly drove past the exit to the 441 bypass and the access road to the lake. Parking in Hugh's driveway, she opened the door, and Willie jumped over her. Her shorts stuck to her legs. She pulled them free and walked around the side of the house to the lawn where Hugh sat in one of the Adirondack chairs. A wonderfully warm breeze smelling of lake lifted the hair from her forehead.

Hugh got up to give her a hug. "So soon? You must have broken all the speed limits."

"No. We left early."

"Go on inside and put on your swimsuit and join me out here. I'll keep an eye on Willie."

She hurried to change, throwing her clothes on the bed. Taking her beach towel, sun screen and book, she went out the glass door.

"Are Suzy and Martin coming?" she asked her brother.

"Nope. They've got some other invitation. The water's great, just the right temperature. Want to go in?"

They waded out to the last sandbar and swam. Willie barked from the shore, then took the plunge and swam with them.

"You always know when I need to get away," she said, treading water, facing Hugh who was doing the same. Willie swam circles around her.

"Willie is trying to rescue you too."

"Do you think I need rescuing?"

"Not anymore." He gave her a big smile and spit out lake water. "Ugh. Let's go in, sis. Tomorrow we'll sail."

They alternated between reading and swimming the rest of the day. Around five, Hugh went inside to fix drinks and make snacks.

"Want some help?" she offered.

"No. You stay put," he ordered. "I'll feed Willie while I'm at it."

The sun spread gold fingers across the water. She closed her eyes, remembering how she had fallen asleep with Paula. It had led to their first night together and their first lovemaking—tentative, shy, satisfying.

"Wake up, sleeping beauty. We have company."

Jarred into consciousness, she turned in the chair. Matt and Natalie stood on the grass with Hugh. They wore swimsuits and carried towels. Matt sported a big grin. Natalie smiled less assuredly. Lindsey got up, looking at them with disbelief.

"What . . ." she said.

"Hi, Mom." Matt enclosed her in a hug as if there had been no estrangement. "You look great."

She knew she didn't look great. She felt like a sun-dried piece of meat. When she attempted to smile, her lips cracked. She licked them and tried again. "I didn't know you were coming."

Natalie took a step toward her. "Sorry, Mom." The blue of her eyes looked liquid as it always did before she cried.

"It's okay," Lindsey said, taking her daughter in her arms. She felt Natalie stiffen, and she let her go. It would take time. Anything worthwhile did.

"Cocktails on the way," Hugh announced.

"I'm going for a swim. How about you, Nat?" Matt said.

Feeling overwhelmed, Lindsey sat down again. She would join them when Hugh came back. Right now she only wanted to watch. She feared if she blinked, they would disappear.

Publications from
BELLA BOOKS, INC.
The best in contemporary lesbian fiction

P.O. Box 10543, Tallahassee, FL 32302
Phone: 800-729-4992
www.bellabooks.com

THE KILLING ROOM by Gerri Hill. 392 pp. How can two women forget and go their separate ways?   1-59493-050-3 $12.95

PASSIONATE KISSES by Megan Carter. 240 pp. Will two old friends run from love?
1-59493-051-1 $12.95

ALWAYS AND FOREVER by Lyn Denison. 224 pp. The girl next door turns Shannon's world upside down.   1-59493-049-X $12.95

BACK TALK by Saxon Bennett. 200 pp. Can a talk show host find love after heartbreak?
1-59493-028-7 $12.95

THE PERFECT VALENTINE: EROTIC LESBIAN VALENTINE STORIES edited by Barbara Johnson and Therese Szymanski—from Bella After Dark. 328 pp. Stories from the hottest writers around.   1-59493-061-9 $14.95

MURDER AT RANDOM by Claire McNab. 200 pp. The Sixth Denise Cleever Thriller. Denise realizes the fate of thousands is in her hands.   1-59493-047-3 $12.95

THE TIDES OF PASSION by Diana Tremain Braund. 240 pp. Will Susan be able to hold it all together and find the one woman who touches her soul?   1-59493-048-1 $12.95

JUST LIKE THAT by Karin Kallmaker. 240 pp. Disliking each other—and everything they stand for—even before they meet, Toni and Syrah find feelings can change, just like that.
1-59493-025-2 $12.95

WHEN FIRST WE PRACTICE by Therese Szymanski. 200 pp. Brett and Allie are once again caught in the middle of murder and intrigue.   1-59493-045-7 $12.95

REUNION by Jane Frances. 240 pp. Cathy Braithwaite seems to have it all: good looks, money and a thriving accounting practice . . .   1-59493-046-5 $12.95

BELL, BOOK & DYKE: NEW EXPLOITS OF MAGICAL LESBIANS by Kallmaker, Watts, Johnson and Szymanski. 360 pp. Reluctant witches, tempting spells and skyclad beauties—delve into the mysteries of love, lust and power in this quartet of novellas.
1-59493-023-6 $14.95

ARTIST'S DREAM by Gerri Hill. 320 pp.When Cassie meets Luke Winston, she can no longer deny her attraction to women . . .   1-59493-042-2 $12.95

NO EVIDENCE by Nancy Sanra. 240 pp. Private Investigator Tally McGinnis once again returns to the horror-filled world of a serial killer.   1-59493-043-04 $12.95

WHEN LOVE FINDS A HOME by Megan Carter. 280 pp. What will it take for Anna and Rona to find their way back to each other again? 1-59493-041-4 $12.95

MEMORIES TO DIE FOR by Adrian Gold. 240 pp. Rachel attempts to avoid her attraction to the charms of Anna Sigurdson . . . 1-59493-038-4 $12.95

SILENT HEART by Claire McNab. 280 pp. Exotic lesbian romance.

1-59493-044-9 $12.95

MIDNIGHT RAIN by Peggy J. Herring. 240 pp. Bridget McBee is determined to find the woman who saved her life. 1-59493-021-X $12.95

THE MISSING PAGE A Brenda Strange Mystery by Patty G. Henderson. 240 pp. Brenda investigates her client's murder . . . 1-59493-004-X $12.95

WHISPERS ON THE WIND by Frankie J. Jones. 240 pp. Dixon thinks she and her best friend, Elizabeth Colter, would make the perfect couple . . . 1-59493-037-6 $12.95

CALL OF THE DARK: EROTIC LESBIAN TALES OF THE SUPERNATURAL edited by Therese Szymanski—from Bella After Dark. 320 pp. 1-59493-040-6 $14.95

A TIME TO CAST AWAY A Helen Black Mystery by Pat Welch. 240 pp. Helen stops by Alice's apartment—only to find the woman dead . . . 1-59493-036-8 $12.95

DESERT OF THE HEART by Jane Rule. 224 pp. The book that launched the most popular lesbian movie of all time is back. 1-1-59493-035-X $12.95

THE NEXT WORLD by Ursula Steck. 240 pp. Anna's friend Mido is threatened and eventually disappears . . . 1-59493-024-4 $12.95

CALL SHOTGUN by Jaime Clevenger. 240 pp. Kelly gets pulled back into the world of private investigation . . . 1-59493-016-3 $12.95

52 PICKUP by Bonnie J. Morris and E.B. Casey. 240 pp. 52 hot, romantic tales—one for every Saturday night of the year. 1-59493-026-0 $12.95

GOLD FEVER by Lyn Denison. 240 pp. Kate's first love, Ashley, returns to their home town, where Kate now lives . . . 1-1-59493-039-2 $12.95

RISKY INVESTMENT by Beth Moore. 240 pp. Lynn's best friend and roommate needs her to pretend Chris is his fiancé. But nothing is ever easy. 1-59493-019-8 $12.95

HUNTER'S WAY by Gerri Hill. 240 pp. Homicide detective Tori Hunter is forced to team up with the hot-tempered Samantha Kennedy. 1-59493-018-X $12.95

CAR POOL by Karin Kallmaker. 240 pp. Soft shoulders, merging traffic and slippery when wet . . . Anthea and Shay find love in the car pool. 1-59493-013-9 $12.95

NO SISTER OF MINE by Jeanne G'Fellers. 240 pp. Telepathic women fight to coexist with a patriarchal society that wishes their eradication. ISBN 1-59493-017-1 $12.95

ON THE WINGS OF LOVE by Megan Carter. 240 pp. Stacie's reporting career is on the rocks. She has to interview bestselling author Cheryl, or else! ISBN 1-59493-027-9 $12.95

WICKED GOOD TIME by Diana Tremain Braund. 224 pp. Does Christina need Miki as a protector . . . or want her as a lover? ISBN 1-59493-031-7 $12.95

THOSE WHO WAIT by Peggy J. Herring. 240 pp. Two brilliant sisters—in love with the same woman! ISBN 1-59493-032-5 $12.95

ABBY'S PASSION by Jackie Calhoun. 240 pp. Abby's bipolar sister helps turn her world upside down, so she must decide what's most important. ISBN 1-59493-014-7 $12.95

PICTURE PERFECT by Jane Vollbrecht. 240 pp. Kate is reintroduced to Casey, the daughter of an old friend. Can they withstand Kate's career? ISBN 1-59493-015-5 $12.95

PAPERBACK ROMANCE by Karin Kallmaker. 240 pp. Carolyn falls for tall, dark and . . . female . . . in this classic lesbian romance. ISBN 1-59493-033-3 $12.95

DAWN OF CHANGE by Gerri Hill. 240 pp. Susan ran away to find peace in remote Kings Canyon—then she met Shawn . . . ISBN 1-59493-011-2 $12.95

DOWN THE RABBIT HOLE by Lynne Jamneck. 240 pp. Is a killer holding a grudge against FBI Agent Samantha Skellar? ISBN 1-59493-012-0 $12.95

SEASONS OF THE HEART by Jackie Calhoun. 240 pp. Overwhelmed, Sara saw only one way out—leaving . . . ISBN 1-59493-030-9 $12.95

TURNING THE TABLES by Jessica Thomas. 240 pp. The 2nd Alex Peres Mystery. *From ghosties and ghoulies and long leggity beasties . . .* ISBN 1-59493-009-0 $12.95

FOR EVERY SEASON by Frankie Jones. 240 pp. Andi, who is investigating a 65-year-old murder, meets Janice, a charming district attorney . . . ISBN 1-59493-010-4 $12.95

LOVE ON THE LINE by Laura DeHart Young. 240 pp. Kay leaves a younger woman behind to go on a mission to Alaska . . . will she regret it? ISBN 1-59493-008-2 $12.95

UNDER THE SOUTHERN CROSS by Claire McNab. 200 pp. Lee, an American travel agent, goes down under and meets Australian Alex, and the sparks fly under the Southern Cross. ISBN 1-59493-029-5 $12.95

SUGAR by Karin Kallmaker. 240 pp. Three women want sugar from Sugar, who can't make up her mind. ISBN 1-59493-001-5 $12.95

FALL GUY by Claire McNab. 200 pp. 16th Detective Inspector Carol Ashton Mystery. ISBN 1-59493-000-7 $12.95

ONE SUMMER NIGHT by Gerri Hill. 232 pp. Johanna swore to never fall in love again— but then she met the charming Kelly . . . ISBN 1-59493-007-4 $12.95

TALK OF THE TOWN TOO by Saxon Bennett. 181 pp. Second in the series about wild and fun loving friends. ISBN 1-931513-77-5 $12.95

LOVE SPEAKS HER NAME by Laura DeHart Young. 170 pp. Love and friendship, desire and intrigue, spark this exciting sequel to *Forever and the Night*. ISBN 1-59493-002-3 $12.95

TO HAVE AND TO HOLD by Peggy J. Herring. 184 pp. By finally letting down her defenses, will Dorian be opening herself to a devastating betrayal? ISBN 1-59493-005-8 $12.95

WILD THINGS by Karin Kallmaker. 228 pp. Dutiful daughter Faith has met the perfect man. There's just one problem: she's in love with his sister. ISBN 1-931513-64-3 $12.95

SHARED WINDS by Kenna White. 216 pp. Can Emma rebuild more than just Lanny's marina? ISBN 1-59493-006-6 $12.95

THE UNKNOWN MILE by Jaime Clevenger. 253 pp. Kelly's world is getting more and more complicated every moment. ISBN 1-931513-57-0 $12.95

TREASURED PAST by Linda Hill. 189 pp. A shared passion for antiques leads to love. ISBN 1-59493-003-1 $12.95

SIERRA CITY by Gerri Hill. 284 pp. Chris and Jesse cannot deny their growing attraction . . . ISBN 1-931513-98-8 $12.95

ALL THE WRONG PLACES by Karin Kallmaker. 174 pp. Sex and the single girl—Brandy is looking for love and usually she finds it. Karin Kallmaker's first *After Dark* erotic novel.
ISBN 1-931513-76-7 $12.95

WHEN THE CORPSE LIES A Motor City Thriller by Therese Szymanski. 328 pp. Butch bad-girl Brett Higgins is used to waking up next to beautiful women she hardly knows. Problem is, this one's dead.
ISBN 1-931513-74-0 $12.95

GUARDED HEARTS by Hannah Rickard. 240 pp. Someone's reminding Alyssa about her secret past, and then she becomes the suspect in a series of burglaries.
ISBN 1-931513-99-6 $12.95

ONCE MORE WITH FEELING by Peggy J. Herring. 184 pp. Lighthearted, loving, romantic adventure.
ISBN 1-931513-60-0 $12.95

TANGLED AND DARK A Brenda Strange Mystery by Patty G. Henderson. 240 pp. When investigating a local death, Brenda finds two possible killers—one diagnosed with Multiple Personality Disorder.
ISBN 1-931513-75-9 $12.95

WHITE LACE AND PROMISES by Peggy J. Herring. 240 pp. Maxine and Betina realize sex may not be the most important thing in their lives.
ISBN 1-931513-73-2 $12.95

UNFORGETTABLE by Karin Kallmaker. 288 pp. Can Rett find love with the cheerleader who broke her heart so many years ago?
ISBN 1-931513-63-5 $12.95

HIGHER GROUND by Saxon Bennett. 280 pp. A delightfully complex reflection of the successful, high society lives of a small group of women.
ISBN 1-931513-69-4 $12.95

LAST CALL A Detective Franco Mystery by Baxter Clare. 240 pp. Frank overlooks all else to try to solve a cold case of two murdered children . . .
ISBN 1-931513-70-8 $12.95

ONCE UPON A DYKE: NEW EXPLOITS OF FAIRY-TALE LESBIANS by Karin Kallmaker, Julia Watts, Barbara Johnson & Therese Szymanski. 320 pp. You've never read fairy tales like these before! From Bella After Dark.
ISBN 1-931513-71-6 $14.95

FINEST KIND OF LOVE by Diana Tremain Braund. 224 pp. Can Molly and Carolyn stop clashing long enough to see beyond their differences?
ISBN 1-931513-68-6 $12.95

DREAM LOVER by Lyn Denison. 188 pp. A soft, sensuous, romantic fantasy.
ISBN 1-931513-96-1 $12.95

NEVER SAY NEVER by Linda Hill. 224 pp. A classic love story . . . where rules aren't the only things broken.
ISBN 1-931513-67-8 $12.95

PAINTED MOON by Karin Kallmaker. 214 pp. Stranded together in a snowbound cabin, Jackie and Leah's lives will never be the same.
ISBN 1-931513-53-8 $12.95

WIZARD OF ISIS by Jean Stewart. 240 pp. Fifth in the exciting Isis series.
ISBN 1-931513-71-4 $12.95

WOMAN IN THE MIRROR by Jackie Calhoun. 216 pp. Josey learns to love again, while her niece is learning to love women for the first time.
ISBN 1-931513-78-3 $12.95

SUBSTITUTE FOR LOVE by Karin Kallmaker. 200 pp. When Holly and Reyna meet the combination adds up to pure passion. But what about tomorrow?
ISBN 1-931513-62-7 $12.95

GULF BREEZE by Gerri Hill. 288 pp. Could Carly really be the woman Pat has always been searching for?
ISBN 1-931513-97-X $12.95

THE TOMSTOWN INCIDENT by Penny Hayes. 184 pp. Caught between two worlds, Eloise must make a decision that will change her life forever. ISBN 1-931513-56-2 $12.95

MAKING UP FOR LOST TIME by Karin Kallmaker. 240 pp. Discover delicious recipes for romance by the undisputed mistress.   ISBN 1-931513-61-9 $12.95

THE WAY LIFE SHOULD BE by Diana Tremain Braund. 173 pp. With which woman will Jennifer find the true meaning of love?   ISBN 1-931513-66-X $12.95

BACK TO BASICS: A BUTCH/FEMME ANTHOLOGY edited by Therese Szymanski— from Bella After Dark. 324 pp.   ISBN 1-931513-35-X $14.95

SURVIVAL OF LOVE by Frankie J. Jones. 236 pp. What will Jody do when she falls in love with her best friend's daughter?   ISBN 1-931513-55-4 $12.95

LESSONS IN MURDER by Claire McNab. 184 pp. 1st Detective Inspector Carol Ashton Mystery.   ISBN 1-931513-65-1 $12.95

DEATH BY DEATH by Claire McNab. 167 pp. 5th Denise Cleever Thriller.   ISBN 1-931513-34-1 $12.95

CAUGHT IN THE NET by Jessica Thomas. 188 pp. A wickedly observant story of mystery, danger, and love in Provincetown.   ISBN 1-931513-54-6 $12.95

DREAMS FOUND by Lyn Denison. Australian Riley embarks on a journey to meet her birth mother . . . and gains not just a family, but the love of her life.   ISBN 1-931513-58-9 $12.95

A MOMENT'S INDISCRETION by Peggy J. Herring. 154 pp. Jackie is torn between her better judgment and the overwhelming attraction she feels for Valerie.   ISBN 1-931513-59-7 $12.95

IN EVERY PORT by Karin Kallmaker. 224 pp. Jessica has a woman in every port. Will meeting Cat change all that?   ISBN 1-931513-36-8 $12.95

TOUCHWOOD by Karin Kallmaker. 240 pp. Rayann loves Louisa. Louisa loves Rayann. Can the decades between their ages keep them apart?   ISBN 1-931513-37-6 $12.95

WATERMARK by Karin Kallmaker. 248 pp. Teresa wants a future with a woman whose heart has been frozen by loss. Sequel to *Touchwood*.   ISBN 1-931513-38-4 $12.95

EMBRACE IN MOTION by Karin Kallmaker. 240 pp. Has Sarah found lust or love?   ISBN 1-931513-39-2 $12.95

ONE DEGREE OF SEPARATION by Karin Kallmaker. 232 pp. Sizzling small town romance between Marian, the town librarian, and the new girl from the big city.   ISBN 1-931513-30-9 $12.95

CRY HAVOC A Detective Franco Mystery by Baxter Clare. 240 pp. A dead hustler with a headless rooster in his lap sends Lt. L.A. Franco headfirst against Mother Love.   ISBN 1-931513931-7 $12.95

DISTANT THUNDER by Peggy J. Herring. 294 pp. Bankrobbing drifter Cordy awakens strange new feelings in Leo in this romantic tale set in the Old West.   ISBN 1-931513-28-7 $12.95

COP OUT by Claire McNab. 216 pp. 4th Detective Inspector Carol Ashton Mystery.   ISBN 1-931513-29-5 $12.95

BLOOD LINK by Claire McNab. 159 pp. 15th Detective Inspector Carol Ashton Mystery. Is Carol unwittingly playing into a deadly plan?   ISBN 1-931513-27-9 $12.95

TALK OF THE TOWN by Saxon Bennett. 239 pp. With enough beer, barbecue and B.S., anything is possible!   ISBN 1-931513-18-X $12.95

MAYBE NEXT TIME by Karin Kallmaker. 256 pp. Sabrina has everything she ever wanted—except Jorie. ISBN 1-931513-26-0 $12.95

WHEN GOOD GIRLS GO BAD: A Motor City Thriller by Therese Szymanski. 230 pp. Brett, Randi and Allie join forces to stop a serial killer. ISBN 1-931513-11-2 $12.95

A DAY TOO LONG: A Helen Black Mystery by Pat Welch. 328 pp. This time Helen's fate is in her own hands. ISBN 1-931513-22-8 $12.95

THE RED LINE OF YARMALD by Diana Rivers. 256 pp. The Hadra's only hope lies in a magical red line . . . climactic sequel to *Clouds of War.* ISBN 1-931513-23-6 $12.95

OUTSIDE THE FLOCK by Jackie Calhoun. 224 pp. Jo embraces her new love and life. ISBN 1-931513-13-9 $12.95

LEGACY OF LOVE by Marianne K. Martin. 224 pp. Read the whole Sage Bristo story. ISBN 1-931513-15-5 $12.95

STREET RULES: A Detective Franco Mystery by Baxter Clare. 304 pp. Gritty, fast-paced mystery with compelling Detective L.A. Franco. ISBN 1-931513-14-7 $12.95

RECOGNITION FACTOR: 4th Denise Cleever Thriller by Claire McNab. 176 pp. Denise Cleever tracks a notorious terrorist to America. ISBN 1-931513-24-4 $12.95

NORA AND LIZ by Nancy Garden. 296 pp. Lesbian romance by the author of *Annie on My Mind.* ISBN 1931513-20-1 $12.95

MIDAS TOUCH by Frankie J. Jones. 208 pp. Sandra had everything but love. ISBN 1-931513-21-X $12.95

BEYOND ALL REASON by Peggy J. Herring. 240 pp. A romance hotter than Texas. ISBN 1-9513-25-2 $12.95

ACCIDENTAL MURDER: 14th Detective Inspector Carol Ashton Mystery by Claire McNab. 208 pp. Carol Ashton tracks an elusive killer. ISBN 1-931513-16-3 $12.95

SEEDS OF FIRE: Tunnel of Light Trilogy, Book 2 by Karin Kallmaker writing as Laura Adams. 274 pp. In Autumn's dreams no one is who they seem. ISBN 1-931513-19-8 $12.95

DRIFTING AT THE BOTTOM OF THE WORLD by Auden Bailey. 288 pp. Beautifully written first novel set in Antarctica. ISBN 1-931513-17-1 $12.95

CLOUDS OF WAR by Diana Rivers. 288 pp. Women unite to defend Zelindar! ISBN 1-931513-12-0 $12.95

DEATHS OF JOCASTA: 2nd Micky Knight Mystery by J.M. Redmann. 408 pp. Sexy and intriguing Lambda Literary Award–nominated mystery. ISBN 1-931513-10-4 $12.95

LOVE IN THE BALANCE by Marianne K. Martin. 256 pp. The classic lesbian love story, back in print! ISBN 1-931513-08-2 $12.95

THE COMFORT OF STRANGERS by Peggy J. Herring. 272 pp. Lela's work was her passion . . . until now. ISBN 1-931513-09-0 $12.95

WHEN EVIL CHANGES FACE: A Motor City Thriller by Therese Szymanski. 240 pp. Brett Higgins is back in another heart-pounding thriller. ISBN 0-9677753-3-7 $11.95

CHICKEN by Paula Martinac. 208 pp. Lynn finds that the only thing harder than being in a lesbian relationship is ending one. ISBN 1-931513-07-4 $11.95

TAMARACK CREEK by Jackie Calhoun. 208 pp. An intriguing story of love and danger. ISBN 1-931513-06-6 $11.95

DEATH BY THE RIVERSIDE: 1st Micky Knight Mystery by J.M. Redmann. 320 pp. Finally back in print, the book that launched the Lambda Literary Award–winning Micky Knight mystery series. ISBN 1-931513-05-8 $11.95

EIGHTH DAY: A Cassidy James Mystery by Kate Calloway. 272 pp. In the eighth installment of the Cassidy James mystery series, Cassidy goes undercover at a camp for troubled teens. ISBN 1-931513-04-X $11.95

MIRRORS by Marianne K. Martin. 208 pp. Jean Carson and Shayna Bradley fight for a future together. ISBN 1-931513-02-3 $11.95

THE ULTIMATE EXIT STRATEGY: A Virginia Kelly Mystery by Nikki Baker. 240 pp. The long-awaited return of the wickedly observant Virginia Kelly. ISBN 1-931513-03-1 $11.95

FOREVER AND THE NIGHT by Laura DeHart Young. 224 pp. Desire and passion ignite the frozen Arctic in this exciting sequel to the classic romantic adventure *Love on the Line*. ISBN 0-931513-00-7 $11.95

WINGED ISIS by Jean Stewart. 240 pp. The long-awaited sequel to *Warriors of Isis* and the fourth in the exciting Isis series. ISBN 1-931513-01-5 $11.95

ROOM FOR LOVE by Frankie J. Jones. 192 pp. Jo and Beth must overcome the past in order to have a future together. ISBN 0-9677753-9-6 $11.95

THE QUESTION OF SABOTAGE by Bonnie J. Morris. 144 pp. A charming, sexy tale of romance, intrigue, and coming of age. ISBN 0-9677753-8-8 $11.95

SLEIGHT OF HAND by Karin Kallmaker writing as Laura Adams. 256 pp. A journey of passion, heartbreak, and triumph that reunites two women for a final chance at their destiny. ISBN 0-9677753-7-X $11.95

MOVING TARGETS: A Helen Black Mystery by Pat Welch. 240 pp. Helen must decide if getting to the bottom of a mystery is worth hitting bottom. ISBN 0-9677753-6-1 $11.95

CALM BEFORE THE STORM by Peggy J. Herring. 208 pp. Colonel Robicheaux retires from the military and comes out of the closet. ISBN 0-9677753-1-0 $11.95

OFF SEASON by Jackie Calhoun. 208 pp. Pam threatens Jenny and Rita's fledgling relationship. ISBN 0-9677753-0-2 $11.95

BOLD COAST LOVE by Diana Tremain Braund. 208 pp. Jackie Claymont fights for her reputation and the right to love the woman she chooses. ISBN 0-9677753-2-9 $11.95

THE WILD ONE by Lyn Denison. 176 pp. Rachel never expected that Quinn's wild yearnings would change her life forever. ISBN 0-9677753-4-5 $11.95

SWEET FIRE by Saxon Bennett. 224 pp. Welcome to Heroy—the town with more lesbians per capita than any other place on the planet! ISBN 0-9677753-5-3 $11.95